THE DEAD

ONE SITS

By DON THOMPSON

ISBN – 13: 978-0615990873

Table of Contents

WARNING: By proceeding further

you may be rendered illiterate.

1 LETS DO THE PIMPADOODLE

You will remember that I told you about the disgraceful happenings at Fenton, Pettigrew and Cohenstein before. Good old F, P & C is one of our most prestigious and highly regarded large law firms here in Chicago. At least its partners tell us that. Yet last year and the year before people had been murdered in its offices. Outsiders of vulgar disposition who were familiar with what really happened there would exclaim, "How lucky can you get!" At least if they ran slaughter houses they would so exclaim. Free bodies! Free meat!

Horrid events indeed! But these horrid events were merely outliers of the past were they not? No. You guessed it. Another one popped up, figuratively speaking that is.

I tell you about this so you may understand that the recent events do in no way reflect on the character and standing of this venerable and honored firm, but are symbolic of the risks all law firms are subjected to due to the vengeful and pugilistic natures of the outside elements they come in contact with. I also wish you to know that if you can understand that last sentence, you can breeze through the rest of what follows. And, as the honored and honorable Chairman of the firm, Graybourne St. Charles said to the cat he keeps in his office, in one of his conversations with that advisor, "Oh dear Pussy, this never happened before we started letting all sorts of people into the firm, like those Jews and foreigners." By 'foreigners' he meant not only the people in the overseas offices, but those here in this country with non-waspy names.

The highly placed can instinctively identify terrorists and conspirators. And some of these miscreants who had become partners were actually plotting against dear Graybourne. But for the moment he was secure because he was the partner in charge of the firm's biggest source of business which was the Swifton family and their controlled companies. His nickname amongst his childhood friends and officially was Graybee. Others referred to him in other terms. Charlie. The Saint. And to many of his partners, Grabby. And in descriptive terms, a bigoted dumb snob.

F, P & C had offices in the Swifton Building, most of which was occupied by The Swifton Bank, one of our great nation's largest banks. The family also had vast interests in other enterprises. The Bank and the other enterprises were the source of a large percentage of F, P & C's revenues. The head of all the family businesses was Arthur Swifton, a comrade in arms of F, P & C's exalted leader. Arthur was proud that he was called Swifty. He took this to refer to his intelligence. He was also proud of his other nickname of Arty, which he took to refer to his artistic sensibilities. Swifty and Graybee were birds of a feather. With similar mental abilities. (As each other I mean.)

Trisha DeLang was the granddaughter of the richest man in Chicago. When her grandfather was found dead in one of Fenton, Pettigrew's men's rooms it was not a member of the firm who was responsible for it. This is what I mean when I tell you that outside elements were responsible. While it is true that he had been murdered, it was one of his own family members who was responsible for it. Trisha was now almost eighteen and she was the hottest teen idol in the business. She was a firm client as were her family's businesses. Naturally, St. Charles was the lead lawyer on the account. Another reason the terrorists were held at bay for the moment. St. Charles did not know what to make of Trisha though, or her bi-racial black-white condition, so other lawyers were necessary to help with the account. One of these was a young associate named John Sweeney. An associate is a lawyer who is not a partner. Sweeney was a Hey Duder and St. Charles certainly did not approve of him, but Sweeney was bringing in an unheard amount of business for an associate and so he stayed. Actually, besides bringing in a lot of business, he was also one of the firm's best associates in terms of legal abilities. He understood Trisha and, besides bringing in a lot of business, Trisha wanted him as her lawyer. So the firm always had him present for any meeting involving her and he was the contact person with her. While St. Charles was the nominal partner in charge of the account, he actually delegated the oversight duties to the firm's Managing Partner, Bumper Lohman.

Bumper was a big nobody. Most people did not even notice him. Even when he was speaking. He didn't speak a lot and when he did he said a lot with few words. If you don't talk a lot you aren't important. He was one of the equity partners. These were the partners who actually owned the firm. The rest of the partners had no ownership interest, but a large part of their pay depended on the profits of the firm. Amongst the equity partners there was a Management Committee, headed by St. Charles, and Lohman was part of this. The members of the Management Committee were the equity partners with the highest billings. Lohman was the Management Committee member with the lowest billings. He was also the one who solved all the problems, although the rest of the equity partners gave themselves credit for it. Lohman was at the other end on the age spectrum from Sweeney, but the two recognized each other's competence and worked well together.

Sweeney often had another associate named Sean Featherbottom helping him out with things. Sean was young, pretty and blonde. He was "wishy" according to the one living name partner, Zenon Cohenstein. Cohenstein called Sean Fluffy on the basis that he was sure Sean had his bottom feathers fluffed a lot, but he could have cared less about who Sean poked, or got poked by.

Sweeny couldn't care less either since he was too busy porking or poking every skirt in sight. Lohman didn't care about Sean's sex life either, but he was busy trying to get Sweeney to confine his activities to women outside the firm.

How did Cohenstein get to be the name partner of an old line waspy outfit? Business. The firm he merged into Fenton, Pettigrew had the business and was growing fast while Fenton, Pettigrew was not growing. They had a lot of big old-line clients, but they were not adding clients. Cohenstein's firm was. In spades.

Lohman, Sweeney, Trisha DeLang, her mother, Wandrasha, and her agent Eben Gohr, were having a meeting in the conference room just outside St. Charles' office. St. Charles had planned to be there, but he had been called away to attend an urgent conference with Swifty at The Bank. The subject of the meeting was the financing of Trisha's new movie. They were discussing who to approach and how and the possible legal aspects thereof. Why would a member of one of the richest families on the continent have to worry about raising money for a movie? They weren't about to risk their own money on movie, that's why. The idea was to get suckers, who were referred to as investors, to finance the movie, and to rake off big shares of the profits with fees and profit percentages and to leave the suckers holding the bag if the movie lost money.

They had been discussing a prior contact with a representative of a so-called private equity firm about an investment in the movie and discussing why he was not showing any further interest. Trisha, who was a bit of a potty mouth, interjected. "I don't like his ass. I saw him at a party after we met and he tried to put the make on me. I told him to go dribble a football." That might explain his lack of further interest.

Just then St. Charles came in from his meeting at The Bank. He was surveying the scene when Sean Featherbottom who was supposed to attend the meeting, but had also been tied up elsewhere, although not in the manner he would have preferred, entered. Sweeney said, "The Queen is here."

St. Charles shot around towards the door and said. "She's here? Where?" He flattered himself to think, or hope, that an actual queen would come and see him some day.

Trisha wasn't too interested in the details of all this and after a while she started talking about the artistic aspects of the new venture. It was to be a vast semi-biographical musical of her career and her climb to the top. Part of the movie would involve introducing new songs to her hit parade. Trisha did everything. She sang, danced, acted. Everything that could be demanded of a modern media star. While Trisha didn't usually write the stuff, this time she had some compositional input. She had developed a new dance and, with a song writer, a song to go with it. The big new thing was that it incorporated some tap dancing, something ancient enough to be new to the potential audience. This new song and dance was called the Pimpadoodle. It involved hip grinding without too much lateral movement while she was singing and vast and fast lateral dance moves in the non-singing intervals.

Trisha was telling those present about the Pimpadoodle when all of a sudden she got up and started into the song and dance. St. Charles was still standing near in the doorway, dumbfounded by what he was seeing and hearing in his own conference room. When she wasn't singing the lyrics she was humming the tune rather loudly. In one of her dance moves Trisha inserted, "Hi Charlie," and then went on tearing about the room. She was humming away and entered a straight move and needed more room. She headed for the door to St. Charles' office which was partly ajar and hit it and danced on it to his office. The others lost sight or her, but could still hear her. She started back on the lyrics. "I pimpadoodle, I doo da pimpa, da pimpa, da pimpa ----, Oh shitty titty!" She stopped. Silence.

St. Charles was already upset about this creature going into his office. He was headed for it and went in. Soon everyone left in the conference room heard St.Charles yelling and screaming all at the same time – so far is permissible for the elder statesman of the snobistic empire. He was alternating a series of high pitched, hyperventilated gasping grunts with exclamations directed to his cat. "Oh dear Pussy! What have they done! What happened?" Yes, he kept a cat in his office.

The others started filing into his office. They saw what St. Charles was screaming about. An apparently young woman was sitting in St. Charles' desk chair. There was a garbage bag over her head, apparently stuffed with something. A little congealed blood was coming down her body from the bag. Other than the bag she was completely naked except for thigh length shiny black high heeled boots.

Everyone just stood there in silence looking at the sight. Except for Sweeney who said, "Man, those ain't no shitty titties." Fortunately for him this comment did not penetrate St. Charles' state of shock.

There is an old popular song entitled, "I Ain't Got Nobody." Well, on Tuesday, January 15, 2013 Fenton, Pettigrew did got a body.

Oh, the monstrous indelicacy of it all!

Lohman stepped forward and put his hand on the woman's shoulder. "She's cool," he said. Then he shook her slightly. There was no reaction. She was slightly stiff. He turned to Sweeney and said, "Call an ambulance. And call the cops. This doesn't look kosher." Sweeney already had his smart phone out to fiddle with, as he usually did, and proceeded to make the calls.

St. Charles gasped. "The police! What do you mean kosher?"

Lohman responded. "I don't think, or at least it's possible that this is not a natural death. At least she seems dead. Kosher – you know – not natural. Not on the up and up."

"Oh, the Jewish word. You mean – not again!" said St. Charles.

"Yes, we have another body to explain," said Lohman.

St. Charles became even more bug eyed.

 Gohr said, "Let's get the bag off her head. Let's see who she is." He stepped towards the desk.

"No," said Lohman. "Leave everything as is. Don't touch anything. Don't move around in here. Let's all just go back to the conference room."

Sweeney said, "Yeah, we've seen the good parts already." Then he turned towards Lohman and said, "Hey Bumps. I called the ambulance and the cops. They're on the way."

"Bumps?" said St. Charles. "Where are the bumps?" No one responded. This is another example of why Sweeney managed to stay on at the firm. St. Charles did not know what he was talking about half the time. Since he did not know what most other people were talking about half the time either, this did not bother him.

Lohman motioned everyone towards the conference room and they started to leave the office. Lohman was going to bring up the rear and as the others were filing out he noticed that there was a fresh garbage bag in St. Charles' waste basket. It was like the bag over the body's head. He also noticed two parallel raised lines on the rug beside the desk, as if something had been dragged there.

When they all got back to the conference room they sat at the conference table. St. Charles sat at the head of the table, as befitted his eminence, but he was speechless.

Lohman said, "Does anyone know anything about this? Does anyone know who she is?" No one said anything. "What about you Graybourne?" asked Lohman. "How did she get there?"

St. Charles just looked at him with a blank state and wide eyes.

"Well, I mean," continued Lohman, "It's your office. How did she get there?"

"How would I know?" said St. Charles.

"When was the last time you were in your office?" asked Lohman.

"Who wants to know? That's confidential," said St. Charles. Idiots understand very well that they do not have to explain confidential matters.

"I think the police will want to know," said Lohman.

"Oh," remarked St. Charles. "I see. Well the last time I was in my office was this morning when I came in and before I went out to my conference at The Bank." He said nothing further.

Lohman asked, "Was she there then?"

"Of course not!" said St. Charles. "Who do you think I am?"

Lohman said, "So if she wasn't there then someone must have put her in your office after that. Or she came in by herself and then died there. But I don't think she would cool down so much that fast. I'm no authority, but maybe the police will be able to go into that."

Now St. Charles was recovering. "Why did you call the police?" demanded St. Charles. "What basis did you have to sully our reputation that way?"

Lohman did not remind St. Charles that he could have countermanded the request to Sweeney to call. "Think of how it would look if we had not called. Then, if it comes out this was not some kind of natural death, we have a story that she was found in your office and you tried to cover it up. I'll call our PR firm and see what they suggest we should say. As soon as I can get back to my office."

Trisha had been silent up to now, but she spoke up. "This is exciting!" She turned to Gohr and said, "Let's add this to the movie."

Gohr thought for a moment and said, "Maybe. We don't know how it's going to play out."

"We've got a while," she said. "If it doesn't play out to a good story or they don't wrap it up by the time we're ready to go, we'll make up our own story. Something like the head of the firm offing whores or like that."

St. Charles looked at her with a combination of horror, contempt and hatred. But what could he say to a major client. He looked at Lohman pleadingly.

Lohman looked at Gohr and Wandrasha. "Does the movie cover the death of Trisha's grandfather here in the men's room?"

"No way!" said Trisha. "I don't want to bad mouth the family. Or me. I'm supposed to be pure."

"Pure what?" asked Sweeney. "Hey just cool it. We don't know what's going to happen here. And you don't want to trash your lawyers. You want to help out our PR. The better the people around you look, the better you look."

St. Charles thought, "Can you talk to a client that way?"

Lohman thought that he was grateful that Sweeny was on the job. He might have thought what Sweeney just said, but he would be thinking about how to say it for a long time before saying anything.

Wandrasha chimed in. "Cool it Hon." That ended the matter.

2 THE COPS COME

At that point the conference room phone rang and a team of paramedics came in through the conference room door at the same time. St. Charles was out of it. Lohman motioned to Featherbottom to get the phone and motioned to the paramedics to go into the office. They did so and the group waited silently in the conference room.

"Who was on the phone?" Lohman asked Sean.

"Reception called. She says the police are on the way up."

No sooner did he finish than several detectives and some uniformed officers came in. Lohman motioned them into the office too. One of the detectives told two of the officers, "Keep them all here and try to keep their hands off everything."

Lohman had seen the detectives before. They had been the ones investigating the death of Trisha's grandfather. He even remembered their names. Detective Smokey Bongwad and Sargent Wilbert Gilbert. Or was it Gilbert Wilbert. He couldn't remember. The detectives went into the office with the paramedics and those in the conference room could hear the sounds of what they were doing and saying, but couldn't hear exactly what was being said. They just sat in silence and waited.

After a while the Sargent came out. He approached Lohman. "Gilbert sir. We meet again."

"Ah yes," said Lohman. "I remember. Sargent Wilbert."

"Gilbert, sir," said the Sargent. "Glibert, Wilbert."

"So Sargent Wilbert," said Gohr, "What's going on here?"

"Gilbert, sir."

"What?" exclaimed Gohr. "So it's Gilbert or Wilbert? Which?"

"Gilbert, Wilbert, sir."

By this time Bongwad had emerged from the office. He said to the assembled group, "He's militarily trained. First name Wilbert. Surname Gilbert."

No one wanted to continue with this anymore. "What happened?" asked Gohr.

Bongwad said, "We're going to ask you. She's gone. We got that bag off and she's been shot in the head. The M.E. is on the way. That's, I mean, someone from the Medical Examiner's office.

We're going to have to ask you some questions, but for now we have to seal off the office and the conference room. We have an evidence tech team coming. Is there someplace else we can go?"

Lohman answered. "We can go to my conference room on 44. Bongwad turned to the uniformed officers and said, "Take them down there. Get a couple of the other officers and keep them there. If they need anything have them call to get someone else to bring it in. If they need to get rid of anything, examine it and if there are any questions, keep it there. If it can go have them get someone to pick it up. And keep them all in sight on the way down there and at all times. Anyone wants to go to the john you go with them." He turned to Lohman and his people and said, "It'll help if you cooperate. The officers have instructions and if it looks like you are trying to avoid observation or get rid of something they know what to do which you don't want them to do. So it'll be a good idea to cooperate."

At this point St. Charles got up and headed for his office. Gilbert was nearest to him. Gilbert stepped in front of St. Charles and put a hand on his chest. "How dare you!" said St. Charles.

"Sir! You can't go in there," said Gilbert.

"But it's my office. I have work to do. My Pussy's in there!"

"Are you serious?" asked Bongwad. "Oh, I remember, you have a cat in there. She's sitting on her perch. She isn't going anywhere."

"But you can't keep me out of my office!" said St. Charles.

"Downstairs sir," said Gilbert with enough of a threatening tone to quiet St. Charles down.

The uniformed officers then escorted the group down to Lohman's conference room. They entered through his office. There was a door directly between the conference room and the hall, but Lohman did not tell the officers that. He wanted to enter through his secretarial area because he wanted to talk to his secretary.

Lohman's secretary was unique. Tina Goblat was her name, although she went by the nickname of Tete. She was six feet tall and weighed 220 pounds. All muscle. She was big boned and big muscled. She talked like a punch drunk boxer. She was rather intimidating which is a talent Lohman often took advantage of when he asked her to tell someone something. They listened to her and did what she said. Period. She called everyone Hon when addressing them. If there was someone who could intimidate the cops if necessary and tell them what to do, she was the person.

That is not why Lohman wanted to go by her. He wanted to get some things done. As the group came into her area, led by one of the uniformed officers, she looked up and said to the officer. "Hi Hon. What's up?" Then she saw the group that was following headed by Lohman. She kept silent.

Lohman said, "I have to talk to you Tete about some things."

One of the officers said, "No. We go to the conference room. No one else comes in or leaves unless we go with and no one goes to talk to someone else. Maybe to the toilet."

Lohman asked him, "Can I talk to her on the phone with you there?"

The officer thought for a moment and said, "OK. From the conference room. Let's get in there."

They all went into the conference room and Lohman pointed out some of its features. Since he was the Managing Partner it was better equipped than other conference rooms. It had multiple phones and a refrigerator with things to drink and cabinets with snacks and it had coffee fixings and a coffee maker. Lohman pointed these out to those present and then asked one of the officers if he could call his secretary. The officer said yes and he did.

"Hi Tete," he said. "What's going on?"

Tete said, "You're asking me? The cops again. That Sean Featherbottom! Who did he kill this time?"

It was true that Sean had seemingly been implicated in prior murders affecting the firm, but it turned out to be more probable than not that others were responsible. Lohman responded. "I doubt he did anything. The body of, well, a naked body was found sitting in St. Charles' office chair. A young woman. Naked except for thigh high boots and a bag over her head. Looked like one of those office waste basket bags we use."

"This'll be fun," said Tete. "The whole place is asking what the cops and the paramedics are doing here. Wait'll they hear this. And in Charlie's office too! What other things do we not know about the Saint. This is going to be fun." Tete was referring to the gossip she was looking forward to. One of her primary assets so far as Lohman was concerned was that she was up on all the firm gossip.

"Don't tell anybody anything right now," said Lohman. The police are investigating and we don't know anything about what happened. No one knows who she is or how she got there. Just call the PR firm and give them a heads up and get them working on it. Then don't tell anyone anything, but if you hear anything let me know. Did you hear anything yet? Has anyone said anything that might indicate who she is or how she got there?"

"Nothing yet," said Tete. "I'll tell you if I hear anything. One thing I hear already is the calls from up there. How many of the equity partners are up there? How many are in? Anyway, the cops rousted them all out and they sealed off the floor. No one knows how long and they are all calling for you to do something about it. And to top that off two have balled me out and McDade too."

McDade was Geeley McDade who was the Business Manager of the firm. He was a non-lawyer who was in charge of some of the non-legal aspects of the firm.

Lohman said, "Tell Geeley to get them set up in some of our vacant offices." In the past most large firms had a good deal of vacant offices available for expansion. These days most large firms had a lot of vacant space because of the recession and a reduction in business. F, P & C, however, was still expanding.

Tete continued. "They're also screaming up there on 55 about the paper towels in the wash room. There aren't any. What happened? Is she the cleaning person for the floor? Did she get killed before getting to the washrooms last night?"

"God knows," said Lohman. "Just tell Geeley to wait until the police clear out and then he can get the matter fixed. By the way, have him get the building log for the past – say – two days so we can see who checked in and when. Have him check the phone log too and assemble it for examination."

"Right Hon." Said Tete. "Too bad we can't see who checked out and when too. You'd think we'd have more than roach trap security. You can check in, but you can't check out. So we don't need to know when the crooks left? I suppose not. We don't let crooks in so how can they leave? Who needs to know that?"

"Don't tell Homeland Security," said Lohman. "Anything else going on?"

"Nothing important," said Tete. "You don't have any appointments scheduled soon, right?"

"Right," said Lohman. "If anything comes up don't come in here. Just phone in." he hung up and turned to look at the others in the room. They were all playing with their smart phones except St. Charles who was staring at the wall in a state of semi-shock.

Eventually the police finished with their business up on 55 and Detective Bongwad and Sargent Gilbert came down to 44 to interview the people in Lohman's conference room. They took them one by one in Lohman's office and released them back to their own offices after the interviews instead of letting them go back to the conference room and compare notes. Eventually they finished and everyone could go back to work.

3 FIRM BUSINESS

The next day the Management Committee was scheduled to meet first thing in the morning to discuss several ideas that had arisen for expanding the firm's business and offices. The Management Committee had nine members. St. Charles was the Chairman. Cohenstein was the Vice Chairman. The other members were Lohman, the Managing Partner, Alan Allen, who had a big municipal securities practice, John Feepot, head of the corporate department, Gooster Fileform, head of the securities department, Jeffrey Wax, head of tax, Peter Freebornstein head of litigation, and Pincus Ruhlman. Pincus was another member of the Cohenstein faction. He had a Rottweiler which he often brought to the office which offended St. Charles and Pussy to no end. But he was pulling in big bucks. What can you do?

The meeting had been scheduled for St. Charles' conference room, but the whole fifty fifth floor was still blocked off by the police. Because of this it had been moved to Lohman's conference room on the forty fourth floor. Most of the other members of the Management Committee had their offices on 55, but Lohman preferred to be more in the center of things. This suited St. Charles since Lohman was not of high social rank or heritage. St. Charles knew he could not prevent some of the equity partners with less than suitable heritage from having offices on his floor, but one less meant he could see that one more suitable person was on the floor. Cohenstein, the Vice Chair, didn't care who was where.

"Fenton, Pettigrew," is how St. Charles referred to the firm. Never would he use the word Cohenstein. But Cohenstein was the reason they were still in existence. He had merged his firm into Fenton, Pettigrew because he could make use of the venerable name. They, on the other hand, were going down the tubes until he arrived. Now the firm was growing while most other large firms were not, due to the recessionary and cost cutting atmosphere that still prevailed in 2013 after the 2008 crash.

Since the 1970s large law firms had grown much faster that the economy in general. A great deal of the growth was due to mergers, such as the one involving Cohenstein's firm. Fenton, Pettigrew had engaged in some of these, but since Cohenstein arrived almost all their growth had been generated without the mergers. Cohenstein could get blood out of a stone. Business too. And so could the people he brought in with him.

In early 2013 the firm had about 425 lawyers, exclusive of a breed of lawyers called contract lawyers. I say the firm had about 425 lawyers because they were constantly entering and leaving the firm. The contract lawyers were lawyers hired on an independent contractor basis to handle routine tasks such as reviewing documents produced in litigation to see what they contained. This task was being taken over by word recognition software, but F, P & C still employed a good number. Independent contractors are not employees and you do not have to pay them the same benefits as employees. These independent contractor lawyers were on a much lower pay scale than the other lawyers in the firm. The other lawyers were called associates and partners. The associates were the junior lawyers and, unlike the contract lawyers, they were said to be "on partnership track". Above the associates were the partners. Most were merely partners in name only. They did not have any ownership of the firm or a right to any of the profits.

However they were paid a share of the profits as well as their base salary. In other words, if the firm did not have a good year, the firm did not have to pay them so much. Some of the people referred to as partners really were partners though. They were called equity partners and they were the owners. There were about 50 of them. Of these, 9 were on the Management Committee. Picked for their expertise? No. They were the 9 highest billers. The firm also had a lot of secretaries, receptionists, waitresses, clerks and paralegals. The latter are people who did the low level routine work. Not really legal work, but semi-legal or para-legal, whatever that is.

The firm had its main office in the heart of Chicago's downtown, called the "Loop". It occupied floors 40-55 in The Bank's building, Swifton Plaza. It also had a suburban office in Highland Park which is in the middle of the fashionable and rich North Shore area of Chicago's suburbs. Other offices were in New York and Shanghai. The firm was in the process of opening a London office too, but that was still in process. Some of the equity partners with high hopes had been talking about getting into Singapore. They wanted to be in all the financial centers of the world eventually. These partners were in the old line St. Charles faction. To them a firm of suitable rank, such as theirs, should be in all the important financial centers. However, according to Cohenstein the firm should be where the clients were. In the future offices in New York and London could lead to clients with a need for legal services in other financial centers, but at the moment few clients were asking for services in Singapore.

So Cohenstein wanted to open offices in Milwaukee, Cleveland and St. Louis. His people had developed a lot of clients in those areas and were wasting a lot of time on travel. The clients also wanted local lawyers. Milwaukee, Cleveland and St. Louis, so far as the St. Charles faction were concerned, were not conceivable. Some of them did not even know where these places were. Or so they pretended. St. Charles had informed everyone that he had once been in St. Louis on a business matter, but the best his hosts could come up with for lunch was the Mid-States Athletic Club. "Think of it," he said, "an athletic club. That is the best club in town. They weren't even dressed properly. And there were people from the stock yards there. They still had stock yards. Imagine that? And they let those people into the club just because they were officers of the place. Imagine having to sit next to a table of people who worked in an abattoir!"

Cohenstein had been trying to get the other members of the Management Committee to descend to reality. His main pitch was money. These offices would generate more money. Lucre sways the highly placed.

The meeting had been scheduled for Lohman's conference room, but he was not the first one there. He was in a conference with Tete in his office, when the others were filing in to his conference room. He and Tete had to straighten out some things with the police who were still working on 55. When Lohman had finished with this he went into the conference room. Most of the Management Committee partners were there, but not St. Charles. On principle St. Charles made people wait for him. It was not that he thought his time was more valuable than theirs, it was just that he could not possibly conceive of scurrying about to suit the needs of lesser mortals. Cohenstein was sitting in the chair at one end of the table, thereby making it the head chair.

Just as Cohenstein had got up to get a cup of coffee, St. Charles came in. Although Cohenstein had a lot of papers spread out where he had been sitting, St. Charles headed for the chair and sat in it. The other partners were getting tired of having to wait through the "Who gets the head chair" routine, but they had no other alternative than to see how it played out.

Cohenstein turned around with his coffee cup and saw St. Charles in the chair. He turned back to the counter and put down his cup. Then he pulled out his cell phone and stepped out into the hall. St. Charles did not use a cell phone. Soon Tete came in and addressed him. "Mr. St. Charles, there's a call for you." She motioned to a phone in the room. St. Charles stepped over to the phone and picked it up. As he did so Cohenstein came back into the room and sat in the chair.

St. Charles was talking into the phone. "Hello! Hello!" He was saying, "There's no one there," as he put the phone down and turned back to face the interior of the room. He saw Cohenstein in the chair. He straightened up and walked out. Tete was still in the room. She observed all this. As St. Charles left she went after him. They both went out into the hall, but after a while she came in again. However, she came in from the door leading to Lohman's office, not the hall door. St. Charles was following her. She went to the end of the table opposite Cohenstein and pulled back the chair for St. Charles. As she did so she said, "The Chairman will sit here. It's too bad we don't have a definite table head here." St. Charles sat down and proclaimed that they could now start the meeting.

Those present began to discuss the possible new offices. Some wanted to keep talking about Singapore and someone brought up Mumbai as a possibility. "Where is that?" asked St. Charles.

"It used to be called Bombay," said Lohman.

"Of course," said St. Charles.

The conversation drifted to discussion of the various Asian economies and a lot of other cities were discussed as possibilities. Lohman realized that these were more wishful thinking ideas than possibilities of real business-generating locations. St. Charles did not think in terms of getting business. He thought solely of what is proper, suitable and of high esteem. He expressed his disapproval of most of the places mentioned. Cohenstein reminded him of how much business they were getting out of the Shanghai office. The U.S. clients wanted some services in China, but mostly the Chinese clients of the office wanted legal services in the U.S.

"That may be," said St. Charles, "but look at the people we have to put up with. You know, because of Chinese law we had to make it an affiliate, ostensibly a separate firm. Just think of the name. Pu, Phu, Po and Pho. I can't even get their names straight. I can get the first names. They are all Dong. Dong Pu, Dong Phu, and so forth."

Cohenstein chimed in, "Dong is their family name. The family name comes first in China. Just think of it this way – in China they have their Dongs in front."

"Well anyway," said St. Charles, "the last time they were over here I came into my conference room to meet with them and they were all sitting there in a trance. I asked what they were doing and they said they were analyzing the Feng Shit of the building. They were trying to see if it was properly placed. They decided they couldn't tell. They didn't want to be in a building unless they knew its Feng Shit. They said they could not take any chances. They knew their hotel had good Feng Shit so I had to go there."

"Do you mean Feng Shui?" asked Cohenstein. "You said shit."

St. Charles just looked at him. St. Charles knew what the word meant, but he also knew that it was not in his vocabulary so he could not have said such a thing.

Cohenstein managed to steer the subject back to the three U.S. cities and the Committee voted to open offices there and told Lohman to get it done.

The Committee had also hired a management consulting firm to advise them on marketing. Lawyers use the term "marketing". They do not use the term "sales". It is vulgar. Ordinarily Lohman would be the contact person for this consulting firm, but hiring them was the idea of the St. Charles faction who thought hiring a consulting firm was the way to get the new business they generally weren't bringing in and they thought for the really important things the consultants should report directly to the Committee.

People from the consulting company were waiting in the waiting area outside Lohman's office with Tete. When the time came, Lohman called them in. The head of the consulting firm himself was there. He was Claybat Whiffle. The firm was CW Solutions. They had done work for F, P & C before and some thought that they created more problems than solutions. Problems without solutions. However, all those in high places who run large organizations and have no idea what is going on hire consultants. Then whatever happens they can say they hired the best there is. What else can you do? Some might say that if you cannot tell whether you should wipe your ass or your nose you are not going to get much help from someone who takes such questions seriously and makes a living from people who cannot tell what to do in such a situation. Others might question why you cannot just wipe both. The problem only arises if there is only one piece of wiping material. At any rate you can see how great problems arise and become bigger problems which require expert advice.

Whiffle had distributed copies of his report before hand and of course no one but Lohman had read it so he proceeded to explain his wondrous conclusions. His task was to develop ways of getting new business. His conclusion was that the firm needed to hold sales and give discounts. After all, that is how American business works these days.

"So we just give it away?" asked Cohenstein. "My parents used to call that giving away the store."

"It's just temporary," said Whiffle. "It's like the phone companies offering discounts on phones or internet service. Then they lock you into a contract and mark you up after the introductory period."

"Yeah," said Cohenstein. "It's starting to show. They have declining profit positions. They are getting to the point where all they get is the new business at the discount and they are eating each other up."

"But they are getting tons of new business," said Whiffle. "Then they mark it up later."

"Yeah," said Cohenstein. "And as soon as the customer can, they switch to another carrier offering a discount for new accounts. Anyway, I've been doing this for years. I offer the discounts and sales, but they aren't real. Who can tell? What we charge our clients is confidential. I charge close to one thousand dollars an hour most of the time. I just tell them I will discount my fees and only charge them whatever it is I want to charge them. Sometimes higher that my usual rate. Same thing for sales. I tell them there's a discounted rate only for new matters in this period only, whatever period it is. It's nice of you to tell us this, but half of us are doing it already. The rest probably don't know how to work it. It doesn't work unless you use the idea to charge more. So how much are you charging us?"

Whiffle sidestepped the question. "Exactly," he said. "It's all about how you do it. It's all in the details. You'll see in our follow up report." Good save Whiffle.

"Yeah," said Cohenstein. "It's all in the details. Like when I say, 'A gentleman always carries a plastic bag with him so he can pick up his poo.' You can see how the details, the little things, count. I left out 'dog's'. 'So he can pick up his dog's poo'."

No one said anything for a while. Then they decided Whiffle should deliver his follow up report soon so those so inclined could learn the techniques of charging more and convincing the client that they were charging less. Whiffle and his crew then left and the discussion turned to the unfortunate events of the day before.

Everyone wanted to hear from Lohman with all the lurid details. Everyone wanted to know how someone like that got into the place and how she got into such a state. Ruhlman wanted to know,

"What were her tits like? Big ones? Firm? What were the nipples like?"

Lohman did not reply right away so Cohenstein said, "Oh crap Pinky! You know, if I didn't know you better I'd think you were trying to eliminate yourself as a suspect. Always with the tits!"

Of course St. Charles did not hear this. It was loud enough and he was right there, but proper ears do not pick up filth. He said, "This is unfortunate in the extreme. Soon what happened will be all over the news media. What are we going to do? How do we get out of this one?" Oh Great Wizard, what do we do now? Give him credit. You gotta ask.

No one had any suggestions except Cohenstein. "It's going to be hard to spin it the way you might like. She came here for some legitimate reason and then died. Maybe. But she took her clothes off first? Or someone else did? Or they took her clothes off after the death? And the sexy boots? And the bag over the head? Even if she came here kosher, things went downhill after that. I don't think we can get away from the fact that it was not St. Peter's widow who came here and died an unfortunate natural death."

St. Charles was turning green. He looked towards Lohman. "Bumper! Get this fixed!" Everyone else looked at Lohman too. The great Wizard had spoken to St. Charles. The same as usual. "Tell Lohman to fix it," he had said.

Lohman was thinking the same way as what Cohenstein had said. He had no great ideas about how to clean up the story. "I have alerted our PR firm he said. They don't have the full details any more than we do so they haven't suggested anything yet. I'll see what they come up with when we can tell them more. Anyway, I think the news is going to come out soon with what is known now and I think Zenon is right. We're going to take a hit."

"Hit, shmit," said Cohenstein. "Remember what the old show business idea was. 'I don't care what they say about me, just so long as they spell my name right.' We are going to get coverage. So some bad guy or guys are around. Even maybe someone in the firm. So, shmoo. Along the way we let people know what great lawyers we are. We are going to have an audience. Get that PR firm to arrange interviews. Get out press releases about how great we are. Let everyone know that the way we do things is perfect. Let them know we are the hottest and best law firm there is. Everyone wants us. Few can get us. We do it right. We will find out who is responsible for this and see that all is made right. Fenton, Pettigrew and Cohenstein does it and does it right, even if it means ferreting out bad guys within. Good and great F, P & C does not tolerate such things or such people. Everyone has bad guys within their organizations, but we do something about it. God! We are good! That's why everyone wants us to be their lawyer."

St. Charles' fear of what was coming up in the media abated. His concern over this was displaced and a new outrage had taken its place. Someone had added "Cohenstein" to the spoken firm name. He suffered in silence.

Just then a phone in the conference room rang. Allen was closest to the phone and picked it up. He listened for a moment and then said, "Send them in." The Management Committee had representatives from The Bank on the agenda. The Bank people wanted to talk to them about new products, in particular Growth Capital Funding Keeps or GCFKs.

Tete opened the door and held it for Swifty and his loyal followers. One was Denton Choudry, Chief Operating Officer of The Bank. Swifty couldn't operate a lawn mower. Also with them was Pulaski Rhodes, head of Swifton Securities. They had a crew of underlings with them too. Everyone got up and greeted the new arrivals and for a while the gathering resembled a cocktail gathering with coffee.

Soon St. Charles invited everyone to be seated. After they were seated he said, "I know we were talking about something else this morning, but I know you want our input in this matter too. What I've heard about it sounds exciting."

"Thank you," said Swifty. "It is exciting. We have a new product we think can generate big revenue and we want to run the idea around with our trusted advisers before getting to work on the details. Of course, when we do get to work on the details we will have to see that we structure things properly according to the law. We're just trying to get feedback on the overall idea just now."

Rhodes added, "Goldboi and Baggs are working on something similar and we'd like to get some unique attributes for our product. Maybe even some copyright or patent protection." A group of younger people had come in with the Bank people and Rhodes turned to the apparent leader of the group and said, "Go ahead." Then he turned to the others present and said, "You may have met Leeto, Leeto McGreggor, before. He is head of product development for The Bank. We use him at the securities firm too." He turned it over to McGreggor.

McGreggor turned to an underling of his own who had a large brief case which he opened. He took a projector out and aimed it to one side of the table towards an open space in the room. Then one of his underlings opened another case and took out a fold up screen and set that up in the open space. They soon had a PowerPoint show operating.

McGreggor talked about how the source of economic growth was small business. He explained about how small business was starved for capital in the best of times, but especially now with the after effects of the recession. Venture capital firms and private equity firms were no longer supplying the capital. Then he explained about how all big fortunes and all exceptional investment returns were produced by small businesses which got large. "So," he posited to those present, "there is a market here for financial services designed to supply needed capital to small business and exceptional returns to investors."

He went on to describe the risks involved and the possible losses as discouraging investment in the area. He pointed out that sophisticated investors took risks in this area, but only after their careful examination of the investments. However, even they were put off by the difficulty of identifying the good opportunities in this area. He explained that the key to success in this area was to find the opportunities for the investors and to find a way to ally their concerns over risk.

The SEC definition of sophisticated investors hinged on the amount of their income and assets. Their ability to evaluate the investment was not part of the definition. So, just because someone has money that makes them a sophisticated investor. This is a myth the legal system has adopted because it favors those in charge who are the people who sell the investments to the investors who, if sophisticated, would not buy them.

McGreggor continued by explaining that The Bank was not in the business of assuming risks. Therefore it would not be investing in the products itself. However, The Bank was going to make loans to the small businesses and buy stock in the companies to begin with. These loans and shares of stock would then be pooled together. Meanwhile Swifton Securities was going to assemble investors into separate companies that would buy the pools of loans and stock. Naturally a lot of the investors would borrow the money for their investments from The Bank. That is, if The Bank found them to be credit worthy and they could put up lots of collateral. McGreggor called this group of investors the "small business investors".

In the meantime, McGreggor explained, the small business investors would want to be secure in their investments so the scheme involved another set of investors who were going to come together in companies that would offer protection to the small business investors against the operating small businesses they had invested in failing or going bankrupt. In essence they were going to sell insurance against losses. Since they would insure a lot of the small business investments, the risk would be reduced. In the meantime they would charge high rates for the insurance. The investors in the small businesses would not mind because they were looking to high returns to begin with. McGreggor called this other group of investors the "insuring investors".

McGreggor went on to explain that the companies offering the insurance were not going to have limited liability. If an individual is committed to insure something then everything he has can be gotten by the insured to pay off the obligation. If the insurer is instead a corporation which the individual owns, only the assets of the corporation can be taken by the insured. The individual is said to have limited liability. A key feature of what the bank was putting together was that the insuring investors would operate through an entity without limited liability because they were going to guaranty the entity's obligations. This point would be used to convince the small business investors that the insurance was really worth something. Naturally, anyone who actually was a sophisticated investor putting his money into the insurance company would do so through his own limited liability vehicle and that would be the real investor in the insurance company and the entity that guaranteed its debts.

What The Bank was going to tell the small business investors was that they were insured against losses by the insurance company. Their protection was not limited to the assets of the insurance company because its owners, the insuring investors, personally guaranteed its debts. What The Bank was not telling the small business investors was that the insuring investors might themselves be limited liability companies or corporations with little or no assets.

At the same time, one of the potential small business investors who actually was a sophisticated investor would know this. Therefore that investor would not consider the claim of no limited liability a plus. That investor would instead see that the seller of the investment was feeding him or her bullshit and would not deal with the seller. So who was The Bank planning to sell these things to?

McGreggor referred to the concept of spreading risk by pooling risks. If you invest in only one company you could lose everything if it fails. Not all the companies will fail so if you invest in all of them you will still have something left after the failures. And the winners will make up for the losers. He explained that the more companies you invested in the higher your chances are of getting the big winner.

Most accountants say lawyers can't count. And most people in the securities business rely on the fact that neither investors nor lawyers can think. However, Lohman could think that the more companies you invested in the more you reduced your rate of return overall when there was a big winner among them. With one company you can lose it all. But, when it is successful you don't have to offset the gains from it with losses on the other companies. It works both ways. People like McGreggor did not explain both sides of the coin. Only the side they want you to see.

The investors in the small businesses or the insurance vehicles were going to be sold loans too. This way they could increase their returns. The Federal Reserve had been drastically reducing interest rates during the recession and money could be borrowed by "sophisticated investors" at low rates compared to the rates charged in the past. If a bank can get money from the Federal Reserve at 0.25% and then lend it out at 3% it makes a mint. It doesn't have to put up any of its own money. If an investor is going into a venture expected to return more than 3% then he can make a mint too. Say the investment is $1000. It is going to return 4% or $40. The investor borrows $900 of the $1000 at a cost of 3%, or $27. He puts up $100 of his own money. The return on the investment is $40. His cost is $27. The net return is $13. That is a 13% return in his $100.

Making money is so easy. The sellers of these products do not tell this to the "sophisticated investors". Instead the sellers let the investors come to this conclusion themselves. The Bank and Swifton Securities were not "sophisticated investors". They sold the crap to the "sophisticated investors". Whatever The Bank put in the small business companies it in turn unloaded on the suckers. And for doing all this The Bank charged large fees for setting up and selling the investments.

But don't the small businesses eventually pay off with large returns? Larger than conventional investments in large established companies? Especially if you invest in a broad cross section to reduce the risk of loss on any one small company? Maybe. Some day. That is the key to all securities fraud. You don't have to deliver anything now. Just a piece of paper evidencing the deal. In the meantime the people who put these things together make out like squirrels in a nut house.

St. Charles was impressed. "Sounds complicated," he said.

"That's a good thing," said Feepot. "We'll have to do a lot of work on these."

Jeffrey Wax added, "We can probably cross sell tax shelters with this." Then he asked, "What are the Keeps?"

Rhodes said, "The interests in the companies. The interests in the small business funding vehicles. These are 'Keeps'. As opposed to something and investor will want to resell. Like a speculator would.

'Keeps' is a product name. Something to interest investors. We'd like to trademark it."

Lohman thought to himself, "Same old crap they have been selling to the suckers for years." He had sense enough not to say this.

Ruhlman didn't. "Isn't this just like all the other products banks and securities firms developed in the boom and sold off to investors like the sub-prime mortgages?"

"Certainly not!" said Choudry.

"No. No," said McGreggor, "this is different. Way different. The products have insurance against losses. And there isn't going to be a crash this time. We already had that. This time it's different."

"Right," chimed in Swifty. "This is a winner. Think about it. Think about what might be the legal ramifications, but above all think about any problems in selling it. Think also about potential customers. We know you have a lot of clients who could be interested in investing or interested in selling the Keeps. We are just floating the idea to you and several other advisers like our accountants. Just give us your feedback, whatever it is."

Just then Tete stuck her head in the door and announced that the police had finished on 55 and the floor was now open again. This was greeted with applause and everyone took it to be a good time to end the meeting, which they did.

4 CLIENT MATTERS

Lohman had a tight schedule for the rest of the day so he had gone to the firm cafeteria and got a sandwich and a drink to take back to his office. He was sitting at his desk eating and reviewing his schedule when the phone rang. It was Wilson Armour, the General Counsel of The Swifton Corporation, the holding company for most of the Swifton interests. General Counsel is the term applied to a lawyer on the payroll of a company who supervises other lawyers on the same payroll doing work exclusively for the employer company. Lawyers like these are called house counsel. Most of the Swifton companies had their own legal departments, but Armour was informally in charge of legal matters for all of them. He was a fried brain idiot just like Swifty and St. Charles and he fit right in. St. Charles was F, P & C's lead lawyer for the all the Swifton companies. In the past the outside lawyers like St. Charles had their relationships with the heads of the client companies and the house counsel lawyers were considered suitable only for low level routine work. The outside lawyers did not report to them and did not take orders from them. These days things were reversed. The number of lawyers on company staffs had increased and they handled every matter they could for their employers. The General Counsel generally hired the outside lawyers and the relationships of the outside lawyers were with the General Counsel, not his boss. With Swifton though, the old relationship held true. St. Charles got the business because he had Swifty in his pocket.

Lohman was not usually involved in Swifton matters so ordinarily Armour would not call him. However, this was the old relationship. Armour chased after St. Charles. St. Charles did not court or pay much attention to Armour. As a result, Armour could not easily get in touch with St. Charles. On the other hand, Armour knew Lohman was the Managing Partner and he knew that, unlike other lawyers, Lohman responded to phone calls. No true lawyer of any significance answers his phone or returns calls. Since Lohman did answer his phone calls and did return calls he could not possibly be of any importance so Armour did not mind making routine use of his availability.

"Hello Wilson," said Lohman. "How are you today?"

"Fine, fine," said Wilson. "Do you know where Garybourne is?"

"No," said Lohman, "but I can try and find out. He probably has a lunch meeting." St. Charles always had a lunch meeting with persons of equivalent importance as he where they discussed things of even greater importance.

"I need help now," said Armour. "I know he's usually tied up at lunch time. I've been calling for him all morning. And I have been trying to find our own people on the job and I can't."

"What's up?" asked Lohman.

'U.S. Reo," said Armour.

"What's that? I'm not familiar with all your companies. Is it one of yours?" said Lohman.

"Yes," said Armour. "It stands for Real Estate Owned. It takes care of properties banks have foreclosed on. It does work for a lot of banks and other lenders. One of our subsidiaries bought it a while ago. I didn't know it was part of our group either until this problem came up. They must have bought it without telling me. Were you guys involved?"

"I would have to search our records and talk to Graybourne and others. I don't know off hand," said Lohman.

"Well," said Armour, "I can't get ahold of anyone. U.S. Reo has a law department and they sent me copies of a complaint they received. The complaint names The Bank as a party too. U.S. works on a lot of properties owned by The Bank. So I tried to call U.S. All morning I've been trying. All I can get are recorded messages. Then I got ahold of a number for their law department and called and it took half an hour to get through to someone who told me I can't talk to anyone direct. She said she takes the information and relays it and then someone will call me back. Not any of the lawyers though. I told her who I was and demanded to speak to the General Counsel. She just told me that was not possible and hung up. This is what they are supposed to do to the customers, not to me. I don't have time for this. I even called the guy in The Bank's law department who is in charge of foreclosure problems. He said - do you know what he said? He said he couldn't get through to them either. And then he added that he and his people don't actually do the foreclosures. They get cheap foreclosure firms to do that. I told him to contact them and he referred me to someone who was on vacation. You guys are going to have to get into this. You'll just have to go down the chain of command till you get some action."

Lohman thought that this is the kind of thing that St. Charles could milk for all it was worth. "What is the complaint about?" asked Lohman.

"Actually, it's more than one, but they are all for the same thing from the same law firm. I got two of them and the letter with them said they are a whole lot more coming. Why can't it be a class action?" asked Armour.

"Well, of course it haven't seen it so I don't know. However, sometimes cases don't qualify as class actions because the damages are quite different for each of the plaintiffs. Then you have the situation you mention where a lot of similar suits are filed by the same law firm. Anyway, what is it about?" asked Lohman.

Armour explained. "U.S. maintains foreclosed properties for the banks and then tries to sell them. It has a subsidiary that is a licensed real estate brokerage and it hires out of work real estate agents who are responsible as independent contractors for maintaining and selling the properties. They have to pay the costs out of their own pockets. They aren't employees so they don't have to be paid. Instead, they are compensated from their commissions on sale. The commissions are rock bottom. Most of them have been out of work for a long time because of the recession and housing bust and they'll take a lot less. The suits allege that U.S. and The Bank are taking wrongful advantage of them and committed fraud in signing them on to do the work. Apparently The Bank is charged with conspiracy in the matter. I don't know. I don't have time to read through all these things. My secretary told me about it."

Lohman thought to himself that this was just another example of the fact that much law is practiced by the secretaries of lawyers.

Armour continued. "This could be big. A lot of other banks are named too. It's a big deal plaintiffs' law firm. This will probably hit the news. I'll have my secretary get this over to you."

Lohman said, "You know that we have no authority over U.S. Reo's law department. If they won't listen to you, it will take us a while."

"Oh you have to get on it now," said Armour. "The ball's in your court."

Lohman said, "Right," and the two said goodbye.

Lohman sighed and put the remains of his sandwich in the waste basket and went out to talk to Tete. He was due at a meeting in St. Charles' conference room, but he explained the U.S. Reo matter to her and told her to look for the complaints and to get ahold of him as soon as she got them. Then he told her to get in touch with the U.S. Reo law department and find out what was going on. No one hung up the phone on Tete and lived.

Lohman then headed for the elevators and went up to St. Charles' office on 55. He was scheduled to meet with St. Charles, Cohenstein and another of the equity partners named Winston Camelman.

Lohman was not looking forward to the meeting. He could usually handle St. Charles and Cohenstein and their little tricks, but he anticipated problems because of Camelman. Camelman was a self-important little turd. Both he and St. Charles thought themselves the most important person in the firm – and the world. They were constantly making catty comments to and about each other and it was no secret in the firm that Camelman was after St. Charles' clients. As for the smallness of the turd – he was five foot three inches tall and weighed about 110 pounds. Therefore, despite his supposed importance, he did not stand out in a crowd. He couldn't even be seen. He made up for this with a big mouth. Maybe no one could see him, but they could hear him.

The meeting involved a delicate matter. Two delicate matters. One was a client complaint. The other was a complaint by St. Charles against Camelman. Camelman was always trying to horn in on someone else's clients and this time the client belonged to St. Charles. The two did not like each other.

The client was American Stocking Corporation. It stocked and shipped products for a lot of companies selling on the internet. It even did so for some of the very large retailers who farmed out this part of the business to American. American employed a lot of minimum wage people to deal with the inventory and ship it. They were part time so no benefits had to be paid and they were not treated too well. For instance, they had to beg for bathroom breaks. It was a very large company and a big client. Ostensibly it was St. Charles's client, mainly because he played golf with the controlling shareholder, Sam Wham.

Part of American's strategy to keep its employees in serfdom was to sign them to agreements that in return for their continued employment they would not go to work for a competitor anywhere near where they worked for American for a year after they left American. These types of agreements were called covenants not to compete. Lawyers sometimes call agreements covenants to emphasize their Biblical significance. American did not need the protection. Any competitor could hire a lot of other people and the

American employees would not be taking any significant information about American or its methods of business or its customers with them. What American wanted was to keep its wages low. If the serfs can't go elsewhere they have to stay put at subsistence wages.

These types of agreements were controversial. Some states had statutes that said they were unenforceable. Some states limited their enforcement. In states where they were enforceable, this particular type would probably not be enforceable. However, regardless of the law, they were usually quite effective because a departing employee did not have the money to fight a law suit. Also, American customarily threatened the potential new employer with a suit for interfering with the non-compete agreement and the new employer generally did not want any part of that expense for someone who was easily replaceable.

Now however, there was a class action suit. Instead of American bulldozing the serfs, the serfs had risen up in revolt along with some of the new employers who had hired some of them and were threatened with suit by American. The suit alleged that the agreements were clearly unenforceable and that American had interfered with the prospective advantage of its ex-employees seeking new jobs and with the contracts between the ex-American employees and new employers when they did find new jobs. The allegation that the non-competes were clearly unenforceable was crucial, because if there was any question about it the law said American had a privilege to interfere with the ex-employees' job hunts or new jobs.

The suit covered ex-employees in all states, even though the crucial question of whether or not the agreements were clearly unenforceable was settled against the agreements by statute in some states. The agreements all contained clauses that Illinois law governed them and that any law suit could be brought in Illinois. Tell that to one of your California serfs where there is a statute saying these agreements are unenforceable.

When an employer sues to enforce a non-compete it asks for an order that the ex-employee cannot work at a certain place. This is in distinction to most law suits where only money damages are given to a successful plaintiff. The specific relief comes in what is called an injunction or temporary restraining order. These enjoin or restrain the ex-employee or the new employer or both from doing something. There are three bites at the apple, in contrast to the single trial of most law suits. First, since the matter may be an emergency where the new employment may irreparably injure the old employer, the emergency relief of the temporary restraining order is available. The old employer may have spent weeks or months preparing for the suit, but the ex-employee is called on the phone one day and told to appear in court the next morning. Few can even find a lawyer that fast or come up with the money. Regardless of the outcome of the temporary restraining order hearing, the next step is a hearing on a preliminary injunction. This is a hearing where there is a little more time to prepare. Then there is the full blown trial to see if a permanent injunction will be issued.

In this case this procedure was reversed. The ex-employees and new employers had a prominent class action firm on a contingent fee basis and now the ex-employees were going to get three bites at the apple. And the first bite was coming quick. Emergency!

The client complaint was on behalf of American. It came from its General Counsel, Gloria Florentino. Gloria was a gorgeous blonde. She was very young for her job, but Wham appreciated her talents, not many of which were legal. She couldn't get ahold of St. Charles. She then called Camelman, which she had a habit of doing when she couldn't reach St. Charles. She complained to him about not being able to reach St. Charles and he brought the matter up to Cohenstein with a reminder that he should be credited with the business because he was the contact person these days. Cohenstein knew a problem when he saw one and he had called everyone involved to a meeting on the matter. Actually, he couldn't get St. Charles either, but when he told Lohman this, Lohman asked Tete to get in contact with him. Tete got St. Charles and told him to be there. He was.

The meeting was rather animated. Cohenstein said bluntly that there had been numerous instances where Ms. Florentino could not reach St. Charles. St. Charles responded that this was of no importance. He dealt with the owner, Wham. Camelman kept saying that the client was calling him and he was taking care of the client's matters so he should get more credit for procuring the business. St. Charles pointed out that the client was Wham and not Florentino and that Camelman was not keeping him informed of what was going on with the client.

Camelman said, "And what would you do about it anyway. You'd just turn it over to someone else to handle."

"Why certainly I would," said St. Charles. "To some junior like you. I handle the important matters, not the details. I have to be kept informed so I can inform Mr. Wham about what is going on. You should mind your tongue when talking to a superior."

"Has your psychiatrist gone nuts!" exclaimed Camelman. "I'm handling the client. I should get the bucks."

"Once again," said St. Charles, "the client is Wham. I am the Wham contact."

"Sam, Wham, whatever," said Cohenstein. "This is a matter for the Management Committee anyway and Winston, you have to realize that you're not on it. And Graybourne. We do have to pay more attention to the General Counsel. How could you not anyway. She's a looker."

"Why?" asked St. Charles. "She seems not to recognize my importance. Always after me for this or that, even though she well knows what other partners we have assigned to her matters. What does she think I am? An answering machine? I don't want to deal in stereotypes, but she is a blonde of vacuous inanity, if you know what I mean"

"What?" asked Camelman?

Cohenstein liked to adopt the new words and phrases he heard these days. "A dumbwad," he said.

"A what?" asked St. Charles.

Lohman chimed in. "He means she's not too bright."

"What do the lights have to do with it?" asked St. Charles.

"She's dumb. Of low intelligence," said Cohenstein.

"So?" said St. Charles.

Lohman was getting tired of this. He said something St. Charles could understand. "She has no social or professional standing to speak of and is of low origin."

St. Charles said, "Well, I know that. What else is new."

Cohenstein said, "so much for that. Graybourne, call her and talk to her and tell her who is assigned to the matter. I talked to Morton Wharton in litigation about it. He'll handle it. He knows it's coming. Tell her he will contact her and then tell him you called. He's waiting to hear that. He'll take it from there."

St. Charles didn't say anything. His facial motions showed he was coming to terms with the stress of the moment. The talk then turned to who each one was going to bill for the conference and how much and what they would say it was for. The others mostly knew what to put on their time sheets and the bill, but they knew Lohman had to be given specific orders or else he would chalk it up to firm management time.

Just then the intercom announced Mr. LaRue who at the same time popped his head through the door without waiting for permission. This was Bungus LaRue, the firm's governmental affairs partner. What this meant was that he was a lobbyist and a fixer. He was an ex-congressman and a lawyer who had been disbarred and then readmitted to practice again when the appropriate authorities had been adequately informed of the egregious mistake they had made.

"Any of you guys seen Needham?" he asked.

Those present just looked at him for a while. Needham was Needham Pompous, the Governor of Illinois. Why he would be trotting around the top floor of the firm, no one knew. And no one was going to ask. No one who had any sense ever asked what LaRue was up to. Lohman said, "He hasn't been in here."

"So what are you guys doing?" asked LaRue. Cohenstein explained that they were discussing a new client matter and he briefly described the suit to LaRue. "I can fix that," said LaRue. "Or maybe not. Who's the judge?"

"It's not that kind of thing," said Cohenstein. "Not now, anyway."

"Ok," said LaRue. "See you all later." He left as quickly as he came in.

"What was that all about?" asked St. Charles.

"Who can tell with Bungus," said Cohenstein.

"So what about that dead whore in your office?" Camelman asked St. Charles.

"What!" exclaimed St. Charles in disbelief.

Just then came another intercom ring and another head popping through the door. This time it was the Governor. "Any of you guys seen Bungus?" he asked.

"Why hello Governor," said St. Charles. How nice to see you. Make yourself at home. Can we get you anything? Lohman will tell my secretary."

"Nah," said the "Governor. I'm in a hurry. Where's Bungus?"

Cohenstein said, "He was just in here looking for you. He's probably still on the floor."

Before anyone could say anything The Rt. Hon. Pompous left through the door to the hall. As he did so, the door from the inner office burst open without any warning and a flustered looking woman shot in just as the intercom rang. She was a big busted red head in 8 inch heels. Everyone recognized her. She was Eleanor Pompous, the Governor's wife. She looked around and asked, "Have you seen my husband?" No one said anything. She then went on through the hall door and disappeared.

Just as she left, LaRue bust in again from the inner office. "Have you seen the Governor's wife?" he asked. "Eleanor. We got word she was coming. And then we got word another young lady is coming. A friend of the Governor, if you know what I mean."

St. Charles certainly did not. The others could guess.

"So why did you let her in?" asked Cohenstein.

LaRue answered, "She was already past reception when we heard about it. I don't know how she got past security in the lobby, but with her looks she could get in anywhere. If you see either one of them hold her and call and page me and I'll get the other two out of the building. Or, I'll just get Eleanor out. She doesn't know about the friend – I think. Anyway, let me know if you find either one of them."

"Eleanor just went through here before you came in," said Cohenstein. She went out there." He pointed to the hall door.

LaRue looked at it and said, "We gotta head this off or his ass is gonna be grass."

Cohenstein said, "Well, it's all relative. In Mexico a grassy ass is an indication that people are quite grateful." He added, "And in hillbilly land it means they are quite satisfied." He chuckled as LaRue turned pale and hurried out the door.

After a brief silence the conversation reverted to the other young "friend" they had been talking about. Camelman said, "So what are we going to do about the little whore?" He didn't really care, but he did want to needle St. Charles

"Oh, leave it!" said Cohenstein. "Let's get out of here and let Graybourne make his call." They all did so.

5 LOHMAN INQUIRES

Lohman got back to his office and talked to Tete. "Did you find out anything about U.S. Reo?" he asked.

"I talked to the General Counsel," said Tete.

"How did you manage that?" asked Lohman. He knew he shouldn't have asked as soon as the words were out of his mouth.

"Oh, I heard some things about him and his secretary. I talked to her and she put me right on to him. It sounded like he didn't have anything to do, but was horrendously busy doing it. He didn't know anything about the matter. Never heard of it. So I told him to find out and get back to me. He didn't even know who was handling things like that. I gave him a hint. I asked who handles litigation. He said a lot of people. I asked who heads the department. He said he would find out. I told him he should do so and quick. So he had a job to do and, well Hon – when the dodos have to move they look for outs. At that stage he asked who I was. I told him and I told him that Mr. Armour was complaining about him. Then he asked me who he was. So I had to tell him. Hon, I think you lawyers make all the legal problems on your own. You don't need the clients except to pay. This guy is probably going to be President some day."

"Of U.S. Reo?" asked Lohman.

"That or the country, Hon," said Tete. "He's qualified for either."

"Did you hear from anyone?" asked Lohman.

"Not yet," said Tete. "You know how these people are. I'll have to keep after them."

Lohman thought for a moment. He would have to get someone on the matter right away. "Well, get ahold of Morton," he said. Morton Wharton was the head of the litigation department. "Tell him we seem to have a big class action suit coming against The Bank and tell him to identify someone who can handle it. Get Morton to head it up himself if he's available. Tell him whoever it is needs to remain available so we can contact him or her as soon as we know what is going on. Did Armour get the complaints he has to you?"

"They're supposed to be in the process of being emailed. I'll have to follow on that too. They have to have someone to remind them to breath over there. I don't know how they manage sex," she said.

Lohman said, "Perhaps their bedroom alarm clocks go 'in, out', instead of 'tick, tick'."

"Yeah, Hon," said Tete, "And next you'll tell me that when the alarm goes off that's the signal for the - you know. But that won't work. Who's going to set the alarm for them?"

Lohman shrugged. "Well, for here and now, cancel my appointments today and tomorrow. We'll talk about rescheduling later." Lohman scheduled his own appointments.

"Right Hon," she said. "In the meantime I've been getting complaints from a few people up on 55. They're saying the cleaning service didn't empty the waste containers at the copy machines up there Monday night. One of the secretaries said someone put their dirty panties in there and a lot of dirty paper towels with dark stuff on them. Maybe they had an accident. Anyway, whatever that was, I checked. I asked some of the secretaries up there and the waste containers were emptied last night. You know, Hon, I've heard that the higher the status, the dirtier the underwear. Which makes sense since it is only the appearance that people can see that counts. Anyway, so goes it with our leading citizens on 55."

Lohman said, "I suppose it's a good thing I'm not up there."

"You're a big wig too, Hon," said Tete, "So don't go showing your undies around here."

Lohman and Tete often got into little snippets. He said, "And what about your panties?"

"You think I'm wearing any?" she responded.

Lohman sighed. He wasn't going any further with that.

Tete said, "Oh, and another thing. They were going over the building log in the business office. McDade called and said they didn't notice anything unusual Monday night. A lot of our own people checked in. Probably coming back from dinner. Levin was one. Camelman too. There weren't any later check-ins except one. Someone from a messenger service came in. They signed in to see Stonegold. You know, Steven Stonegold. The check in time was a little after 10."

"What messenger service?" asked Lohman.

"Not ours," said Tete. "Some outfit called Zoom Shot. The messenger printed her name as Wendy Laymen. And in case you want to know, I had them look for Charlie too. He didn't check in late on Monday, but he did check in twice Tuesday morning. The first time around 8 and then later just about when you had your meeting up there. Is he one of the early set?"

Lohman answered, "I don't think so. He spends a lot of time on evening entertaining. But we all have varied schedules. He had an early meeting at The Bank so maybe he had to get in early to prepare for it."

Tete scoffed. "Him? Prepare? Fat chance!"

Lohman said, "It's just a thought. Anyway get ahold of the cleaning service and ask them what was going on with the waste containers. And get the time records for Camelman, St. Charles, Stonegold and everyone on 55. And check the phone records for Monday night too." The lawyers billed for their time so they kept records of what they did and when. The firm also had a computer system that tracked where all calls, both in and out of the firm, came from and went, so far as possible. "And one more thing. Check with the night receptionist to see what she knows." After hours the firm had only one receptionist and that was on the 40th floor where everyone entered.

Lohman then went into his office to review his client matters and check what he had to do and when. One thing he did was to get Stonegold on the phone and make an appointment to see him Thursday morning.

Thursday morning they met in Stonegold's office. Most big shots had people come and see them. Lohman preferred to get out and around and to see people in their offices. This is just one more reason why no one considered him important. No one who considered themselves important that is.

They greeted each other. Then Lohman said, "I suppose you have heard what happened Tuesday with that body in Graybourne's office?"

"I heard," said Stonegold, "But it doesn't seem like anyone really knows what happened."

"Yeah," said Lohman. "We don't know how she got there. But she may have been a messenger. A messenger from a Zoom Shot messenger service was logged in around 10 Monday night. She logged in to see you. Her name was Wendy Laymen. What was she delivering?"

"I don't know," said Stonegold. "I hate to tell you this, but I was supposed to get a delivery. I think it was supposed to come by Zoom Shot. But I wasn't here. I was in Seattle. Lincoln asked me to get the delivery for him. Lincoln Beale, you know. But he was not going to be here. He got called away. So he asked me to get the delivery for him and to authorize her entry."

"What was it?" asked Lohman.

"I don't know," answered Stonegold. "He just said it was a certified copy of something. Something were we needed the original for the next day. It wasn't even for him. He said Wanzer needed it."

"Wanzer Levin?" asked Lohman.

"Yes," said Stonegold. "Wanzer needed it for a hearing on Tuesday. But then he got called away and he asked Lincoln to authorize the entry and get the document. They – well I told you already. He got called away too and passed the job on to me. It isn't easy to always find someone who will be in at that hour. Anyway, I had to go so I left a building pass at reception to let her in and I told the receptionist about it. I had my secretary do the pass."

"Why didn't Wanzer just do that in the first place?" asked Lohman.

"Lazy, I guess," said Stonegold. "Or he may not have known how he could do it. Who knows."

"Where did Lincoln and Wanzer have to go?" asked Lohman. "Do you know?"

"Don't know," said Stonegold.

"Where were you in Seattle?" asked Lohman.

Stonegold replied, "I was just out there for the day. I flew out and back. I didn't get home until around midnight. I was at one of our clients who supplies carpeting to Boeing for the planes. There was a contract problem and I had to see how the goods are made. Goodman Fabrics. I was there with their plant foreman."

"Who's that?" asked Lohman.

"Jerry Goodman," said Stonegold. "It's a family company."

Lohman took his leave and returned to his office, greeting people along the way. When he got back he told Tete to call Goodman Fabrics and talk to Jerry Goodman and check to see if Stonegold was there on Monday and when. She wrote down the information and then said, "I checked with the cleaning service about Monday night. They say they emptied the copier waste basket. The woman who is assigned there spoke to me. She says she usually empties them around six or seven. She says she emptied them again Tuesday night. She said there was a lot of paper – crumpled paper – on the top and she heard some hard things go in to her container. She didn't examine the contents though. They don't spend their time doing that. She said she just emptied the containers as usual and put new garbage bag liners in the containers. Same as Monday night. No one told her there was anything unusual about them."

She continued. "I looked up the Zoom Shot service in our records too. We don't have anything on them. We never paid them for anything. There are no payment records. And I had IT look in all our computer records for them. Nothing. And I checked phone records that night. Nothing unusual. The Saint got some incoming calls, but messages were left."

Lohman asked her to check out calls for Stonegold, Beale and Levin too and let him know what she found. He then went into his own office.

6 A LOOK AT THE ZOO

Tete had left some of the time and phone records on Lohman's desk. He started to go through them. He could only find three of the 55th floor lawyers who were billing after 8 p.m. Lohman started calling them. One said he was working at home. He said he was reviewing the briefs for a motion that was going to be heard the next day. Lohman could see that he had checked into the building early the next day. He picked up the phone and asked Tete to check with the other lawyers assigned to the case and see if anyone could corroborate his story. Lohman then called the other two lawyers. He could only get one and that one said he was working on a deal at another firm. Lohman asked who else was there and he mentioned the lawyer at the other firm and identified the associates they had with them and other people who were present. One was an accountant who Lohman knew and trusted. Lohman called the accountant and found him in. The accountant confirmed what the lawyer had said. Just to be sure, Lohman called Tete again and asked her to check with the associates who were supposedly there.

When Lohman had finished telling Tete to do this she said she had talked to the night receptionist about the lawyer who was working at home and she said she remembered him leaving the office around 7 p.m. Lohman then looked at the check-in records again and did not see him logged back in that night.

Lohman had noticed a lot of associates checking in after 6 p.m. Many associates worked late and they were probably coming back from dinner. Nevertheless Lohman asked Tete to have the firm's head investigator find out where they were later that night. She said a lot of them probably wouldn't even talk to him. Lohman said, "Well, convince them." He felt confident that they would talk or die.

The time records also showed Beale was in a conference. Lohman called him again and got him. However, he told Lohman he couldn't talk just then and they made an appointment to meet late Friday.

The records did not show anything else of note except the building log. This showed that Levin and Camelman checked in late on Monday. There were no billing records for Levin on Monday or for the whole month before that either. Nor were there any billing records for Camelman on that Monday night. There could have been other equity partners who did not already have their time in for that Monday too. Many of the firm's equity partners did not record their time as they put it in. They put it in the time sheets later when they had to be submitted to the business office for billing. The lesser lawyers could not get away with this because they had to get their time in at the end of each day and if they did not the business office contacted them. If they repeated the offense, their boss talked to them. And if they still did not comply, Lohman talked to them. Or worse, Tete did. On top of this, their time records, which were kept in the firm's computer system, were checked randomly throughout the day.

Equity partners, however, did not have to put up with this incursion on their freedom. Big Brother does not have some Super Big Brother watching him. They also liked to write fiction at the end of the month when they had to get their time in. This they could get off their ass to do, because the time records were necessary to create the bills and if the bills did not go out the firm did not get paid and if the firm did not get paid they did not get credit for the billings and soon they would not be such big deals anymore.

Lohman called Camelman, but he wasn't in. Then Lohman got Levin on the phone and told Levin he was coming up to see him. Levin allowed as how, even though he was extremely busy, he would set aside some time for Lohman. Levin did just that. He put aside his crossword puzzle just a little before Lohman arrived.

Levin was a big shot. He was, if you asked him, extremely important. He was 50 years old, one of the top billers, six foot two and 280 pounds. So, whatever he was, he was a big one.

Lohman came into his office. They greeted each other. "So Wanzy," said Lohman, "I suppose you can guess why I'm here."

"No," replied Levin. "I'm supposed to play guessing games?"

"I guess not," sighed Lohman. "It's about Monday night. I'm trying to find out who was where. I am told a messenger was going to deliver something to you then, but you couldn't be there so you had someone else let her in. Is that right?"

"Yes," said Levin. "It was a certified copy of a document I needed for a hearing on Tuesday. An affidavit it was. I couldn't be there, I thought, so I was talking to Lincoln and he said he was going to be there so I asked him to let her in."

"Yes," said Lohman. I talked to Lincoln. "But the building log says you checked in that evening."

"Wadda you doing?" asked Levin. "You're spying or something?"

Lohman looked at him for an instant. Then he said, "Sort of. The Management Committee has told me to find out what is going on here."

"So go find out. What I'm doing is none of their business," said Levin.

"Yeah," said Lohman. "We just run the place. So you can tell that to the police too when they get around to you."

"What!" That got to Levin. "Keep those creeps away from me. That's your job."

"So, if I can't, what are you going to tell them?" asked Lohman.

Levin thought. Then he said, "Well it's no big deal anyway. I was going to go to a show with my wife, but she had a cold so we didn't go. I went to dinner with Winston. Then I came in to pick up the document myself. I got it, checked it out, prepared it for Tuesday, and then I went home."

"Who was going to deliver the document," asked Lohman.

"How do I know," said Levin. "Probably some messenger service."

"Do you know which one?" asked Lohman.

"No," said Levin.

"Did you see the messenger?" asked Lohman.

"No," said Levin. "I don't deal with messengers."

"Why didn't you just tell the lobby to let her in and tell the receptionist she was coming?" asked Lohman.

"I told you," said Levin. He was irritated. "I don't deal with things like that. Beale said he could handle it. Christ!"

Lohman asked, "Who was the document coming from?"

"You are aware of the attorney-client privilege?" said Levin smugly.

"Yes," said Lohman. "And I am aware that it does not prevent attorneys within the same firm from talking about a matter. I am also aware that if you used the document in a hearing it is no longer covered by the privilege because we made it public."

Levin didn't like this kind of treatment. "It's confidential," he said. The Devil seldom wants anyone to know what he is up to.

Lohman said matter-of-factly, "I'll tell the Management Committee."

"Seladora Bruce," said Levin. She was the General Counsel of a large Levin client. "I needed it for a settlement conference I was going to have with the SEC."

"Thanks," said Lohman. He took his leave, this being the most pleasant part of the meeting.

Lohman had noticed another partner in the firm offices billing late on Monday night and he had made an appointment to see her next. She was on a lower floor and as he left Levin's office he headed for the elevators. He saw a little lump of black scurrying towards him at about 50 miles per hour. This was an instantly recognizable character within the firm, even though she was one of the newer associates. Tambola Cook was her name. Second in her class at Yale. Tops at looking up the law, crafting legal arguments and writing briefs and memos. And a little weird. She was five foot four and weighed about 180 pounds. She generally wore resale shop clothes and running shoes and was usually covered with a black cloak that almost reached the floor. She often wore a black conical hat which she usually forgot to remove indoors. She always walked on the left and had earned the nickname of Miss Leftwitch.

Today she was zooming at Lohman. She was on her left of the hall and was entirely engrossed in whatever was on her smart phone which she held in front of her. Lohman was aware of her ways and he moved to his left. No sooner did he do so than Tambola crossed over to her right and whammed into him. Her little conical hatted head almost put a hole in his belly.

She bumped off of him and looked up. "Oh, hello Mr. Lohman," he said.

Lohman didn't really know what to say and he realized that whatever he said probably wouldn't have registered on her. So he brushed it off. He said, "Well, if distracted driving is OK, so is distracted walking I guess."

Tambola gave him an odd look. Why not? He said such odd things sometimes. The she volunteered, "I'm going to see Mr. Levin. He sent for me."

"Well, I suppose he's waiting for you," said Lohman. "I just met with him." Then he stepped aside to let her pass and continued on his way.

The partner Lohman was going to see was Goola Woolaman. She was one of the partners who had been billing on Monday night and

Lohman knew she usually did her late night work at the office. She was also one of the people who were available to see Lohman that afternoon so he had arranged to meet with her. She was in the litigation department and the litigation people usually worked some of the longest hours. Lohman knew her fairly well and used her on some of his own client matters.

When he got to her office they greeted each other and asked about their respective families. Then Lohman said, "I'm here to talk about Monday night."

Goola said, "So who isn't talking about Monday night? But what do I know about what happened up there? I was tied up."

"What were you working on?" asked Lohman.

"The Suspender Railway of Chicago," she said. "That's the client."

"Who?" asked Lohman.

"See," said Goola. "They're a client of ours and you never heard of them. Even if people know anything about railroad matters they never heard of Suspender. It's one of the switching railroads. All the rail lines from the east and the west meet here in Chicago and the cars have to be switched from one railroad to another. And they are all going to separate trains too. So the switching railroads carry a lot of traffic here. If anyone has ever heard of them all they've heard of is the Belt Railway of Chicago. The Suspender used to be called the Chicago Terminal Transfer Road, but they thought they could get some publicity if they changed their name. Didn't work. No one ever heard of them."

She continued. "Their stuff. That's what I was doing. We had a hearing for them Tuesday morning and I was working on that. It is not the usual kind of matter we handle for them. Or for anyone else either. It isn't really a business matter. It's kind of legal malpractice. I don't know what to call it. There's this lawyer – Igor Stein. He's kind of big. 350 pounds. He was representing The Suspender in an accident case. They were insured so we weren't handling it. His insurance defense firm was."

In the distant past large law firms defended insured clients in accident matters covered by the insurance and that was a major part of the business. As time went on though, the insurance companies discovered that they could get other lawyers a lot cheaper for a job that did not usually require top legal talent and the insurance defense firm developed. Substantial and important business firms like F, P & C no longer handled such matters.

Goola continued. "So Stein was in court for a motion just before a trial was set to begin. The court was hearing some motions in other cases that morning before beginning the trial. The trial lawyers had already set up and were there waiting for the court to finish the motion call. Stein came in and, without looking, sat down in a chair where the trial plaintiff's lawyer had left his brief case. He squashed everything in it. Including the reading glasses. The plaintiff lost the trial and now they are suing Stein and the Suspender Railway for the loss. They claim it was caused by their lawyer being unable to read his notes and documents during the trial."

"So why isn't a defense firm handling this suit?" asked Lohman.

Goola answered, "There's an exclusion in the insurance policy dealing with legal matters. It's an odd thing in small print in a subordinate clause in the back. So we got the case. At our rates. It's a big money case. Louis Wavidson is the plaintiff's lawyer. You've perhaps heard of him. He's about the biggest in town. At least he gets most of the publicity."

"I've heard of him," said Lohman. "Sounds like a mess. Anyway, what do you know about Monday night? You were here. Did you hear or see anything? Anything you noticed when you left?"

"No," said Goola. "I left a little after eleven. I just left on 40. The receptionist didn't say anything. Just 'Good night'. Wait. There was an associate I was talking to about a memo he prepared on the case. He said he had been in with St. Charles on a deal that day. What was his name – Henry. Henry Dolin. That's it. Maybe he knows something. It was up there."

"See if you can get him," said Lohman. She could and Lohman told Dolin he would see him right away.

Lohman bid Goola goodbye and went off to see Dolin. Dolin was new and once he figured out that he was not in trouble he was very impressed by Lohman. The Managing Partner came to see him. Wow! Lohman put Dolin at ease and then asked what he had been doing with St. Charles. Dolin explained that he had been with the firm only a few months and had just heard of St. Charles the week before when one of the partners took him into a meeting with St. Charles where a big case was being discussed.

Dolin said, "I didn't know anything about the case. I just went in with my boss and they were talking about possible settlement of the case with the other side. I didn't know who Mr. St. Charles was. I didn't know who any of them were. They were all talking about some patent matter and royalties. From what he was saying, I thought Mr. St. Charles was on the other side. I didn't know who he was or what his name was until Monday when I was called up there and he gave me some instructions for something he wanted me to work on. I was kind of surprised. Boy he sure has some super negotiation strategies if he can make people think he is on the other side. I mean, he seemed so contrary and dumb. He had us all fooled.

"Did you hear anything about Monday night? Did anyone say anything about Monday night? Did Mr. St. Charles?" Lohman asked.

"No," said Dolin. "You mean about the whore upstairs?"

"Who told you there was a whore upstairs?" asked Lohman.

Dolin replied, "That's what everyone is saying. That Mr. St. Charles had a whore in his office. A dead one. Did he?"

Lohman realized that the rumor mill was off and running. "Well, I think the rumors are getting out of hand," he said. "There was a dead young lady in his office, but he appears to have nothing to do with it. And there is nothing to indicate that she was a whore, as you put it. She probably was working for a messenger service. If you hear anything more, let me know will you."

Lohman then left and went back to his office.

A large law firm is often called a law factory. By this time, dear reader, you can see that it could just as well be called a zoo. A special kind of zoo for the mentally afflicted denizens. A psycho-zoo.

7 THE GUN

Friday morning Lohman was in his office reading a legal memorandum prepared by one of the associates. Tete rang him and said she was coming in. She did. "Get this, Hon. They found the gun."

"What gun?" asked Lohman.

"The gun that killed the Saint's little playmate," said Tete.

Lohman asked, "She was killed with a gun?"

"Well, I'll bet she was and that this is it," said Tete. "You know where they found it?"

"No," said Lohman.

"In his cat box," she said. "The box is cleaned every night by the cleaning crew, but it isn't until Thursday night that they change the whole thing. They did it last night and found the gun. I just heard. It's a little gun and they say it looks like it has a silencer on it."

"Who says?" asked Lohman.

The head of the cleaning crew. She's here during the day. She says the cleaning person assigned to the Saint's office called her today and told her about it. She said the cleaning lady left the whole thing there in his office. She just dropped the whole thing where it was when she saw the gun. It's sitting on the floor in his office. Then he calls and starts complaining to me about it. I told him not to touch anything and wait till he hears from you. He said, 'Where will my Pussy go?' To Hell I hope. You think he did it?"

Lohman didn't know and said so. "Get the police and tell them about this."

Tete said, "The cleaning crew also found some fingerprints in the 55th floor men's room. On the wall. She told me they look like finger prints made with blood. They're on some of the wall tiles."

Lohman said, "I'll go up there. And get me somebody who can watch the place until the cops come. See if Wiggy can do it. Anybody. Get some of the associates if you have to." Then he took off for the 55th floor.

Wiggy was Wiggy Rodriguez, head investigator for the firm. Wiggy was not his real name, but described his obvious wig of which he was supremely proud.

Lohman got up to 55 and went into St. Charles' office. "Good morning Graybourne," he said.

"Not to me," said St. Charles. "Look at this mess they've made. Where will Pussy go?"

Lohman asked, "Did you touch anything? Whatever this is, the police will probably want to see just how it was found and take fingerprints."

"Of course I did not touch anything!" exclaimed St. Charles. "Who do you think I am?"

By this St. Charles did not mean to suggest that Lohman might consider him a murderer or someone who might tamper with evidence. He meant that no one in their right mind could possibly think he would stoop to manual labor, much less stoop to clean up the kitty poo.

Lohman looked at the litter box. It still had a little of the granular material in it with some lumps which he took to be the litter. The gun was lying on the bottom of the box in plain sight. It was a shiny silver automatic pistol and it appeared to have a silencer on it. The handle looked very fancy and had what appeared to be distinctively colored plastic sides. Lohman knew St. Charles well enough to suspect that what he took at first glance to be plastic was more probably pearl. He looked at St. Charles. "Did you ever see this before?" he asked.

"It looks like mine," said St. Charles. "I used to have such a weapon and it had a silencer. I kept it over there." He motioned to a cabinet with a series of drawers in it. "It was in the top drawer. It's not there now. It's been gone for some time."

Lohman asked, "Why did you keep a gun in the office? How long has it been gone?"

"Oh," said St. Charles, "I looked for it last week. It was gone then. I thought I misplaced it. In any event, I got it because I was robbed once. Some infernal hooligan robbed me as I was going over to the Pullman Club for lunch. It was in bad weather so I had my chauffeur drive me and it happened just after I got out of the car. Fortunately he was carrying my coat and my wallet was in there when it happened. It was extremely demeaning and I vowed that it should never happen again."

Lohman looked at him for a while without speaking. He wanted to ask if St. Charles knew how to use it or if he ever had used it, but he knew better. He would ask, St. Charles would say he did know how, even though he didn't and he would be annoyed with Lohman for having asked. Why ask questions when you already know the answer.

St. Charles took the pause to indicate that Lohman was thinking something else. "Don't be surprised. Lots of the partners have guns here. I know. We have talked about them.

"With silencers?" asked Lohman. He couldn't help it.

"Of course," said St. Charles. "Actually the silencer was the idea of the dealer. I told him I didn't want a noisy gun. Nothing obtrusive. He was the one who suggested the silencer."

"I see," said Lohman. "Where did you get it? It looks sort of unique."

"From Jon Won," said St. Charles. "He sold it to me."

Lohman said, "I don't know anything about gun dealers. Is he downtown? Are there any gun dealers downtown?"

"I don't know if there are any dealers downtown," said St. Charles. "He was a caddy at Olgosia. I was telling him about the attack on me one day while I was at golf and he suggested it. Quite a few of us at the club bought guns from him. Very convenient, don't you know. And we did not have to register them."

Lohman had thought all guns had to be registered. "How did you manage to avoid registration?" he asked.

St. Charles waived a hand at Lohman. "I don't bother with that kind of thing. He knows about these things. He's a dealer."

Lohman's silence was taken by St. Charles to mean Lohman accepted this.

Lohman asked, "How long ago was this?"

"Not long," said St. Charles. "I got the gun last summer. I can't remember exactly when."

Lohman said, "Maybe your checking account records would tell us when."

St. Charles straightened up at that. "My financial records are confidential," he said. "Besides, I paid him in cash. He told me that all gun dealers operate that way."

"Did you get a receipt?" asked Lohman.

"I don't bother with things like that," sniffed St. Charles.

"Where is he now, he's still a caddy there?" asked Lohman.

St. Charles said, "Oh, he left a few months ago. I don't keep track of people like that. You know Bumper, you really have to clear this up. The whole thing is very inconvenient. And think of the effect on my Pussy with these horrors going on in her presence." Then he picked up his cat and fondled her. "Oh, if only my Pussy could talk!" Then he put Pussy back on her pedestal and said, "Now, if you will excuse me, I have to go over and see Swifty."

As they were turning to leave the office Lohman said, "I'll just ask your secretary some things about these events if you don't mind."

"If you must," said St. Charles in a pained manner. He proceeded out of his office and past his secretary into the hall and headed for the elevators.

Lohman stopped by the secretary's desk. She was a well-mannered, even-tempered lady in her mid- fifties. Her name was Catherine McKeigan. She had been St. Charles' secretary for years. "Catherine," said Lohman. "I want to ask you some things if you don't mind."

"Of course, Mr. Lohman," she said.

"Catherine," asked Lohman, "you're aware of the gun in the cat box, are you?"

"Certainly,' she said.

"Did you see it?" he asked.

She said she had. Then Lohman asked, "Did you know he had a gun?"

"Oh, yes," she said. "He showed it to me when he got it. And he told me where to find it in case that would be necessary. There were a few people in his office and I was coming in with some papers when he was telling everyone about it and he asked me to listen too. He was showing us the gun and showing us the drawer where he kept it. He was talking about the need to protect himself and he told us about the time he was robbed over by the Pullman Club."

"Who else was there?" asked Lohman.

Catherine thought. "Let me see.   Mr. Stonegold. Then, Mr. Camelman. And Mr. Beale, Mr. Levin and some associates. Now let me see – Mr. LaRue, Mr. MacLeish and Mr. Nath. And the associates. Let me think. This was just a little while ago. They were all there in the conference room to start with and then he evidently took them into his office. The red dress – yes, Portilla Bush. Then Adronica Velez. She goes to my church. Then that Grant Germaine. He is up here lot. He's quite tall. And then that nice Sean Featherbottom. That's it. Those were the people."

As they were talking Zenon Cohenstein had walked in. He listened to them a while and then asked where St. Charles was. Catherine said she thought he went to see Mr. Swifton and Cohenstein said he would call over there after a while. Then he said, "So what is all this about the gun? He showed it to me once. Camelman was there too. He showed us both."

Lohman said, "Apparently the same gun has been found in his cat box. They clean it every day, but they do not change the whole contents. They do that weekly on Thursday night and in doing so the cleaning lady found it in the box. Sounds like his. He says he lost it a while ago."

Cohenstein just looked at Lohman for a while. Then he said, "So we'll see if our little lady was shot and if she was shot with his gun. Great. Well, at least we'll get a lot of publicity. Maybe we can say the cat did it." Cohenstein thought for a moment. Then he said, "I can see the tabloid headlines now. 'Pussy kills whore!' Whadda ya think?"

Lohman headed back to his own office suite. As he entered Tete told him that McDade had followed up on the phone calls on

Monday night. The firm computer had no records of any calls to or from Stonegold, Beale, Levin or St. Charles after five. There were no records of calls to or from them with outside persons and no inter-firm calls involving them. Of course, the firm's system did not record cell phone calls so they couldn't be sure that there were no calls at all involving these people.

As Tete finished telling this to Lohman, she added that the police had already arrived and had been up on 55 for a while. She said that Bongwad and Gilbert were on the way down to see him. "Or Wilbert," she added.

Lohman moved towards his private office, but just then Sargent Gilbert came in. Or was it Wilbert? His mother probably couldn't remember so, dear reader, why should I?

He was followed closely by Bongwad. There were some chairs and a couch in the outer office with Tete and Bongwad pointed to one of the chairs and said, "May I," as he sat down. Gilbert remained standing rather stiffly. Lohman greeted them and asked if they wanted to come in to his office, but Bongwad said, "No thanks. This is fine here. And we can talk to both of you at once."

Lohman asked, "Did you go upstairs? Did you see the gun and the cat box?"

"Yes," said Bongwad. "We have secured the place and some officers are up there with the evidence techs. What do you two know about this?"

Tete and Lohman told them what they had heard and what they had seen about the gun, the cat box, the fingerprints on the 55th floor men's room wall and the copier waste baskets. Lohman also told them what he knew about who was on 55 Monday night and about the delivery to Levin.

"We'll check it out," said Bongwad. "Here's what we found so far. She was shot in the head. It was a small caliber weapon and the bullet didn't go all the way through, but it killed her. She was shot from the side. Right above the left ear. There is residue there that indicates the gun was right up against her head. The gun we saw upstairs is the type that would produce these effects. We'll see what the techs have to say, but I'll bet we have the murder weapon there. And we'll have to check out Mr. St. Charles and his story that his gun went missing."

Bongwad continued. "She was killed around midnight. The time of death was probably between 10 and 4 in the morning. We found some interesting fingerprints in Mr. St. Charles' private washroom too. Not only that, but one was in the same type of blood as the victim's. Guess who it belonged to?"

"I don't want to know, do I?" asked Lohman.

"Well, I don't know," said Bongwad. "Anyway, we already have prints on file from a lot of the people in the firm because of the prior murders here. Guess who it was?"

"Who?" asked Lohman. "It couldn't have been the dead woman, could it?"

"Nah," said Bongwad. "It's Mr. St. Charles. Of course more blood work has to be done. We don't know his blood type. It could be the same. Then there are some other tests that are being done. They can test blood for more things than the type you know."

Tete looked at Lohman with an "I told you so" look.

Bongwad then said, "We found other prints in his washroom too. There are a lot of his that are not in blood. There are some we can't identify. One set that we could identify belonged to that kid we thought killed that old guy in the wheel chair last year. What's his name?"

"O'Brien," Lohman volunteered.

"Nah. The kid. What's his name? You know that little blond kid."

Gilbert held out his arm and flapped his wrist. "That kid, Sir," he said.

"Sean Featherbottom," said Lohman.

"Yeah," said Bongwad. "His prints were there. We're going to have to get prints from a lot of other people too, not that that will necessarily clear anything up. A lot of the prints you get in these situations aren't good enough to do anything with or are just partial sets of prints that can't definitely be tied down to anyone."

Lohman asked if they knew who the victim was. Bongwad said they weren't sure and were working on it. He said, "That messenger service you mention. Zoom Shot. I think I've heard about them before. I think I heard rumors they are running around like a transport service for illegal stuff. Like maybe drugs. We'll check them out."

8 FURTHER INQUIRIES

Late Friday afternoon Lohman met with Lincoln Beale. Levin had asked Beale to receive the delivery for him, but Beale had passed the task on to Stonegold who just left a building pass to let the messenger in. Lohman wanted to find out what Beale knew about the matter and, in particular, where he was on Monday night. He was billing then. Lohman asked Beale about these matters and Beale told Lohman that he, Beale, had been in New York at a dinner meeting with lawyers for a company that was in default in paying back a loan it had received from The Bank. It was a large company and a large loan. As usual with large loans, The Bank had sold off parts of the loan to other banks. However, the Bank remained responsible for administering the loan for all of them. Beale was representing The Bank and trying to negotiate some sort of arrangement for payment with the borrower's lawyers. He gave Lohman the names of the lawyers he met with, the F, P & C lawyers he took out there with him and the places they were at and other details.

After they parted Lohman called McDade, the business manager, to see if he was in. Then he went to McDade's office and told him what he had learned from Beale and asked him to check it out by looking at the other lawyers' billing and expense records and asking them to confirm what Levin had said.

As they were finishing up McDade said, "Lincoln may have been in New York, but when he's around here he's a pain in the butt. He's always complaining about things. He seems to have a fetish about neatness. He is always saying something hasn't been cleaned in his office or on his floor or that someone moved something from its proper place. And if there is anything in his waste basket he wants it cleaned right away. Someday the cleaning people are going to tell him the way to see that his waste basket is always clean and empty is to take anything he sees in it and shove it up his ass. Of course that might be full too so maybe that wouldn't work."

McDade continued. "And Monday night. I heard the little whore had a waste basket bag over her head. Guess what. Beale called me and started complaining about the cleaning service again. He said there was no liner in his waste basket on Tuesday. So do you think that's where the bag came from? Does he know about the bag over her head? Did he put it there? Is he complaining to try to hide his involvement?"

"Lord knows," said Lohman. "Why do you call her a little whore?"

"I know I shouldn't spread it around. I'm sorry. It's just that 'little whore' is the term everyone is using. Haven't you heard everyone talking that way?"

"I've heard it from a few. But I didn't know it was all over. I guess I'll have to get Tete to tell the rumor mill to tone it down. And you might put out a firm directive to everyone to watch how they talk about this matter and to whom because, as they say in England, everything you say will, not may, be used against you. And as I tell my clients – if at all possible. Make sure you do not phrase it as a directive to cover things up. Just frame it as reminding them about PR matters and not coming to conclusions when they do not know the facts."

"Sure," said McDade unenthusiastically. "Anyway, I wouldn't think Lincoln was the type. Who knew."

"And who does know now," said Lohman. "That's my point. And come to think of it, who is the type around here? You can never tell. I am constantly being surprised about what my trusted partners and associates are up to. And you, Geeley. What are you up to behind the scenes?" Lohman waived a scolding finger at him.

"Don't worry," said McDade. "I'm not up to what I'd like to be up to. The only thing that'll ever save me form Hell is that I seem to lack the ability to commit the sins I lust after."

Lohman scolded him again. "There are those who commune with God frequently who proclaim that sin is in the head. You sound to me like you are doomed." They both smiled.

Saturday morning Lohman was in the office as he usually was. He was trying to get in touch with more of the people whose time records showed they were billing on Monday night. He had had Tete call most of them to see if they were working in the firm offices or elsewhere and he had a list of people who were billing in the office. He was calling the partners on the list and he actually got in touch with most. As opposed to the associates, there weren't that many of them.

Talking to high powered lawyers can be a pain in the ass. At least that is what Lohman usually felt. He did it because it was his job. Of course some of the people in the firm were his friends and some were great people who were pleasant to talk too. Most, however, were people he did not know too well. After all, there were so many people in the firm that he could hardly know them all well. At any rate, his inquiries revealed noting of importance. Some talked about what great and clever leading edge, sophisticated things they were doing. One went on forever about an annuity contract he had created. One hundred fifty pages long and with no actual promise to pay in it. Who would notice? Who would even read it through? Naturally his client was the insurance company that was supposed to pay. Others talked about how great they were too. Some, since they had Lohman on the phone, asked him to solve the problems they were supposedly hired at great expense to solve. They were charging clients all get out because of their expertise which apparently was in asking other people about the matter.

9 WHAT THE COPS FOUND

After talking to as many lawyers as he could stomach, Lohman was reviewing a client's file when he got a call from the receptionist that the police were down in the lobby and wanted to come up to see him. He asked her to see that they got in. He went down to 40 to meet them when they came in, which they soon did. They exchanged greetings and Lohman asked them to come up to his office. They took the firm elevator up to 44 and went into Lohman's private office. Bongwad seated himself, but Gilbert remained standing, half at attention.

After some small talk Bongwad said, "We know more now. We don't know who did it, but we know more. We id'd her. She has a record. Prostitution and drugs. She was 18. Wendy Laymen must have been a new name. We have her under Sally Strokenutz and one arrest under Ivanna Rubbadem. Nothing under Laymen. As I told you before, she was shot. There was a garbage bag over her head. It was stuffed with bathroom tissue and towels. Probably to absorb the blood. And it had clothing articles in it. Probably for the same reason. Clothing articles. They all seemed to be like things from a sex store. There was one pair of little lace panties that was rolled up and with a corner of the fabric stuck in the hole in her head. Or partially. Naturally it couldn't fit. We don't know where the garbage bag came from. The waste basket in the office had a bag in it."

Bongwad continued. "None of the clothes we found were anything she could wear in the street. So we are still looking for the clothes she came in with. Then she had those, well — those boots - they were -."

Gilbert chimed in, "Sexy sir."

"Yeah," said Bongwad. "Well, she seems to have been working, if you know what I mean?"

Lohman's head rose up a little and his eyes moved around a bit.

"Yes, here in your firm," said Bongwad. "Sometimes big shots do it in the office. Anyway, we'll find out. And we did find out already who that blood print in the 55th floor men's room belongs to. Mr. Stonegold. It's his. And it's the same blood type as the victim's. There were also some prints in her blood in Mr. St. Charles' washroom. They were partially wiped out, but we could identify them. We have his prints on file from last time. You know, when that O'Brien guy was killed here. And then there are Featherbottom's prints and a few others that aren't in blood. We haven't tracked down the others yet, except for the cleaning lady. So it seems more than one person is implicated by fingerprints, even though we haven't got around to checking out everyone yet."

"We haven't found any other prints we can identify yet," said Bongwad. "Sometimes that tells us something though. That drawer where the gun was kept was wiped clean of prints for instance."

Lohman said, "This is a mess. Maybe for you it's standard stuff, but for us it's a mess."

"You seem to have one a year, Sir," said Gilbert.

Lohman did not reply.

"We checked out Zoom Shot a little bit too," said Bongwad. We couldn't find much, but we got their phone. It's just an answering service in India. They say they don't know anything. They just take orders they say. For what, they won't say. For who, they won't say. We'll try to follow up with our Indian police contacts, but from my experience we don't usually get much out of them. Anyway, a legit messenger service usually doesn't operate that way."

Gilbert then added, "Tell him about the jewelry."

"Oh, yeah," said Bongwad. "There was a purple thing in her boots. I think it's called a brooch. It's round and has shiny stones or glass set in it. They are all set in a metal backing. And in the same boot there was a slip of paper with a U and P on it. They appear to be a user name and a password for a web site, but we haven't found out for what site."

Bongwad paused and Lohman thought out loud, "I suppose we are stuck with the sex angle," he said, followed by, "Ah – crap!"

Bongwad and Gilbert exchanged glances. It was not any big deal to them.

Then Bongwad said, "It does look like we have a sex angle, but who knows. You can't assume things."

"Sure," said Lohman. "She could have been coming here to see her lawyer."

Gilbert said in disbelief, "Sir! You have clients like that?"

Lohman thought to himself that many of the firm's clients were called whores, but not like this. Then the thought came to him that many more of the firm's lawyers were called whores.

"Look at this," said Bongwad. "Here's the stuff that looks like a user name and password. Can we check it out with your computers?"

"Of course," said Lohman, "but we'll have to do it because of the attorney – client privilege.

"I know," said Bongwad. Then he showed Lohman a sheet of paper with a business card copied on it. It said only -

U: PuSsY-4U.XTc

P: SuKYou2Man.

Lohman's whole face squeezed a little tighter.

Bongwad said, "So what we want to know is what happened to her clothes. If you find out anything, let us know."

"Of course Detective Bongwad," said Lohman. "Is there anything else?"

"No, no," said Bongwad. "We'll be looking for the clothes too." Bongwad then asked where he could find McDade and Levin. Lohman told him and then he turned to Gilbert and said, "Let's go."

The officers left and Lohman went to see Henner Pigman who was the manager of the firm's IT workers. They handled all the computer and software problems. He explained what the police had found out and what they wanted. Then he gave the paper with the U and P on it to Pigman.

Pigman laughed. Then he said, "No site. We have to know the site. But sometimes computers save passwords. We'll see."

"While you're at it," said Lohman, "Check out everything you can about Stonegold, Camelman, Levin, Beale and an associate named Sean Featherbottom." Pigman asked Lohman to repeat the list while he entered the names in a laptop. Lohman wondered if he could write. Lohman added, "And Mr. St. Charles too."

"He'll can me," said Pigman.

"We won't tell him," said Lohman. "Anyway, see what you can find. Computers, phone records, time records, file information, at the least the parts on our system. Check it for, say, a week before and after that Monday."

After this Lohman left and went back to his office.

10 SEX FOR SALE

Lohman was set for a conference with John Sweeney. Sweeney was Trisha DeLang's lawyer, but the firm insisted that a partner be responsible for all matters and Lohman was the responsible partner for DeLang matters. One was pending that Sweeney and Featherbottom had been working on and they were going to come in soon to discuss it. Trisha wanted Sweeney as her lawyer. He had the business getting magic in the show business, media and arts areas and he had the magic with her. So the firm set up Sweeney as the lead lawyer on her account, and others too, even though he was an associate. Featherbottom was an even more junior associate, but he was good and Sweeney wanted Sean working with him. A lot of work in large firms was done this way. In effect there was a salesman on the account who did the talking and show parts and then there were other lawyers who did the production work. This very often meant that some fool big shot partner would promise the impossible to the client or potential client in order to get the business and the backup lawyers actually delivered the impossible. Who do you think got the credit?

Sweeney was not the incompetent who promised the impossible. He was good too. He knew what he was doing and he knew how to do it and he knew what was possible and what was not. And he knew how to say, "I'll have to check that out Dude," in a way that engendered confidence in the client instead of a feeling that Sweeney was not an expert. Usually this approach did not sell to big shots who believed that everyone knew everything in their fields like they did. However, it did sell to people who knew what they were doing and how they did it. They knew that every new task involved looking in to things. And it did sell in show business where a lot of the clients had no idea what the lawyers were talking about anyway and just went by whether or not they liked the lawyers.

The firm did not ordinarily allow associates to operate on their own so Lohman was the supervisor for Sweeney on the DeLang matters. And when they had to deal with someone who wanted a big shot partner to deal with he fulfilled that role.

This time Sweeney and Sean, besides reporting on what they were doing on the matter, were asking Lohman what to do. After discussing the matter, Sweeney said, "Bumpy Dude, you gotta tell us what's happening with the interesting events last Monday"

Sweeney was a Hey Duder and often a nicknamer to the named person's face. Lohman was used to it. Actually, he never minded it, although at first he was not used to it. It is not the type of talk one encountered at the refined, dignified and sedate F, P & C. Or is that sedated?

"What do you mean by the 'interesting events'?" asked Lohman.

"You didn't see the email from McDade, Man?" said Sweeney. "He says we have to watch what we say about the little dead whore."

"Well, you're not watching it," said Lohman dryly.

"Oh Man!" said Sweeney. "I did. I didn't say little dead whore. I said 'interesting events' and you didn't know what I was talking about. Anyway I was trying."

Lohman did not want to pursue this any further. Actually it did seem like they had a dead little whore on their hands and dealing with reality is preferable in the long run to living in a fantasy world.

"So what happened, Dude? Did something happen while our exalted leader was getting his nuts off?"

Lohman squeezed his eye a little. Or rather they did it themselves. He was thinking how he would explain this kind of talk to the Management Committee. Many of the other lawyers talked in similarly disrespectful terms about the head of the firm, but they were equity partners or they were talking only to others with the same opinion. Then it occurred to Lohman how he always dealt with any questions about Sweeney. He reminded the complainers about how much money Sweeney was bringing in. And he remembered that there were often no complainers because most of the older lawyers did not know what Sweeney was talking about half the time.

Lohman told Sweeney and Sean what he knew. Why not? They might know something.

As soon as Lohman came to the name of the messenger service Sweeney interrupted with, "Dude! Oh shit man! You mean it? They – you know what they do? Dope and sex. That's what they deliver. A lot of my people use them. I even give their name to prospects I'm working on."

Lohman looked at him for a moment. Then he said, "You never cease to surprise me. Are you using them?"

"No Man," said Sweeney. "You know by now that a lot of my crowd does dope and sex and a lot of weird new combinations of both. I don't sell that stuff. I don't supply it. But I let them know how to get it. And I keep up with how people can get it. It gets clients Man."

"Have you ever dealt with Zoom Shot directly," asked Lohman.

"No Dude," said Sweeney. "I deal direct with the dames. And I don't need to pay. And I don't do dope. Maybe I ought to. Do you know how difficult it is to deal with someone who's high? And boring Man! All I can say is sooner or later you can leave and they don't' even know you're gone."

"I've seen Zoom Shot messengers," Sean volunteered.

"Dude!" said Sweeney. "What were you doing with Zoom Shot? I know they have guys too, but is that what you are doing?"

"No," said Sean. "But I have seen some. They're cute."

"Where?" asked Sweeney.

"Around," said Sean.

"Where around?" demanded Sweeney.

Sean pursed his lips to one side a little and looked that way and wiggled around in his chair a little. Then he looked at Lohman. Then back at Sweeney and he said, "Well, I've had them pointed out to me. At bars and once at a party. Two of then showed up as we were leaving."

"Whose party was that?" asked Lohman.

"It was a party some of Mr. Goren's clients were having," said Sean.

"Figures," said Sweeney. Mr. Goren was Winter Goren a partner who was known as the Firm Fruit. He was an old timer from the days when such terms were used and when being such was not acceptable. He was a wrist flapper and a lisper. He was a cream color suit and lavender tie wearer and even someone in deep denial of the presence of gay men in 1960 would have thought he was possibly a homosexual. Except of course St. Charles, who thought he was artistic. One thing stood out about Goren at F, P & C. He brought in a lot of business. So, whatever sort of degenerate he may have been, he was OK.

Sean continued. "And at the party I remember one of the guys there put his hand on my – you know. Well, the back side—"

"Your butt, Dude," Sweeney added.

Sean just gave him a glance. "He said, 'So you're a Zoom Shot boy are you?' I didn't know what he was talking about. I didn't even know what was going on there. Mr. Goren just happened to invite me when he saw me in the hall earlier that day. He said it would be clients. I don't know why he was pawing me that way."

Lohman was from the old days. His language was from the old days. "You know who Winter's clients are. He was pawing you because you're queer – or homo – gay, that's it. I forgot for a moment."

Sweeney jumped in. "Hey Dude, that's like saying 'nigger' in the White House."

Lohman couldn't help himself. "So this is the Palace and he's the Queen?"

Sweeney exclaimed, "Hey Man, you blew a funny!"

Sean just pursed his lips and moved them and his nose from side to side as he looked from one to the other.

Lohman went on. "Just think of all the changes I have had to make to keep up with what is the correct thing to say. Then think of when you get to be my age and you have experienced an ever greater rate of change in the PC language. Just think of how out of it you'll be." Then he added, "So like, Yeh."

Lohman then said, "The messenger was there to deliver a document. Mr. Levin needed it for something the next day."

Sweeney said, "I never heard of them delivering anything except dope, but I suppose they could do documents."

"What do you two know about it?" asked Lohman.

"Nothing by me," said Sweeney. "Sean and I were both here that night. We were working on the same thing. We went out to dinner together and came back in around 9. I remember we were talking – when we were in the lobby and coming up the elevator – about this femmy brooch Sean had pinned to his bag. Sooo queer Man!"

"Why do you always keep saying I'm gay?" asked Sean. "I don't go around saying you're straight all the time."

"I didn't say gay," said Sweeney. "I said femmy."

"Well, same thing," said Sean.

"Ok, so queer Dude. All right?" said Sweeney. "Anyway it looked nice. Remember I told you?"

Sean said, "It did, didn't it. Have you seen my new one?" Sean held up his bag so Sweeney and Lohman could see the brooch pinned on it. "It's by one of the best known costume jewelry designers there was. Gloria DiTurbo. She worked in Boston for Filene's. Her jewelry is in high demand amongst those in the know. See how pretty it is. See the little amber colored glass pieces here. See how well they fit in the bronze colored backing."

He started to go on about DiTurbo and her history and where her pieces could be found until he realized that his audience was not really interested.

"So what happened to the purple one you had last Monday?" asked Sweeney.

"I'd like to know," said Sean.

"Purple?" asked Lohman. "You had a purple brooch?"

"Yes," said Sean. Did you see it? Did you find it? I wasn't by anybody special, but it was pretty."

Lohman said, "A purple brooch was found in the one of the messenger's boots. And I hate to tell you this, but one of your fingerprints was found in Mr. St. Charles' washroom."

Sean didn't say anything. He started turning red in the face and looking form side to side and wiggling in his chair. Finally he said, "Well, I've used it. Mr. St. Charles said I could when he had me up in his office to ask me about something and I had to go."

"When?" asked Lohman. "Was that on Monday?"

"No. It was before that," said Sean. "I could look it up in my time records."

"Do that and let me know," said Lohman. He knew that associates had to enter their time records in the computer as they went along and that the computer could tell when they were entered and when they were altered, if that was done. "What did you do after coming back in on Monday?"

"I went back to my office," said Sean.

"Me too Dude," added Sweeney.

"But I did go up to 55 later," said Sean. "I had to deliver something up there. Mr. Levin wanted a memo on a contract matter and I put it on his desk. He wanted it as soon as I could get it to him. He wasn't there. This was just before I went home. When I was leaving his office I saw the messenger in the hall. Or at least I assume it was her. She looked odd. Gorgeous in messenger clothes." Then Sean went on about how her hair and nails were done.

Lohman stopped him. "Then what happened?"

"Oh, yes," said Sean. "She asked me where Mr. Levin was. I pointed out his office to her and went on to the elevators. She had this big wheeled bag with her. The same thing you see people going to the airport with. I assumed it had things for Mr. Levin in it."

"What do you know about all this?" Lohman asked Sweeney.

Sweeney looked at Sean and then back at Lohman. "Not much. I didn't know he was up there. Me, I just finished in my office and went home about nine." Then he turned to Sean and said, "Shit

Dude, you're always offing someone around here. I gotta give you credit though. You always get rid of the right ones."

Sean was speechless, unless you could understand pursed lips moving from side to side and chair squirming.

Lohman added, "John, you know darn well he didn't do those other things. Probably not this one either."

The meeting then broke up. Lohman reviewed his matters and decided he could leave everything till later and went home.

Lohman lived in a street called Dearborn. Swifton Plaza was also on Dearborn. Lohman's house was about 2 miles straight north and he often walked home. This Saturday he had the time and the weather was nice for January so he decided to walk. When he walked home he often went circuitous routes so he could see the sights. He decided to do that. He decided to go up the North Branch of the Chicago River. He often did this in the summer, but he had never done it in the winter and he was curious to see how it looked. Instead of going straight north he headed one block west to a street called Clark and headed north. He went a few blocks north and headed between the old court house on his left and the new one on his right. Then he arrived at a cross street called Randolph and headed to the northwest corner where the whole block was filled with the State of Illinois Building. This was a mid-rise building sheathed in shinny glass with muddy blue and muddy salmon colored panels. The building had been designed by a famous architect and he had called for panels of a better color, but supposedly they cost too much so the grand poobahs who were in charge of the project cut costs by changing to the muddy colors. After all, most of the money had already been allocated to the proper contractors who all had to recover the costs of the kickbacks they gave the politicians to get their contracts.

This corner of the building was rounded so there was a little plaza in front of the entrance. This had a sculpture by a famous modern artist in it done in white with black outlines. Lohman headed past it and went in to the building. The major part of the building was taken up by a central atrium which went all the way up to the roof. The building was a monument to the Illinois politician. What are the working parts in other buildings were entirely empty. Just as were the politician's heads. Actually, the building should have been sheathed in blonde colored glass. Anyway, the parts around the edges, like pockets where the wallets were, were all filled in with offices.

Lohman entered and walked through the building. This way he could walk diagonally through the block and go one block north and one block west at the same time. He came out of the building just under the elevated tracks surrounding Chicago's central area. This was on Lake Street, one block north of Randolph, and just a little east of LaSalle, the street west of Clark. The elevated tracks carried Chicago's L, as the trains and system were called. Newer parts of the system used subways, but the original system was all elevated. Lines came in from the north, west and south and then they circled around the central area on the elevated tracks which surrounded the area. Many people will tell you that is how the area came to be called the Loop, but that is not so. Before the L and before electric street cars the system used cable cars. Cable cars operated with a continuous cable that at some point had to turn around and come back to the power house. Because the cable cars circled around, the downtown area got called the Loop.

Lohman was not thinking of what the area was called or why. As he came out of the building one of the trains was passing overhead and what he was thinking was that the noise was unbearable. He headed for LaSalle Street and went a block north. There LaSalle Street met the main branch of the River, which went east and west. There was an elevated two level street called Wacker along the River and Lohman headed west. There was a bridge over the River where LaSalle met Wacker. That was one of Chicago's newer downtown bridges. Originally there was a tunnel under the River there. Cable cars entered the Loop on LaSalle and they could not go over a bridge that opened. Or at least the cable could not. Therefore a tunnel was built under the River for the cable cars and other traffic.

Lohman headed two blocks west on Wacker. He headed past a building that once had been occupied by the Chicago Times. He looked across the River to a large newer building that now housed the Chicago Sun-Times which had acquired the Times long ago. The Times went into the Sun-Times not too long after the Times building was built. He wondered if anyone at the Times could have foreseen then what would happen. He thought too about the history of all the Chicago papers and recalled that one had its building on the block where Swifton Plaza now stood. It had been called the Chicago Inter Ocean.

As Lohman was mulling all this over in his head he was passing by what was once the largest building in the world to his right on the other side of the River. Marshall Field & Company had built this to serve as the headquarters for its wholesale business just as the Depression hit and it decided to get out of the business. Old Joe Kennedy, father of the esteemed (or terrible, depending on your point of view) President Kennedy, then acquired it and made a good deal of money on it. The building stood on what once had been the passenger terminal and yard of the Chicago and North Western Railway.

Lohman got to a street called Franklin that ran north up to Wacker at the River and then went diagonally northwest across the River and became Orleans Street. As Lohman crossed the river he went by the building housing the Sun-Times. Just then he saw one of his friends coming out. This was one of the reasons he liked his walks. He knew a lot of people and he ran into a lot of them on the walks. His friend was Marshall Kogen, one of the reporters. They greeted each other and exchanged some elucidating and important words before Kogen told Lohman that he had to hurry off to a local TV show where he was being interviewed. Before running off, however, Kogen jabbed, "Hey, talk to me later about the dead whore. I'll call. Looks like you're doing one a year now." He was headed south, but he turned and added, "And if you can let me know who gets it next I can sell some papers. Talk to you."

Lohman just stood there and shrugged. "The Hell with it," he thought. "Maybe Zenon's right. At least people are talking about us." Lohman then continued a short distance north to the next east-west street which ran under Orleans. He took some stairs down and walked west about one block to the River. Here it was going north. Just west of where Lohman had crossed the River it split into two branches. One going south and one going north. Lohman was now headed for a bridge across the North Branch. At the east end of the bridge there were some steps leading down to a walkway along the River. This went between the River and something called The East Bank Institution, ostensibly called such because it was on the east bank of the River. Lohman wondered if in reality Israel had something to do with the name. He had a little air in his head just like everyone else and he figured that he may as well enjoy it.

Across the River was a town house complex on land that originally was a freight yard for the North Western. The area where he was walking once had a bridge across the River where the Milwaukee Road trains crossed and then went north along the east side of the River serving what was then an industrial area. Now the whole area was part of Chicago's Richtown. The great MeTown. Where the deer and the antelope play and where the humans display their wealth. This part of the north side was called River North.

It all looked rather bleak in the winter with no greenery. The walkway ended a block north and Lohman had to come up to the street level and go another block north until he could go back to the River through a little park where another bridge had once crossed the River. Lohman got back to the River and stopped to watch the ducks and geese. This area had a ledge of rocks along the side of the River where they congregated. Lohman thought how pleasant they were to watch. If only they didn't leave their calling cards all over the grass.

Lohman went up the River path and soon there was a long old building on his right. This was part of the old Montgomery Ward complex. That company had its offices and warehouse along the River. The buildings had all been converted to residences. He went further up to the Chicago Avenue Bridge. Chicago Avenue ran from east to west between the Montgomery Ward buildings. The bridge roadway was higher than the path along the River, but here

Lohman did not have to come up the stairs. There was a walkway through the bridge under the roadway. This was one of the interesting areas of the walk. The working parts of the bridge were exposed and one could see how it worked. Not that it opened much anymore. Chicago once had the busiest port in the world in the River, but there was hardly any traffic there now, other than pleasure and tour boats which did not require bridge lifts.

Lohman went through the bridge and past a riverside restaurant and some other businesses which had openings on the walkway. Then on north past some town houses to where the path ended. Here Lohman was about three quarters of a mile west of his house, since the River went a little west as it went north. From here he went a few blocks east and north through more town houses till he reached a street called Division. He headed east on Division. To his left was a lot of vacant land that had once been occupied by a housing project that was torn down. He walked further east and approached some new buildings where once the meat packing company Oscar Mayer had a plant next to a public vocational school. He went a little further and came to a north-south street called Wells.

In the mid to late 1960s Wells Street was the hottest night life street in town. In the 1960s Lohman could stay up at night and was out there with the rest of the town. Now it was just a commercial street on the west side of the Gold Coast, a residential area along the Lake. Lohman turned to his left to go up Wells and as he walked along he remembered which night clubs, theaters, bars and restaurants were where, He recalled the shops. And he recalled that in the middle of it all were a bicycle and shoe factory. For almost every building he passed he recalled what shows and performers he had seen and what things had happened to him there.

Lohman was walking north on the west side of the street. He passed a street called Goethe. This was named after the German poet whose name was pronounced something like Gerte. In Chicago it was pronounced Gothee. On his left was a small park. Across the street he remembered the Plugged Nickel and Mother Blue's night clubs and some of the big name acts he had seen there. As he crossed the next street he remembered a large store that came in after the 1960's and was now gone as well. He crossed the next street and went on reminiscing about the restaurants, bars and tourist oriented mini-malls that had been in the block he was on. He remembered the Pickle Barrel, the Crystal Pistol, the Fire Place Inn, Antonio's, El Griffon, La Strada and the Beef & Bourbon. He remembered everyone dressed up in the 1960's clothes. And he remembered the different color schemes of the era and the then modern style of décor that looked like some Soviet designers crafted it.

Soon Lohman came to an east–west street called North Avenue. Actually, this is where the Old Town area actually began. Those associated with it were very particular about pointing out that it was called the Old Town Triangle and was bounded on its east by Wells Street north of North Avenue. This was just ahead of Lohman. Another boundary was North Avenue from Wells to the west. This was to Lohman's left. The other boundary was a diagonal street named Ogden Avenue that went between North and a few blocks north of Wells. It ran from southwest to northeast. It no longer existed, but it did in the 1960's. Much of the action in the Old Town area of the 1960s was thus south of Old Town proper, although there was still some action north of North Avenue on Wells. The Second City bar and theater was at the north end of Wells where it ended and some other night clubs and restaurants were also north of North like the Earl of Old Town, the Oxford Pub, Moody's Pub, The Sphinx and the Bratskeller.

Some of the action was also on North Avenue, like the Old Town Ale House a block to Lohman's left. Lohman also remembered a Brewery with its restaurant further west. It was not in Old Town proper or on the strip, but it was part of the action too. Sieben's Brewery was the name. It was one of those old pre-Prohibition breweries that were all over Chicago that had survived Prohibition, probably through the efforts of the Syndicate. Capone and his descendants kept pouring out the beer during Prohibition and even after it ended they continued to operate some breweries that bars found they better purchase beer from.

Lohman looked west on North Avenue and contemplated his memories. He saw St. Michael's church in the distance. This marked the southwest corner of the Triangle. A corner of it had been near the diagonal Ogden Avenue. In space where Ogden Avenue had been, not far from St. Michael's, was the Midwest Buddhist Temple which Lohman had often walked past. He contemplated what people in the 1960s would have thought about that. He then remembered the times before the 1960s when the whole area was an old working class area of Chicago and wondered what the residents of those days would have thought of the 1960s night life. Or, he wondered, what would they think of the area now? It had turned into just another area of Richtown. Any blue collar in the area would certainly be some designer creation.

Then Lohman looked north up Wells and contemplated the more northeast section of the Triangle. In that area was another landmark of the era before the 1960's, the Menominee Boys and Girls Club. It was still there in the old building.

After contemplating all this Lohman came to. He had been standing on the southwest corner of Wells and North. His house was three blocks east on Dearborn and several doors south of North Avenue. Lohman headed east on the south side of North. One block further on, he came to LaSalle. He remembered how in the old days there were gas stations all over the place. North and LaSalle had a gas station on each corner. Now there was only one on the northeast corner. Most of the rest of the block it was on was taken up by a large church, the Moody Church, founded by an evangelist named Moody. It had a theology school further south on LaSalle.

Lohman crossed LaSalle. He went a block east to Clark. He remembered an event his father took him to at the Plaza Hotel at this intersection when he was a child. The Plaza Hotel was an apartment hotel on the southeast corner. An apartment hotel was a hotel with permanent residents living in rooms or suites with small kitchens. There were restaurants in the hotel too as well as other facilities found in transient hotels. The Plaza was about eight stories tall, although Lohman could not remember exactly how tall it was. He remembered how fancy the lobby was. It was decorated in turn of the century (1900) style and he remembered all the potted palms. He also remembered vividly the sign on the corner. There was a restaurant there called Hasty Tasty which had its name on a big old fashioned neon sign out front on the corner.

At the northeast corner of North and Clark was Lincoln Park which went north along Chicago's lake front for about five and a half miles. This was the southwest corner of the Park and it was also the location of the Chicago History Museum. It had been called the Chicago Historical Society for years, but for some reason the dumbos running it and spending down its endowment in recent years had to change the name. Lohman remembered an outing his family had made to the Society when he was a kid. Afterwards they had come to the Walgreen's which was then at the southwest corner of North and Clark for refreshments. He recalled the old style soda fountain and the Green River carbonated lime drink they mixed for him. He also remembered looking out the window and seeing the streetcars. Streetcars came east on North Avenue to Clark. The line ended there. The cars would stop and the motorman would get out and put down the pole that went up to the electric wire at the west end of the car and put up the pole on the east end and then set a switch on the tracks so the car could switch over to the tracks on the north side and go west. Then the streetcar would cross over and go back the other way. Soon after that Chicago got rid of streetcars. On North Avenue they were replaced by trolley buses. Trolley buses did not have poles and controls at both ends so some way of turning them around was needed. In this case a turnaround was built in the Park just south of the Museum on the north side of the street. This was still used by the buses that had replaced the trolley buses.

The Plaza Hotel was long gone. In its place had been built a large building housing The Roman School of Chicago. Lohman walked across Clark and passed this building. He crossed the alley behind it and came to another building the School had built in recent years at the southwest corner of North and Dearborn. He turned south on the west side of Dearborn and got to his house. He let himself in. His wife, Gloria, was not home, but the dog, Louie, was. Louie was a Great Dane and he was quite happy and excited to see Lohman. A Great Dane in such a state can be hard to handle, but Lohman knew the right moves.

Now, having had his walk, Lohman realized that it was time for Louie's walk, so out they went to see the world and, so far as Louie was concerned, to shit on it.

11 MORE INQUIRIES

Monday morning Lohman got in early and conferred with Tete about some things. He asked her to set up a meeting with him, her, Wiggy Rodriguez and Henner Pigman to follow up on what he had been told by Beale and Stonegold about their whereabouts the previous Monday. He also asked her to contact the Building Manager and the head of the cleaning crew to see if the cleaning service did Beale's office that night, and in particular, whether they changed the waste basket liner. Wiggy Rodriguez was one of the firm's investigators. Usually he was trying to find out things about the other side in litigation, but he often helped Lohman out with internal matters. Wiggy was not his real name, but it is what everyone called him and it was a name he was proud of. It came from his rather obvious wig. Pigman was the firm's IT manager.

In the meantime Lohman had to see a client about a new matter. It was someone who had been referred by The Cardinal Samuel or, as everyone called him, Cardinal Sammy. The firm members took care to cultivate the local religious leaders and they often picked up business that way. All Lohman knew about the new client was that the Cardinal had mentioned at a party that he had referred the fellow and that the client wanted to start a substantial entertainment venture, part of which would involve making religious films and videos for various religions. The client came in and he and Lohman talked. It turned out that the client did intend to make religious films and had considerable experience doing this while working for other producers. Now he wanted to get in on the business himself and he had rounded up some investors that wanted to back him. What the client had not told Cardinal Sammy was that he contemplated that his main money makers would be religious porn. This would involve people in religious settings veering off into sexual activities. "After all," he said, "someone screwed Mary."

Lohman learned all he could about the venture and after the client left, he called some of the junior lawyers in the firm and set up a meeting where he could explain the matter to them and get them started on the work.

After that Tete, Rodriguez and Pigman came in along with the Building Manager and the head of the cleaning service. Swifton Plaza was managed by a company called Swifton Realty. The Building Manager was Toola Swifton. She was a younger member of the Swifton family and she really did not need the job. Usually Lohman, head of one of the biggest tenants, could not get in touch with her. He had to do everything through her secretary. However, this time Lohman had told Tete he wanted to see Ms. Swifton. What Tete commands, people do. The head of the cleaning crew, Wanda Polchaskowski, came in too.

First Lohman went over what Beale had said about his waste basket not having a liner in it on Tuesday. Toola said she never heard anything about it and that she did not ordinarily deal with such trivial complaints. Wanda said she had heard about it from Toola's secretary. Wanda said she talked to the cleaner who did Beale's office and she said she replaced the liner last Monday night. The cleaner had said she often got complaints about his office not being done right. She said she often was told to go there direct to replace the liner. She had told Wanda that there was no way in Hell she was not going to see that his office was done right, particularly the liner. Lohman then went over what he had heard about the copier waste paper basket liners with Wanda and she confirmed what he had been told. Then Toola and Wanda left.

Lohman then reviewed what he had been told about where Beale and Stonegold were on that Monday and got Wiggy and Henner started on checking it out. He asked them to check out where St. Charles and Levin were too. He also told Pigman to search through the firm computer records for anything involving Zoom Shot. He acknowledged that they had already looked for bills, but he asked Pigman to look for anything.

After this Lohman asked them to wait a moment and he picked up his phone and called Levin. He got lucky and Levin was in and answered. That is two separate things. Just because Levin was around when his phone rang, does not mean he would answer it. He must have been bored. Lohman asked him where he was last Monday night.

"Didn't I tell you?" said Levin. "I told you I came in to get a document."

"Yes," said Lohman, "but what did you do then?"

"What do you mean?" said Levin. "What is this, the Inquisition?"

"No," said Lohman. "But remember what I said about the police? What if they ask you? And what if I tell the Management Committee you won't answer questions?"

"I get the document and then I went home," said Levin. "I was going to go to a party with my wife that night, but she came down with a cold so we decided not to go and I came in and got the document, prepared for Tuesday, and then went home. I had been out getting something to eat since we weren't going to the party. I left about ten thirty. Satisfied?"

"Who was the document from? What was it?" asked Lohman.

"It was an affidavit I needed for Tuesday. It came from Seladora Bruce. You've met her," said Levin.

Lohman thanked him and hung up. Then he told Rodriguez and Pigman what he had heard and asked them to follow up on it.

"What about Mr. St. Charles?" asked Wiggy. "He's not going to talk to me."

"Well, just check the other things. Any records. Any people who might know where he was. Ask about a lot of other things too and if Mr. St. Charles objects I'll say it was the other things I told you to go into and inquiries about him were just incidental."

They left and Lohman got back into his regular routine.

Tuesday Lohman went to the business office and followed up with McDade and Pigman on Zoom Shot. There were no records of F, P & C having hired them to deliver or pick up anything. The firm always used a messenger service named Ready?-Sent!. Pigman had found a few records of sign-ins by Zoom Shot in the building log, but the building office had not been too helpful. He had seen those records and there were two sign-ins after hours to a lawyer who had left the firm. They were trying to locate him, but so far could not. McDade had talked to his former secretary who was still with the firm and she did not know his whereabouts. She never heard of Zoom Shot. The firm itself did not have any check in records. If messengers came in during the work day they came up in the freight elevator and whoever was in the firm's back office that the freight elevator opened into would take the delivery. No records were kept. If the messengers came in after hours, they used the regular passenger elevators and came in on 40 and either left their materials there with the night receptionist or were directed to the recipient's office if that is what the recipient wanted.

Pigman had checked the old billing records for the lawyer who left on the nights when the Zoom Shot sign-ins were recorded. Nothing was mentioned in the records for one of the nights and on the other night he did not bill anything.

McDade had got one of the corporate department people to look up Zoom Shot. Nothing was found. The Secretary of State's office created corporations and other legal entities, but that office did not have any records of an entity by that name. Surprisingly enough, there was a listing in the White Pages for a Zoom Shot, but it turned out to be a photography service. McDade had had Wiggy check it out and there actually was a guy operating as a photographer for hire who used the name. He didn't know anything about a messenger service, except that he sometimes got calls from people who wanted delivery who wouldn't tell him of what.

Lohman went back to his office and called Seladora Bruce. She knew Lohman and took his call. They greeted each other and talked. Then Lohman brought up the subject of what had happened. "Well, Seladora, you probably have heard about the death here last week."

"Oh yes," she said. "The little whore."

Lohman cringed. He realized that the undesirable "little whore" wording was getting around. "Well, we don't know that," he said.

"Then, what was going on?" asked Seladora. "From what I've read and seen on TV it doesn't sound like she was there to deliver. Uh, a document, I mean."

"Yes, the circumstances are suggestive," admitted Lohman. Why not admit it? He wasn't going to get around it. "Anyway, we are trying to find out what happened. Apparently she was here to deliver a document you sent to Wanzer. An affidavit, he said."

"To Wanzy?" she said. "Yes, there was something. Let me think. Yes. I remember. I sent him and affidavit."

"By Zoom Shot?" asked Lohman.

"How would I know," said Seladora. "I gave it to my secretary and told her to get it to him. What's the big deal anyway? What did he have to do with it? I can't understand this. The police called me up and asked me this too."

"We're all just checking everything out," said Lohman. "This is hardly the only thing being asked about. We're going into everything we can about what happened that night."

"Well, for what it's worth, my secretary says she can't remember anything about it. She had a ton of papers to deal with that day. She never heard of Zoom Shot either," said Seladora.

Lohman bid her goodbye and hung up. He got back to his regular work and soon he forgot all about the little whore.

12 WHAT THE CLEANING CREW FOUND

Thursday morning Lohman went straight from home to a client's office in the area a little north of the Loop. From there he went to the office and got in about 10. No sooner had he got settled in his office than he got a call from Geeley McDade.

They greeted each other and then McDade said, "Guess what the cleaning crew found?"

Lohman said, "Another dead body? Maybe a dead elephant in the vault? Or a dead mouse. We could take that."

"Why would we have animals around?" commented McDade. "Other than cats and dogs and such pets," he added.

"So, what? You asked me to guess," said Lohman.

McDade said, "They found a big wheeled bag in one of the hall closets on 55. It was in that closet up there next to the entrance to the east copy room. You know the place across from Levin's and Beale's offices where there is that back entrance to the copy room. It had blood on it. They also told me they found a lot of messy stuff in Stonegold's office Tuesday night – the Tuesday after our little girl was found. The next day."

Lohman thought that "our little girl" was better than "little whore" or "dead little whore", but not too much. He asked, "What kind of mess?"

"The service says there were a lot of papers all over the place. They weren't there Monday night when the office was serviced so the mess must have happened after that. They tell me he isn't usually so messy. And we went over all the other questions you were talking about. The woman who does Beale's office repeated that she did the waste paper basket liner Monday night. She replaced it. She does the copier room on 55 too and she remembers the full copier waste basket on Tuesday night with dark paper towels. She didn't think much of it. She emptied them and heard some solid stuff and that's about it."

"She didn't think that odd?" asked Lohman.

"No," said McDade. "Why should she? You ought to hear what happens with the waste baskets and garbage bins. They find a lot of strange stuff. And looking through it is not their job anyway. It would just take time. I mean, they see the strange stuff a lot of the time without looking for it. Once they even found a midget hiding in one of the big bins down on 43 that had been placed in one of the large conference rooms behind a bar that was set up in there. Some of the partners were having a reception and there was going to be a surprise show and the midget was part of the show. The cleaner was in there just before the event started."

"So how come I never heard about this?" asked Lohman.

"Sometimes we don't tell you all the odd ball stuff. You want to hear it all?" McDade asked.

"I guess not," said Lohman. "What I hear is enough. We really need to add some psychiatrists to the staff."

"Or maybe attendants," said McDade. "That's what they call them in the mental hospitals. Anyway, I sealed off the closet where they found the bag and I called the cops. They're on the way here they said."

13 NO POOFS ON MY DEALS

No sooner had Lohman and McDade bid each other goodbye than Tete rang and said one of the partners was in her waiting area and wanted to see him. The partner was Chesterton McWilliams, one of the old-line, snobby, waspy, St. Charles faction. Lohman told Tete he would see McWilliams and he went out to do so and take McWilliams into his office.

Lohman and McWilliams walked back into Lohman's inner office. They greeted each other and got seated and then McWilliams started in. He wanted Sean Featherbottom fired. He couldn't even remember his name. He just called him, "That pansy blond kid." McWilliams was angry.

"What did he do?" asked Lohman.

"I said fire him," said McWilliams with a raised voice. I don't have to say why. Just fire him. I'm a partner. Fire him."

"We can't just fire people without giving a reason. No one would work here if we did." Lohman was trying to be reasonable.

McWilliams said, "My clients don't like queers. I don't want Poofy on my deals."

"Now, now, Chesty." said Lohman. "As I recall he made your last two deals. You were stuck on some tax issues on both of them and he came up with the solutions and then when you couldn't convince the other side of the solutions he did it."

McWilliams was offended. "I solved those problems. He just did the paperwork. And who needs him. We have a lot of other kids around here to do that. Normal ones. What am I supposed to tell my clients when he flaps into the room?"

"You don't have to tell them anything," said Lohman. "If we had a monkey doing the job all you would say is that he is good at the job. If the client said, 'But he's a monkey', all you'd say is 'Yes'". Anyway, it's against the law in Chicago to fire someone because of their sexual identity. I think that's what it's called. Anyway, you can't fire someone because they are gay."

"Why not!" exclaimed McWilliams. "You got rid of that black bitch for me."

"I remember her," said Lohman. "You said get rid of her because she's black. But you remember that you're the one that hired her. You didn't go through me or the Management Committee. You were saying that since we had so few – uh – African-American lawyers, we should get some. You just offered her a job. Rather than negate that and perhaps get bad publicity, we kept her. Then you and she -," Lohman's voice trailed off because he and she were doin' the heshe.

"Anyway," Lohman continued, "she couldn't do anything right. She couldn't write an intelligible sentence. Then you decided that you wanted to get rid of her. We got rid of her. Not because she was black, but because she couldn't do the job. Sean can do the job."

"No he can't," said McWilliams. "The little prick cost me I don't know how many billable hours,"

Normally saving time is a virtue – a good thing. However, some lawyers feel that if what you are selling are hours, then the more hours you produce the better. So, whereas in the rest of the world how much you get done in a specific amount of time is the measure of productivity, to some lawyers the reverse is true. In their world, the more time it takes you to do something, the better.

"What happened?" asked Lohman.

McWilliams explained. "I was selling an auto dealership. Big one. Poofy is on the deal. You wouldn't let me have anyone else. I had to go out of town on an emergency matter and while I'm away he gives away the store and the deal closed."

"How did he give away the store?" asked Lohman. "Didn't the client have to approve it?"

"The client didn't know what was best," said McWilliams. "Poofy let the client warrant that there were no liabilities other than those disclosed in the financial statements."

"Business sellers ordinarily warrant that," said Lohman.

McWilliams responded, "Sellers do a lot of things. So do buyers. But you don't just agree to them. Not until you have negotiation time on the books. Good Heavens Bumper! How do you produce your hours?"

Lohman almost said, "I get the deals done," but he thought better of it. Instead he said, "Merely because of what you have said, I cannot fire Sean. You have asked to fire him because he's - well – in a protected category. So, even if his work is insufficient, we would be in a bad position if we fired him."

McWilliams had to prove he was a lawyer. He said, "So who will know what I said? We aren't going to tell them."

Lohman ignored this. "I'll talk to him," he said.

"He's already killed two people around here," said McWilliams. He probably did it again. He shouldn't be around here."

"Apparently someone else did the killings," said Lohman dryly.

"Well, get him off my deals," said McWilliams.

"Can't do that either," said Lohman. "That would be a decision based on sexual preference. On the other hand, I think he is assigned elsewhere for a long time so the issue will not arise."

McWilliams stared at Lohman in silence for a while. Then he started lifting himself from his chair and as he was doing so said, "I'll talk to Graybee. He'll understand." He left.

Lohman then rang Sean to see if he was in. Sean was and Lohman went to his office. Sean's office was the usual associate's office with its piles of files and other papers, even in this so called paperless age. There was one difference. He had a set of shelves with all sorts of arty little knickknacks, including some of his jewelry, some china and silverware, some small sculpture pieces, some small framed photos and other items of artistic and collectible interest.

The door was open, but Lohman knocked. Sean told him to come in. Lohman entered and sat down. They greeted each other.

Lohman said, "I just talked to Mr. McWilliams."

Sean pursed his lips.

Lohman continued, "He tells me you closed one of his deals while he was away. An auto dealership sale. He says you agreed to have the seller, our client, warrant that there were no liabilities not disclosed in the financial statements. Do you remember that?"

"Yes," said Sean simply."

"Well….," said Lohman.

Sean paused. Lohman paused. Sean said, "He was angry. He wanted to know why I closed the deal while he was away. I think I cut off his billing, if you know what I mean."

"What happened?" asked Lohman.

"Well," said Sean, "the thing was going on forever. Mr. McWilliams and the buyer's lawyer were going around and around about it. They had been negotiating the point for two weeks. Meetings about three times a week. Every time we got to the issue Mr. McWilliams would say he couldn't agree to it unless they gave back something we had already agreed to. The clients were there too for some of the meetings. They he had to go out of town. The client called me and wanted to know what was holding things up. I told him the warranty issue was involved. He told me he had already agreed to the warranty with the buyer and he told me to get the deal closed. I didn't think it was important so I did it."

"You didn't ask McWilliams about it?" asked Lohman.

"I thought I did," said Sean. "He called in to see what was going on and I told him. I told him what the client said and he said he knew the client had agreed to the matter. I took that to mean I could close it. I was the one going to do that anyway. When he got back and asked about the deal again I told him it was closed and he exploded. He told me just because the client agreed to something did not mean he told me to close it. Well, he didn't explicitly tell me to close, I guess. I don't know. Sometimes I forget how important it is to produce hours here. I'm just supposed to get 50 things done at once and I am trying to minimize the time."

Sean looked like he was about to cry. Lohman took sympathy on him. "Look Sean. You did right. Remember the old hill country joke about the boy who came running home on his wedding night and told his father in disbelief that his bride was a virgin. His father told him, 'You did right to come home son. If she's not good enough for her own family, she's not good enough for you.'"

Sean's eyes widened as he looked at Lohman in wonderment. No one else around the firm talked that way. Was he in even bigger trouble than he thought?

"That's a joke," said Lohman.

"Oh," said Sean.

"Well, anyway," said Lohman, stay away from him. He wanted me to fire you. The first thing he said was he wanted me to fire you because you're – uh - gay. When I told him we can't do that he went on about the deal. That's probably his real problem anyway. So just don't worry about all this. That's what I want to tell you. You're still in good standing here. I'll talk to the head of the department to assign you elsewhere and if McWilliams wants you to do anything for him just get ahold of me. Don't do anything for him. Tell him I told you so. Tell him to call me too. And don't think he won't ask you to do things. He doesn't have to like you to want something done."

Lohman took his leave and went back to his office. When he got there Det. Bongwad and the Wilbert or Gilbert, I forget which, guy were there waiting for him. They talked to Lohman about the bag in the 55th floor closet and other things. Lohman learned nothing new, except that they could not trace the gun beyond the fact that it had originally been made by a manufacturer in Mexico that was no longer in business. They guy who sold it to St. Charles, Jon Won, was gone. They had not been able to find him, although he had a record as a fence and St. Charles had identified the photos they had of him.

Lohman then told them about the wheeled bag found in the closet on 55 and the copier waste baskets and what had been seen there.

At this time Lohman had a little debate with himself. Should he tell the cops about Sean or should he just forget about it? What if they found out about it and found out that he knew about it, but didn't tell them? What if they would never find out? What if they found out about Sean, but didn't find out that he knew about it? Lohman didn't go much further with this because he bored even himself. He opted for the best policy which is honesty. While this was not the general policy in law firms, at least it was his. "While you're here," he said, "I learned something the other day about what happened up there Monday. First, Sean Featherbottom was up there. He saw the messenger come in. He was up there to deliver something to Mr. Levin who was not there. He put it on Levin's desk. He says he saw the messenger coming down the hall as he was leaving. He says she asked for Mr. Levin and he pointed out his office to her and then he left. Also, he had a purple brooch which he seems to have lost. Now...."

Bongwad interrupted. "Him! This time we got him. Where is he? Is he in?"

Lohman replied, "Well hold on now. I know it sounds like he is implicated, but why would he tell me about this if he had anything to do with killing the woman?"

Gilbert interceded. "Sir. Maybe he knew we could place him there and he made up the story to cover. We have his prints up there."

"Why would he be there other than to deliver the document to Levin?" asked Lohman.

"Dope. Sex," said Bongwad.

"I doubt that," said Lohman. He is, what do they say now – gay."

"Bi maybe," said Bongwad.

"What's that?" asked Lohman.

"Bi means both, Sir," said Gilbert. "Sex with both men and women."

"At the same time?" asked Lohman.

"Could be," said Bongwad. "Or it could be that someone else involved was bi and Featherbottom was the male part of the party."

"Well, he doesn't use drugs that I know of," said Lohman.

"How would you know?" asked Bongwad.

"He doesn't act like he's under the influence whenever I see him,' said Lohman.

"That isn't the way to tell," said Bongwad. He got up to go. "We're gonna get him."

"Wait," said Lohman. "You mean arrest him? You don't have it narrowed down to him do you? There were other prints and other people involved. And the messenger checked in downstairs to see Mr.Levin. That confirms Sean's story."

"Yeah," said Bongwad. He motioned to Gilbert and the two left.

Lohman immediately picked up his phone and called a junior partner he often relied on when the going got tough. This was Joe DiBello who just happened to have an office on the same floor as Sean. Lohman got lucky and got DiBello. Without any ceremony he said, "Joe, this is Bumper." He didn't bother asking DiBello if he had heard about the dead woman. He continued. "Joe, the police were just here. That Monday night Sean says he, you know Sean Featherbottom, says he was up on 55 about 10 and saw the messenger come in. He says he had just left a document on Levin's desk and then he saw the messenger in the hall and she asked for Levin and he pointed out the office and went on out. And Sean had a purple brooch which he lost and it was found in the dead girl's boots. Or one of the same color. His prints were found in Graybourne's wash room. But so were other prints. Graybourne's were found there and they had been made in the dead girl's blood. And according to Sean, the messenger had a wheeled case and one like it was found in the hall closet. I just told all this to the police and I think they are on the way down there to arrest Sean. Go there and fend them off. Pretend they are interrupting a conference between Sean and you."

"So he did it again?" asked DiBello.

"You know he didn't do those others," said Lohman.

"Well, at least whoever did them did us a favor. But what about this time? He was there?"

"So maybe he did have something to do with it, but let that proof be developed. Right now there are other definite suspects," said Lohman. "Get going. Hold them off. I'll try to get Bungus to do something."

He hung up and then called Bungus LaRue, the firm's governmental affairs partner. Bungus wasn't in, but Lohman got him on his cell phone. Bungus was at the barber shop getting his hair cut. Lohman briefly explained the situation to Bungus and then asked him if he could do anything to delay the possible arrest – quickly. Bungus just responded, "Sure," and hung up.

How Bungus did things, neither Lohman nor anyone else asked. But Lohman relaxed since Bungus usually delivered.

14 WHAT ARE THE BIG SHOTS UP TO

Friday morning Lohman met with St. Charles and Cohenstein. Stonegold was also there because he and St. Charles were practicing their putting on St. Charles' rug when the others arrived. Stonegold was one of the equity partners officed on 55 and he and St. Charles often practiced their putting not just on the rug, but on some poor client's bill.

Lohman explained the unfortunate facts about Sean and St. Charles.

Cohenstein said, "So why is Fluffy always mixed up in these things? Do you think that kid has something to do with it? On the other hand, what would he be doing with the little whore? And you Graybourne? What's with your fingerprints? What did you have to do with it? What were you doing with a prostitute in your office?"

St. Charles stood as straight as he could. He put his nose up in the air as far as he could. He breathed in as far as he could. He reached for Pussy and took her off her pedestal. He held her and stroked her. He said, "This is an outrage! There are no grounds at all for the suggestion of prostitution. And why would my prints not be in my bathroom?"

"In her blood?" said Cohenstein.

"Oh, I doubt that," said St. Charles. "There must be some mistake. Anyway Sean Featherbottom was there. He admits it. And his prints were there. And his jewelry was found on the body. What else do we need?"

"That's our story!" said Cohenstein. "I can see the headline at the supermarket checkout counter rack. 'The Gay Deceiver.' We were misled by him, but now that we are informed we have nailed him like the honorable and truthful protectors of society we are known to be by all the major companies who are devoted clients of ours because of our superior expertise and character."

St. Charles was a bit relieved. "Quite so," he added.

Lohman then tried to bring them, or at least St. Charles, back to reality. "Gentlemen. Maybe Sean is involved. But maybe he is not involved or, if he is involved, maybe he is not the only one. And maybe the police are not mistaken about your prints Graybourne."

At this St.Charles interrupted. "Of course they are. Get an expert to demonstrate that Bumper."

"My point is," continued Lohman, "that some explaining will be in order along the way. Saying the police are mistaken is not a good public story. Let's approach it from another angle. Where were you on Monday night Graybourne?" he asked.

St.Charles turned a little green. He puffed his cheeks out. He took a deep breath. He stroked his Pussy. He put her back on her pedestal. She licked her forelegs and then sat looking out the window. "I do not have to explain my whereabouts," he said.

Cohenstein said, "That's not a good story for the police."

St. Charles stared the death ray at Cohenstein. Jews are so – you know.

"Well" asked Lohman.

St. Charles finally relented. "At the Pullman Club," he said.

"With whom?" asked Lohman.

"Alone. I was eating alone," said St. Charles.

Lohman and Cohenstein both looked at each other. It was almost unheard of for someone to have a late dinner alone at the Pullman Club, especially St. Charles.

"Can anyone confirm that?" asked Lohman.

"Oh Heavens, I don't know," said St. Charles. Then he seemed to brighten up. "Actually, I did eat there. Go get the bill. That should confirm it. And I stayed there Monday night. I have my regular room there you know. I was there all night until I came back here Tuesday morning early to get a conference call."

"So what about Fluffy?" Cohenstein asked Lohman. "What's our story when he gets pinched?"

"For the moment," said Lohman, "I'm trying to keep him from getting arrested. An arrest of any of our people wouldn't look good. On top of that, I don't think there is a definite case against him. After all, the messenger didn't check in to see him. She checked in to see Levin and Sean says that is who she asked for when he saw her. And, well, we do have other people implicated."

Everyone sat there in silence for a moment, each looking at the others. Stonegold did not have anything to add. He had remained silent through the whole meeting and he said nothing further. Lohman got up to go and said, "Well, that's it then."

Lohman and Cohenstein left and St. Charles and Stonegold got back to their putting.

Lohman went back to his office and found Bongwad and Gilbert waiting for him. He led them into his inner office and they talked about further developments. The police told Lohman how they had taken prints off the wheeled bag found in the 55th floor closet. They found prints containing some of the victim's blood. The prints were on the handle and its extensions and they belonged to St. Charles and Stonegold. The victim's prints were also on the bag in a lot of places.

It was big bag. The kind that would barely fit into an overhead bin in a plane and needed to be pushed in and compressed. It was mostly empty, but it had a few things in it. "Like what?" asked Lohman.

"Like sex shop things," said Bongwad. "There was a penis pump and some sexy little panties and a few other lacey clothing items. And get this. Her blood was all over everything. Now maybe the bag had been full of her equipment when she came in and then it got emptied out. We haven't found the other contents though."

Lohman said, "Maybe the waste baskets have something to do with it. Remember that someone said they saw dirty panties in the copier baskets. And they talked about dirty towels in there. Also, the cleaning crew said they heard the sound of something solid coming out. And someone said the washroom towels had run out. And Mr. Beale said his trash basket liner was missing. It sounds to me like someone took the towels and put them around her head to soak up blood and put a trash basket liner around her head to hold it all in. Maybe they put the bag's contents in the copier waste baskets."

Bongwad said, "Probably. We're still working on it. There weren't any prints that we found on that bag over her head. So we get no help there."

"So did you talk to Sean Featherbottom?" asked Lohman.

"Yeah," said Bongwad. There was some guy there, DiBello I think, and he kept saying he needed Featherbottom on an emergency matter so we didn't get much out of him. Anyway, the Captain called and said we should wait till we get better proof. We'll do it. We'll nail him this time."

The police took their leave. They had wanted to talk to St.Charles and Stonegold, but Cohenstein had suggested to St.Charles that he should go out of town for a rest and Stonegold couldn't be found just then so the police left the building.

Lohman then asked Tete to get the file Levin had been working on. A little while later one of the firm's clerks brought in to Lohman. Lohman went through it. It was a new matter and not too important so the file was not too thick. He soon found what he was looking for. It was the affidavit. The file showed that it had been presented to the SEC on Tuesday after the death. What it also showed was that the affidavit was notarized with Tuesday's date, not Monday's and there was also a document from a messenger service showing delivery early on Tuesday to Levin. The messenger service was the firm's regular service, Ready?-Sent!

Lohman didn't have time to talk to Levin about this. He also didn't want to just then. He wanted to think about what he had found. He had his own clients' matters to attend to and he did just that until late that night and then went home.

15 PANSY'S PARTY

Saturday morning Lohman was in the office working on a client's EPA matter. The client used ink to print its own labels for the goods it manufactured. The ink was an environmentally unfriendly substance and had to be disposed of properly. The client had hired a licensed waste hauler to dispose of the empty ink barrels, but some of the barrels had been found in a waste dump that had tons of harmful waste in it, mostly from large waste producers like oil companies. In cases like this the law provided that each company that had any identifiable waste at the site was liable for the entire cost of cleaning up the whole place, regardless of how little of the mess they had contributed. Of course, each polluter could obtain contribution from the others for their share of the costs, but how much did a small company whose share of the costs might be $1,000 and whose yearly sales might be $25 million want to spend on suing 100 large companies and 500 smaller ones when the litigation costs could be more than their yearly sales? What usually happened is that the large companies were identified by the EPA which then took action against them. They then formed a clean-up group which did work at the site and identified all the smaller polluters. The group then put the squeeze on the small polluters and demanded far more than their fair share of the costs in order to reach a settlement where the big guys would agree to hold the small guys harmless in return for a payment from the small guys.

The small guys usually had never heard of the law involved. It is called Super Fund. Every time this happened to one of the small guys they just could not believe that they had millions of dollars of liability to clean up the entire site, even though they had hired licensed waste haulers and only a tiny amount of their materials had been found at the site. They consulted their lawyers who then told them the sad truth about the law. Once the client had accepted the situation, the cheapest way out was usually to submit to the blackmail. Sometimes there were other approaches, but in view of the amounts involved it was usually not worth it to go into them. So, as is often the case in our great legal system – you name me a better one, etc. – when you win, you lose. So just go ahead and lose. It is cheaper.

In this case Lohman's client had just heard about the matter and Lohman had explained what was involved. The client had recovered from the shock and Lohman was now going through all the details so he could wrap the matter up. The large company group handling the site wanted $35,000 from the client, even though only seven of the client's empty ink barrels had been found. Lohman had explained how it could easily cost way more than $35,000 to fight the matter and that the chances of much success were small. Lohman's clients were usually more realistic than the clients of other lawyers and so Lohman got to the settlement stage more quickly. That is what he was doing Saturday morning.

Lohman finished earlier than he had thought he would. It was a little before noon and Saturday evening Lohman and his wife, Gloria, were set for a party. He had time on his hands for once. Idle hands are the tool of the Devil so Lohman, the great walker, took a bus home and barged in to his house without warning and molested the occupant. Later, Gloria told him how happy she was that he could get away from the office early.

Now, I told you that Lohman took a bus. That is confidential. Please do not tell Mr. St. Charles.

The party was at the Chicago home of Lady Elizabeth Fitch-Bennington. Everyone addressed her by her nickname which was Pansy. She was a member of the English aristocracy and had extensive American agricultural interests. The Wealth Management department of The Bank handled these for her, but she spent a lot of time in Chicago overseeing their overseeing. She was a snob. But she was a natural one. She was an aristocrat and did not know anything else. She was also one of the nicest snobs you could ever meet. Everyone liked her.

Pansy had an enormous two story condominium at Michigan Avenue and Delaware Street. Michigan Avenue was the street that bordered Chicago's downtown on the east. Between Michigan and the Lake, which was farther to the east, was Grant Park. As one went north on Michigan from downtown there would be Grant Park on the right and the buildings of the Loop on the left. Then the park land would stop and buildings would appear on the right as well. As one went further north one came to the Chicago River which ran east and west, coming in from the Lake and going west to a point where it split into a branch going north and one going south. Going further north on Michigan one went over the River on a bridge and Michigan then became Chicago's fancy shopping street. About one mile further north Michigan came to an end where the buildings on the right also came to an end. Here the Lake came a little further west. The street continued straight north where Michigan ended, but here it was called Lake Shore Drive. As you went north on Lake Shore Drive you had a major road on your right and further beyond that the Lake. On your left you had the

Gold Coast residential area. As we have seen, Lohman's house was several blocks further west towards the north end of the Gold Coast area. Pansy's apartment was on Michigan just two blocks south of where Michigan turned into Lake Shore Drive.

Looking at it from the point of view of the Lohman's, to walk from their place to Pansy's they had to go three streets east and about three quarters of a mile south. And the Lohman's were walkers. They were going to head east to Lake Shore Drive and then south on Lake Shore and Michigan until they got to Pansy's.

The whole area used to be occupied by a cemetery and sand dunes and the Lake used to come farther west at that time. Not too long after the Chicago fire which was in 1871 someone called Potter Palmer was involved in real estate development. He had originally been in the dry goods business and had been the guy in Chicago who hired Marshall Field. Field went on to buy the business and it became the Marshall Field & Company that was once a household name. Palmer went onto real estate. He bought a large part of what eventually became the Gold Coast and started building houses and selling lots and houses there. A lot of the houses were big mansions. One of them was his own house which covered most of one whole block on Lake Shore Drive. This went up in the mid-1880s. It had a lot of castellated little towers and was called Palmer's castle. It lasted until about 1950 when it was torn down and a non-descript apartment building built there.

The whole area had gone through a great deal of change since the Fire. First there were the big mansions. Then around the turn of the last century people started building apartment buildings with very large apartments. By the time of the Great Depression the area was a mix of the mansions and the buildings with the large apartments. During the Depression and the World War II housing shortage some of the houses and apartments were divided into smaller units, but the appearance of the area remained the same through World War II. After the War the modern building boom started and new buildings with smaller apartments started filling up the area. Smaller, but not cheap. It was still the Gold Coast.

When the time came, Bumper and Gloria headed to the south end of their block and turned east to head for Lake Shore Drive. There, they turned south and headed for Pansy's. Sometimes in the distant past people who lived in the Gold Coast walked to places they were going, but no more. Bumper and Gloria were headed down a mostly empty sidewalk along the Drive. They did run into a few dog walkers that Bumper knew from his dog walking, but most of the people in the area who owned dogs now hired people to do the dog walking and Lohman didn't know most of them due to the fact that there was a big turnover in the hired dog walkers.

They headed on south past the site where Palmer's castle stood and then reached the block south of it which was empty until well after World War II. The block at that time held the field hockey area used by the Girls' Roman School. The Lohmans lived across the street from a building that once had held the Boys' Roman School Of Chicago. Sometime in the 1950s the two were merged and now the coed school occupied the old Boys' school building and others which had been built near Lohman's house. The old Girls' school building no longer existed. An apartment building had gone up there. It was a one block south of the field and one block west of the Drive. As the Lohmans went by the field and one more block south they came to the block that had been directly east of the

Girls' school. It held a large postwar apartment building too. When the Girls' school had been to its west it had held and oddity in the Gold Coast. It held a three story structure with a mansard roof that had originally been built to house an insurance company. Eventually the U.S. Court of Appeals had taken up residence there until a new building was built for it and the other Federal courts downtown.

The Lohmans passed on by this and came to Division Street where one of the old fancy large apartment buildings still stood. The apartments had been subdivided and were now a lot smaller, but it was still an elegant building. Oddly enough this site originally held the house of another real estate developer named Gross. This guy was no Potter Palmer. He built working class houses all over in large quantities. Some areas still were named for him such as Grossdale. His house was not stone castle. It was wood. Big. On the Lake and big, but wood.

The Lohmans proceeded further south till they got to Oak Street where the Drive went into Michigan Avenue. The high speed outer lanes of Lake Shore Drive turned east here and proceeded for a short distance east until they turned south again, but if one were walking down the Inner Drive on the sidewalk on its west one would be looking straight ahead into Michigan Avenue. At Oak Street and the Drive is where another prominent mansion once stood. It belonged to a member of both the Rockefeller and McCormick families. The Rockefellers you have heard of. The McCormicks were associated with McCormick reaper works which made farm machinery. It merged with other farm equipment makers into International Harvester which was once the biggest industrial company in the world.

The Lohmans crossed Oak Street and went two blocks south on Michigan to Delaware where Pansy's building was at the northwest corner. At the south west corner was the Seventh Presbyterian Church where the Lohman's were members. So were all the other social climbing devout Presbyterians who passed up lots of other Presbyterian churches to get there every Sunday. After all, it is at Seventh where God sits in the second pew. The Lohmans were members out of habit. They had both been raised in the Presbyterian Church and had continued to associate with the Church, but they took it with a grain of salt.

Here they turned right and entered Pansy's building. Pansy was always having parties and the Lohmans went often so the lobby attendant knew them and passed them through to the elevators without getting clearance. They went up and got off at Pansy's floor. The first one of her floors. She had a huge apartment on two floors. Pansy's butler James was there greeting the guests.

He knew the Lohmans and greeted them by name. "Good evening Mr. and Mrs. Lohman," he said, "Lady Bitch is so glad you are here." No one who was familiar with Pansy took any notice of this kind of statement. James was dyslectic. He took their coats and led them into one of the reception rooms where they saw Pansy herself. James led them over to her.

Pansy was accompanied by her boy toy, Johnny Miller. When the Duke's away, the Duchess will play. Or is it that when the Duchess is away, she will play? Anyway they broke in on a conversation where Johnny was explaining scat music to Pansy. "Scat?" she asked as she turned to James as she always did in times of doubt. "What is that?"

"Scatological m'Lady," said James.

"I see," said Pansy as she turned inquiringly to Johnny.

"What's scatological?" he asked.

Interruptions often save the day. Pansy noticed the Lohmans. "Hello Bumper. Hello Gloria. I'm so glad you could come. Aren't we?" she turned towards Johnny. He nodded.

"Now I can find out all about that, well ---"

Just then St. Charles and Swifty came by and greeted the group. Since Pansy was involved with The Bank and St. Charles was her lead lawyer, her parties were well attended by Bank and firm people. St. Charles was almost always there as he was anywhere he could mix with the upper classes.

"Oh hello you two," exclaimed Pansy. "What a coincidence. Now that you are all here you can tell me all about that unfortunate incident at your place. You can tell me all the details about that little.....", she looked at James who was standing by.

James said, "Prostitute," he said.

"Oh I thought she was called something else. They were telling me about it at the spa. Now what did they say she was..?"

"Prostitute is the accepted term m'Lady," said James.

"And naked," said Pansy. "And eighteen was she? Right there in your office. Yours Graybee. It was your office wasn't it? A naked, teenage prostitute. Whatever are you up to?"

St. Charles just stood there. Swifty tried to look wise and important. Lohman interceded. "Well maybe naked and maybe she was younger. But we don't know she was a prostitute and we don't know what she was doing there. So far as we can tell she had no connection to the firm."

St. Charles had recovered. "Absolutely. No connection at all."

"So she wasn't really there?" asked Johnny.

St. Charles stared at him. All of a sudden his expression changed to a happy one. "Maybe," he said. He looked at Bumper hopefully.

Lohman did not pick up on this. He knew she had been there. "All we know is that she was supposed to be delivering something. She was from a Zoom Shot messenger service. No one had ever heard of them. We never use them. We never heard of them before. After all, you would think anyone who used them would remember that name." He looked around. "Did any of you ever hear of them?"

All those present shook their heads. Except Johnny. He raised his hand with the finger pointing up and then let it fall. Lohman asked, "What? You heard of them?"

"No. No," said Johnny. "I would never hear of an outfit like that."

Lohman realized he better not inquire further.

Just then Pansy saw some other new entrants and excused herself. St. Charles and Swifty went off to get something to drink, leaving the Lohmans by themselves. Gloria spotted another firm partner nearby standing with some other people. It was Winter Goren, the Firm Fruit. Actually these days any large law firm had a lot of delectable edibles on their menus, but Goren was from the old days when anyone who dressed, acted and talked like him was called a fruit. There he was in a lavender suit with a cream colored shirt and a lavender tie the same color as the suit and with cream colored patent leather shoes. Naturally his coat pocket was stuffed with a cream colored silk handkerchief. He had white rimmed glasses on that had sparkle on the rims.

Goren had a lot of show business and media clients and was there with some prospects he was trying to get business out of. They weren't front stage people so no one would recognize them. They were two people who controlled a large private production company. Lohman had met them before and recognized them, but hardly anyone else at the party would. One of Goren's sales methods was to introduce prospects to the kind of people who were at the party. Since Sweeney was in with the show business people too and since Sean worked with him they were often working with Goren. Tonight they were with him and the prospects. Sweeney had also brought Trisha DeLang along for the same type of networking.

The prospects had run into several guys they knew and the whole group was talking. The Lohmans went over towards them. They passed several couples on the way and heard some of their conversation. One phrase they heard along the way was, "So the great snake finger of evil has pointed at F, P & C again." Lohman looked at where it came from and recognized a prominent member of the bar from another firm. They were not best buds, but they recognized each other and they nodded.

The Lohmans got over to the group where Goren was. He and his prospects and Sweeney, Trisha and Sean were listening to the conversation of two prominent Chicago sports casters who the Lohmans recognized. Greg Schulztwasser and Jordan Wackhead were their names. They handled the sports reporting for the news casts on two different local TV channels. They were macho guys and they were enthusiastic about their fields. They took sports seriously. Their wives were with them.

Schultzwasser was saying, "The Bears get rid of a quarterback if he's any good. Go all the way back to Halas. If the quarterback starts to go well he's gone. Wham, bam, gone!"

"So what's the big deal!" said Wackhead. "They can just do without a quarterback. They can just have the center come back with the ball. He comes back and at the same time the two guards converge on the middle and block the center rusher and two backs come in to block and the center throws or hands it off."

"Illegal man," said Schultzwasser. "Stupid!"

Wackhead said, "Show me in the rules where it is illegal. The minute the center touches the ball and moves it back to the quarterback's hands he's legal. Why can't he just keep it?"

As this was going on Sean, who had a decorative bag hung over his shoulder, pulled his knitting out of the bag and started working on it.

Schultzwasser noticed this and said, "Freak!"

Goren leaned over and made a point of making a whisper to Sean that everyone could hear. He said, "Don't worry, Sean. He won't hurt you. His attention will probably be diverted by a hot dog first."

Schultzwasser said, "Queers!"

Trisha said, "Hey big sports guy! Go get a squirting insert in your nether regions."

Sweeny, Goren and Sean stared at her in amazement.

Schultzwasser turned to his wife and asked, "What did she say?" He often had to ask what people had said, not because he had not heard them, but because he did not understand them.

His wife looked at him and said, Well, dear, she said.....oh my....."

"Come on, let's go," he said. He and Wackhead and their wives headed for the bar.

The Lohmans started talking with the Goren group. After a while that broke up and they all went off to other contacts. Gloria saw some of her friends and went off to talk to them and Bumper spotted the religious crew. One of them waived him over and he went.

On the way he passed by The Three Stooges. This was a nickname people had given to a certain group of three behind their backs. The Three Stooges were Swifty, St. Charles and one of their friends called The Biffster. Biffster was the guy's real first name. Biffster McCain was his full name. His intimates called him Biff. Everyone else referred to him as The Biffster. He was an old line social register sort who headed a large company and was a client of the firm. The three of them often hung out together.

The Three Stooges were laughing it up. The Biffster said, "Well have you heard this one? Why do elephants fly upside down?"

No one should have ever tried to tell a joke to St. Charles. He said, "They do?"

Then The Biffster said, "They do? Really? I didn't know that. How do they do it?"

Swifty chimed in. "It's a joke isn't it Biff?"

"It is?" said The Biffster.

"So what's the punch line?" asked Lohman.

The Biffster just looked at him blankly for a while. Finally he said, "I forgot."

This did not surprise anyone there.

The Lohmans went on to the religious group. Pansy invited all the big shots to her parties, including the religious leaders. It was customary for her to entertain the Archbishop of Canterbury at home in England so why not have all the religious leaders of Chicago at her parties.

Tonight she had a lot of them. The wives of the married ones had gone off to gossip by themselves. When the Lohmans got to the group they were telling each other dirty jokes.

The group included The Prophet Andy, Angelic Leader of the Evangelical Congregation of the Angel Gabriel and also Cardinal Sammy. His name was Cardinal Brandon Samuel, but everyone called him Cardinal Sammy. They had some lesser lights with them, but they were lesser only in religious terms. In terms of social rank they were way up there. They were pastors of two of the most fashionable churches in Kenilworth, one of the toniest suburbs of Chicago's North Shore. The Lohmans knew them. They were John Cooper, pastor of the Church of The Holy Quilt and Timothy West, pastor of the Church of the Unnamed Redeemer. Lohman sometimes had little systems for remembering names, but his system sometimes failed him. He remembered the name of Cooper's church by thinking of a comforter. However, he could never remember which was the hint word and which was the real word he was trying to remember. After greetings he asked Cooper, who was nearest him, "How are things at the Holy Comforter?"

Cooper was usually pissed off by this, but tonight he was pissed in another way so he ignored it.

The Cardinal said, "Bumper, tell us what is happening at your place. Seems like you have one murder a year. Is God punishing you?" All the religious ones chuckled. The Cardinal continued. "Or maybe God has something good in store for you. It is amazing how God arranges for the righteous to make use of the sinful on the pathway to Heaven." He looked around at the others who all nodded knowingly. They were all a bit lit. "And tell us about this, what would you call it? The little – what are they calling her? Anyway, what are you doing with that kind of mortal sin in your firm?"

Lohman felt like asking him what he was doing with the altar boys, but he restrained himself. Instead he started to tell the group about the girl being a messenger delivering something. He explained that she was from a messenger service they didn't ordinarily use and she was there to deliver a document for use the next day.

"Some messenger!" said The Prophet. "What service uses messengers like that?"

"Zoom Shot was the name," said Lohman.

"Who ever heard of them," remarked The Prophet. "Any of you?" He looked around the group.

"Not me," said Cooper.

"I never heard of them," said West.

They all looked at the Cardinal. He just looked flustered. After a while he said, "No. No. Not me. Never. I never head of them. Why would I use a service like that?"

"Like what?" asked The Prophet. He liked to needle the Cardinal. They hung around a lot, but only to keep an eye on each other while they competed for souls.

No one said anything for a moment. Then Lohman saw Sweeney motioning to him to come on over to where Sweeney was and he headed that way, leaving those who know how to commune with God to do so unhindered by the presence of a sinner.

Sweeney left his group and came out to Lohman and said, "Hey Dude. Trisha stuck her foot up some guy's cunt."

Lohman moved his head back and looked at Sweeney. By now he was not too surprised at anything Sweeney said, but sometimes he wasn't ready for it at all.

Sweeney continued. "We were talking to that guy over there." Sweeney pointed to someone who was standing with Goren, Sean and Trisha. "Trisha tells him what she does and he starts telling her he knows all about business and he starts telling her how to promote herself and she up and tells him to mind his own business. Then they get into it and he says, 'Look little girl, if you would take my advice then you'd come up the ladder. With sufficient improvement you could be a bitch.' We were talking to him a while. He's really touchy. If you say anything, anything at all, he takes it the wrong way and he goes all fainty poo. Know what I mean Man?"

Lohman looked over at the man. He recognized him. He said, "He's from Northwestern. He's head of the NU Meth Lab."

"No Man!" said Sweeney. "They got one?"

Lohman realized that they were thinking about different types of Meth. "That's short for Methodology Lab. It's part of the Business School."

"Yeah, well, we need help. Maybe if you know him you can do something. You know how Trisha is."

"OK," said Lohman. "I'll go over and say hello and you take your people away. I'll tell him it's Trisha's fault, not ours. I'll tell him this happens in show business. He'll buy that."

Ordinarily Lohman would not get involved with this stuff, but Pansy's parties were big networking opportunities for the firm and they were trying always to make a favorable impression on prospects. The guy himself didn't have any business, but being on the faculty of a prominent business school he had many good contacts.

The party continued until late in the night and most everyone had fun. Good company, or at least highly ranked company, good food, good booze and dancing.

The next day the Lohmans had the family over for dinner and then they all went out to a show. After that Lohman indulged in one of his favorite activities which was to take Louie, his Great Dane, out and around.

16 FRANCHISING

Monday Lohman got in early. He had an appointment with one Helvar Kaplinskewski who ran Aunt Mamie's Donut Shops. This was a potential new client who had been referred to Lohman by one of his other clients. Lohman was due to see the guy at 9. But the guy did not show up. Lohman waited until 9:30. Then he got on the phone to Aunt Mamie's to see where Kaplinskewski was. He was told that the guy had gone to see him a lot earlier. Then Lohman talked to Tete and had her look into it. Soon she reported that the guy had entered the building a little before 9 and that he had checked in on 40. The receptionist there said she had told the guy where to go and that Camelman was coming in at the same time and volunteered to show him the way. She said they went off to the elevators together. Tete said she checked with Camelman's office and his secretary said the two of them were in Camelman's office.

If Camelman would steal clients from St. Charles he would certainly steal them from Lohman. Lohman headed for Camelman's office. He went in and introduced himself. Kaplinskewski said he was glad to meet one of the people who worked for Camelman.

"Who told you that?" asked Lohman.

"Winston," was the reply. "He told me."

"I see," said Lohman. "I work with him sometimes. Not for him. He meant 'with'. I'm the Managing Partner. I run the place. He works here." Lohman did not ordinarily talk like this, but this time he enjoyed it. After all he thought, "What was Camelshit going to say?"

Lohman then got into a conversation with the two of them. Kaplinskewski had an up and running franchising business that had over 500 stores across the country and it was growing fast. Businesses like that already have lawyers. However, Kaplinskewski was looking for new lawyers. He was not at F, P & C looking for a new lawyer for a specific problem that had arisen. He was looking for new lawyers in general. He was dissatisfied with his current law firm because they kept telling him he could do things and then he later found out that he could not. Everywhere he operated he was in trouble with the franchising regulators and franchisees and even state Attorney Generals who handled fraud matters. He wanted someone who could handle the legal aspects of his franchising without getting him in trouble. Lohman was familiar with the firm currently handling the business and he had had dealings with them. They operated on the principle of telling the client anything he wanted to hear and leaving the consequences till later. Lohman referred to this method of business getting as the "Mother Killer" advice. Your client consults you and asks if he can kill his mother and get away with it. You say, "Sure. You came to the right place." No one else will advise the client this way so you get the business. The client kills his mother and gets charged with murder. You tell him, "We'll beat it. It'll be expensive, but leave it to me. I can handle these things." The client is then convicted. So what? You got a ton of money out of him and you really didn't have to do anything except talk.

Lohman was aware that this method of practicing law could be applied to all kinds of clients. The guilty as well as the innocent.

Some clients merely want to help their mother across the street and when some errant driver runs their mother down they are charged with murder. The trouble with the "Mother Killer" approach here is that this client is convicted of murder too. Of course that trouble befalls the client and the lawyer is still better off.

As kaplinskewski continued on about his situation, Lohman began to see trouble. Kaplinskewski was the guy who really did want to kill his mother, although he talked as if he was merely God's agent on earth sent here to be of service to the franchisees who needed his help. What Lohman heard was that Kaplinskewski was increasingly being accused of fraud for selling franchises that could in no way make any money for the franchisees. Many of the franchise sales were re-sales of franchises that had failed. Aunt Mamie would repossess these and resell them. The disclosure materials said the franchisees made money and gave an average profit figure. When the failed franchises were re-sold the materials stated the operations had been profitable.

Kaplinskewski did not tell Lohman and Camelman that the franchises did not make money. He did not tell them the failed franchisees had not made money. He told them that these were unfounded allegations the franchisees, regulators and Attorney Generals were making. What he did tell them was that he required financial statements from all the franchisees and he had them audited at random by his accounting firms and the statements showed the franchisees were all making money. Every last one. He told Lohman and Camelman that the trouble was that the franchisees were lying about their sales because a large part of the franchise fees were a percentage of sales.

As for the franchisees who went out of business, Kaplinskewski maintained that they did not fail. He claimed that they had run some of the most profitable franchises and had not declared all the profits to Uncle Sam and were using the purported failures as a cover. After all, if they would cheat him on the franchise fees, they would cheat Uncle Sam.

Lohman decided that he really did not want Kaplinskewski as a client. The guy was headed for the slammer and along the way he was going to require huge amounts of time and he was going to stop paying. Lohman determined to urge the Management Committee not to accept him as a client, and he also decided to let Camelman be his lawyer if the Committee did not veto the guy.

Now if you, dear reader, are thinking that the clients of our most prestigious law firms are the most prestigious, the most meritorious and the most pure themselves, be aware that this is not always so. We can pause here while you assimilate and process this shocking fact.

Pause. Relax. Breathe in slowly. Exhale. Again. There. Feel better now?

So Lohman decided to take a pass. "Well, Winston," he said, "what do you think you can do?"

Camelman lit up. He was hearing that Lohman was going to fade. "Resolve these problems. The baseless, unfounded accusations. We have audited financials. We will stop this. Cold. You came to the right lawyer Helvar."

Good old Helvar bought it before and he bought it this time.

The conversation then gradually changed to personal things like their families, interests, hobbies, who knew whom, gossip and a lot of other things that demonstrated the expertise and good faith of those present. In the course of these meanderings it was revealed that Helvar was a car collector. He had heard that some guy running a big pizza shop franchisor was a renowned antique car collector and he noticed how much publicity the guy got for it. He determined to do the same thing with new cars. He was going to have a stable of all the new high priced cars.

If Kaplinskewski was interested in cars, so was Camelman. Camelman was interested in anything a prospect liked. If he was trying to get business out of Hitler he would tell Hitler how much he liked killing Jews. This time Camelman actually had some interest in cars. He didn't know a thing about them, but he knew that having a fancy car impressed people so he was always taking about his fancy car of the moment. His fancy car of the moment was a Deutschbanger B24.

"I'm trying out a DB," he said. "DB" was the way those in the know referred to Deutschbangers. "I've had it about two weeks. I picked it up a couple of weeks ago. Monday." Here he looked at Lohman and said, "The night – you know…"

Kaplinskewski knew. "The day the little whore was killed here?"

Lohman noticed that the concept of a little whore being killed on the premises was not discouraging this prospect at least

"Yes," said Camelman. "I have it on try out." Here he paused and then leaned forward towards Helvar and lowered his voice, "I buy so many from them they deliver them to me for tryout. They had put it in the building garage and delivered the key up to me. I went down and picked it up about ten o'clock and then took a spin and went home. A DB B24 coupe with that seven speed manual/automatic. What a driver! Smooth, if you know what I mean. Hit the pedal and before you know it you are going whatever speed you want and loafing along in seventh. That car can do 0-60 straight up hill in 4 seconds I think. I might just buy it. I don't know though. Right now I have three Mercs and a Lambo in the garage."

Lohman had seen his garage. He had not seen what was inside it, but it was a two car garage. Helvar took all this in and said, "Yeah. I have a B24 too. But where did you get a coupe? With seven speeds? They only make a six speed."

Camelman said, "Well, well, I mean, he said it was special for me. It's an option, he said."

"They made it specially for you?" asked Kaplinskewski incredulously. "Or it's just an option? I didn't know it was available."

Camelman said, "Option maybe. I'm not sure."

"I need that," said Kaplinskewski. "If I get special cars I'll get special publicity. Where did you get it?"

Camelman said, "Midwest Luxury Motors."

"Who do you deal with there?" asked Kaplinskewski.

"Jay Cooke," said Camelman. "I get all my cars from him."

Kaplinskewski said he was going to contact Cooke and see what kind of special cars he could get. "How much did you pay?" he asked.

"I haven't finally decided to buy it yet," said Camelman. "He wants $280,000 he says, but after all, it's a car. I think I can get it for about $250,000."

The conversation continued at this level until they all got bored with it. At that point Lohman excused himself and left the other two to wind up the meeting.

Lohman made his way back to his office. When he got there he found that Sweeney had just arrived and wanted to talk to him. As he as coming in to the outer office and greeting Sweeney and Tete, Cohenstein came it. Lohman asked them what they wanted and both of them wanted to talk about Camelman. Lohman asked them to step into his office and said he would be right in.

Cohenstein gave a glance to Sweeney and said, "Ah, the kid with the business. Let's go." He led the way.

Lohman turned to Tete. "Me too. I just was in Camelman's office. Maybe I should talk about him too. On the other hand, I'd rather forget him. When you can, I want you to check out something. Camelman said he had a Deutschbanger B24 coupe the Monday night the messenger was killed. He said a Jay Cooke from Midwest Luxury Motors gave it to him to try out. Winston said they put it in the garage and delivered the key to him. He was telling all this to a potential client up in his office. The prospect is Helvar Kaplinskewski. They're both car nuts. Winston says it was a coupe and had a seven speed transmission. Kaplinskewski said they don't make a seven speed or a coupe. See what you can find out about that car. You know how much they cost? Almost $300,000. Thank God I'm not hooked on that kind of stuff."

"Your horse probably agrees," said Tete.

Lohman just went on in to his office. A Horse! They cost more than DB's. But he realized that Tete was not talking about the horses owned by the rich horsey set these days, but the horse she was suggesting Lohman used with his buggy.

When he got into his office he found Cohenstein and Sweeney talking about the best ways to approach strangers at gatherings at religious functions. "Maybe in a temple, but you can't do that in a cathedral Dude," said Sweeney as he looked over to the door where Lohman was coming in.

Cohenstein walked over to Lohman and put a hand on his shoulder as he followed him to his desk and then released the hand and let Lohman sit. As he let go he said, "Camelman. I want him fixed. Put it on the agenda for the next meeting."

"Me too Dude," said Sweeney. "Oh Man, the guy told Trisha I'm a second level junior and I have no authority to deal with her stuff. He told her to call him from now on. He actually told her not to contact me at all."

Lohman asked, "When? Where? He doesn't have anything to do with her does he?"

"No he doesn't," said Sweeney. "She's my client. So, like, I'm not a partner. I run everything through you. I get someone working on her stuff, I clear it with you. You know everything. You know everyone working on her stuff."

Lohman asked, "So how did he get involved?"

"In the hall Man," said Sweeney. "Get this. I'm walking down the hall with Trisha and he stops us and takes us into a room and starts telling Trisha he is a partner and I'm not and the firm wants her to have a, he said, 'real lawyer' in charge of her affairs. "

"When was this?" asked Lohman.

"Earlier this morning Dude," said Sweeney. "We were down on 40. Trisha had just come in and I was there to meet her and he was there and he was talking to some guy he was taking to his office. They were talking about donuts or something Man. So he just stops and greets Trisha like a long lost friend. I think they have met before, but she wouldn't think of him as a friend. Not her type. Not long lost. More like she would long for him to be lost. So we went into one of the meeting rooms and he starts up. He had this other guy in there with him. Called him Helvar. Then after he has told Trisha this he told the other guy that he was sorry for the delay but he thought the guy would like to meet one of his prominent clients. Helvar, or whatever his name was. He obviously knew about Trisha. He was having fun meeting with a star."

Lohman said, "Helvar is Helvar Kaplinskewski. He owns Aunt Mamie's' Donut Shops. He was referred to me, but Winston picked him up on the way in. Winston told Kaplinskewski that I work for him." Lohman shrugged his shoulders. "Just as well. After finding out about the matter I really don't want the guy."

Cohenstein said, "The schmuck did the same thing to me. I have this new client that makes Mexican food. Pretty big company. We're at a party at Graybee's house and Camelman is there. He and me and the client are talking. My client is Mexican. A Mexican citizen. They're setting up plants here, but they are based in Mexico City. The wives are there, but they're off somewhere else. We're talking about this lawsuit with a distributor. My client is worried about the hassle with this guy. I say, 'Don't worry, his ass is gonna be grass, just like you Mexicans say. Grassyass, right?"

Neither Lohman nor Sweeney thought Cohenstein was trying to make a joke. He just talked that way.

"So there we are," Cohenstein continued. "But before we could get into it any further Winston says, 'Oh Zenon, you're so anti-Mexican. You're anti-Hispanic.' Then he grabs the client and says, 'Come with me over to the buffet and you'll meet some of our people with a better attitude.' As he leads the client away I hear him saying how they all work for him."

Lohman said, "He's been busier than usual. I get a lot of complaints like this about him, but not all at once. He also seems to have taken a client from Graybourne recently. The client contacts him instead of Graybourne now. He is working on another client of Graybourne's. One that is starting to call him too. I was in a meeting with Winston and the first client recently and found out that Winston told him that Graybourne is just a figurehead and doesn't really work as a lawyer. The client seemed to think that Winston had always been doing his work and that Graybourne just acted as a go-between."

"That's another thing," said Cohenstein. "We can't have people going around telling the truth about Grabby." Every once in a while the members of the firm used the more popular name for the Saint. "So what are we going to do?" asked Cohenstein.

"I'm no wizard," said Lohman. "I think what we have to do is analyze his billings and ask around to see whose clients he has been contacting and how. What has he been telling them? We have to be able to answer the question of what will be the consequences if we dump him. What will be the consequences if clients learn about all this? Can he walk off with the business? How much business does he have on his own? I'll get to work on it and try to get something ready for the next Management Committee meeting. Then, in the meantime Zenon, you should be asking people what Winston has been doing to them. What do they know about what he is doing in general? Me too. I'll ask around. And I'll have Tete work the non-lawyer grapevine to see what she can find out."

Lohman thought for a moment and then said, "We can search the phone records too. Our system has a record of all land line calls – from where to where. We can run his numbers and the clients' through there. I'll ask Pigman to work on it."

"What I'd like to see," said Cohenstein, "is you tell Tete to go smash his head in."

"That'd be like assault with a deadly weapon," smirked Sweeney.

"So you ask around too," said Cohenstein.

"Right, Dude," said Sweeney. "Man, he's such an asshole, all the toilet paper manufacturers must love him.'

Lohman remarked dryly, "No. He couldn't be an asshole. If he were, all the toilet paper around here would have run away and hid. I hear no such reports."

Cohenstein and Sweeney got up and started to leave. On the way out Sweeney moved to fist bump Lohman. Lohman knew enough by now to at least put up his hand. This time he remembered to make a fist. Cohenstein said, "Kids these days! Come on John, let's go." He put his arm around Sweeney and they walked out together with Lohman following. In the outer office with Tete looking on they all said goodbye and parted.

After they left Lohman turned to Tete and explained what he wanted to find about Camelman's clients and contacts and billings and what he had been doing with other lawyers' clients.

"Will do Hon," she said. "You know, he's not winning the guy of the week award around here too often. Anyway, I found out something about the car. I got that Jay Cooke guy. He's not just a salesman there, he owns the place. Midwest Luxury Motors. They sell a lot of different makes. He says he knows Camelman from selling him cars over the years. He says they don't make a coupe B24 and they don't make a seven speed. I told him Camelman said he got it from them and he said he didn't give one to Camelman. He also said they don't give tryout cars to people. They give the cars to people when they buy them. Anything else, any other test drive arrangement, has a salesman present."

Tete continued. "Then I talked to people in the building garage. Nobody there saw a car like that that Monday, but the place has automatic entry and exit. The building people assigned to it aren't in the parking area too much. At least not constantly. Then I got

166

lucky and got Camelman's wife. Or I got Monica to talk to her. Monica says she said she doesn't know anything about that Monday because she was away visiting relatives." Then Tete squinted her eyes a little and looked directly into Bumper's eyes and said in a pointed, somewhat disapproving voice, "You know Monica."

Monica was Monica Platt, one of the firm lawyers. Despite her being best friends with Bumper's wife, firm rumor had it that she and Bumper were getting it on.

Lohman allowed as how he did and then asked Tete to check on one more thing. He asked her to get St. Charles's billings at the Pullman Club for that Monday night.

"I'll try," she said. "You know they have that twerpy little manager over there."

"Well, if he gives you any trouble, just ask Mr. St. Charles to get them."

"Will do," said Tete.

Lohman started to turn. He said, "I don't know. It's a little, well I feel bewildered. Dead people every year. I'm supposed to practice law for a living, but I have to deal with this kind of thing all the time."

"Maybe it's inevitable," said Tete. "Somebody was going to wack 'em."

"Here? Why here?" asked Lohman. He went back into his office.

17 LOHMAN CONFRONTS STONEGOLD

In his office Lohman finished up a few things and then rang Stonegold and told him he wanted to see him. They made an appointment for after lunch. In the meantime Lohman went to lunch with some of the officers of a client company. After lunch he came back to the office and saw Stonegold. What he wanted to do was hear what Stonegold had to say about his prints being on the messenger's bag.

"Steven, how are you?" Lohman asked as he entered Stonegold's office.

"Fine thank you Bumper. And You?"

"Fine thanks," said Lohman. "Have the police been talking to you?"

"No," said Stonegold. "Why should they?"

"They didn't talk to you Friday or on the weekend?" asked Lohman.

"No," said Stonegold." Actually I was feeling under stress and Zenon suggested I needed to get away so I went to Hawaii for the weekend."

"What stress?" asked Lohman.

Stonegold did not respond. Lohman asked him again. He said, "Well, you know. What with the work load around here and all the recent events."

"I see," said Lohman. "Did you hear that they found the messenger's bag one of the hall closets on 55?"

Stonegold did not respond.

Lohman continued. "And it had your fingerprints on it in the messenger's blood – did you hear that?"

Stonegold did not respond.

"So the police didn't ask you about this?" Lohman asked.

Stonegold still did not respond. Silence is golden so Stone cold silence must also be Gold.

"Crap!" exclaimed Lohman. "They are going to talk to you. What happened?"

Stonegold just glanced up and down at Lohman and the floor. He licked his lips. Then he looked at Lohman again. Then out the window. Then at his desk. Then he said, "Well...." He stopped.

"Well what Steven?" asked Lohman.

"I didn't do it," Stonegold finally blurted out. "She was in my office, but I didn't kill her. I came in Tuesday morning around, well a little before 9. I had got a flight back from Seattle the afternoon before. She was in my office. In that bag. The zipper was partially open and I unzipped it all the way and – she was in there. I felt her. I could tell she was dead. I didn't do it. I would never do a thing like that. You know me Bumper. I'm happily married and everything anyway. What are they going to do to me? I didn't do it. You've got to help me! Please!"

"So is that how your prints got on the bag? They were in her blood. How did you get that on your hands before opening the bag? And how did she get into Graybourne's office? Out of the bag." Lohman wanted to know.

"Oh help me, Bumper! I didn't do it," said Stonegold.

"How can I help you without knowing what happened?" said Lohman.

Stonegold finally came to rest. He took a deep breath. "I don't know what happened," he said. "I came in. My office was a mess. A lot of the papers had been thrown on the floor. There were tracks made by the bag on the carpet. I saw the bag and opened it. All I can say is that I panicked. All I could think of was getting her out of there. I wasn't thinking. I couldn't go down the hall with her. And where would I put her? I saw the door. The door between my office and Graybourne's. I took her in there. I didn't want to leave any tracks from the bag so I took her out and carried her in there. She was little. Light. I carried her. She had a plastic bag on her head. It felt like it was full of paper. I was just going to throw her on the couch, but she was naked and – well – that would be – well, naked on the couch. I thought it would be better if she was covered up a little so I put her in the desk chair. Then I went back to my office. What was I going to do with the bag? I couldn't think well. I was panicked. I zipped it up and took it down the hall and put it in the closet when no one was looking. I didn't know what to do. I washed up and left and spent the rest of the day at home. My wife was out of town so no one would see me there. I didn't even tell my secretary where I was. She called several times. I could see it was here from the caller id, but I didn't answer. Oh, Bumper, what is going to happen to me?"

"I don't know," responded Lohman. "The police are going to be talking to you. You know what you can do. Either you respond to their questions or you refuse to talk to them and refuse to answer their questions."

Stonegold gave Lohman a deer in the headlights look.

"Look," said Lohman, "Do this. Get ahold of a criminal lawyer. Then talk to Bungus. You might talk to him about what lawyer to contact. Bungus may be able to hold off any arrest until we find out who put her in your office."

"I didn't have a gun. That's it!" said Stonegold.

"It was next door," said Lohman dryly. He did not necessarily think Stonegold did it, but he was not trying to figure it all out just then. Maybe Stonegold was telling the truth. Anyway, he was probably in Seattle at the time of the murder. Lohman was thinking more of what he had to do next. He took his leave and headed back to his office.

18 AND WHAT ABOUT FEATHERBOTTOM?

While he was at it, Lohman decided to see what Sweeney knew about Sean Featherbottom. He was no sooner in his office then he got Sweeney on the phone and told him he was coming to his office.

Lohman came in and sat down. After they had greeted each other he asked, "What do you know about Sean? You heard that about his brooch. What was he doing Monday evening? What do you think of him? Why is he always mixed up in these things?"

"Got me Dude," said Sweeney. "I wouldn't worry about him though. I work with him a lot. I even get him out to some of the parties for clients. You know he does good work. He works for you too. He's a nice guy. Maybe you don't see it, but he's a little intimidated by you big shots. But he's more natural with me. And what would he do with a woman Dude? He doesn't even seem to play around too much with the guys. He says he's got a boyfriend, but I never met him. He still goes to parties with that Tammy Fine. You know the lesbian doll doing consumer plaintiffs' cases. Now there's a lawyer Dude! Drops the F-bomb all over the place. She's nice too, though. Except I think the defense lawyers don't think so. So there. Sean's a great guy, he does great work, and so far as I'm concerned every gay guy means there's one more doll hole for me to fill."

Lohman said, "Not if they're lesbians."

Sweeney said, "Well sometimes you want to plug all the holes in a dyke, Dude. Like that Tammy Fine. Yeah Dude!"

Lohman looked at Sweeney in silence for a moment. Actually he wished he could be so uninhibited.

After a while Lohman said, "So you aren't thinking he did anything wrong I take it. I don't really see it either, but he sure gets mixed up in things. Hey, are you going to the ASPS fundraiser weekend after next? We want a lot of firm people there."

"Yeah, Dude," said Sweeney. "Sometimes the parties are more work than the law stuff. This is gonna be one. American Serenity Providers Association. ASPS. Bull! Asspiss is more like it. It's nothing but a feeder for ECOTAG. More like American Stupid People's Society. Why do those fools buy their stuff?"

ECOTAG was the Evangelical Congregation Of The Angel Gabriel, led by The Prophet Andy, its charismatic leader. It was a worldwide religious organization and a rich one. Its headquarters were in the tallest building in Chicago. ASPS was a gathering of all the religious organizations in Chicago and its ostensible purpose was to foster interest in religion and God in general in a nondenominational way. In practice it was dominated by ECOTAG and the Catholic Church which was led by Cardinal Brandon Samuel who everyone called Cardinal Sammy. The Cardinal and The Prophet talked a good game of peace and cooperation, but in reality they were in fierce competition for the local souls, at least the rich ones. Pious and devout F, P & C got a lot of business from both of them.

"And, Man, you should look into them too. ECOTAG, I mean," said Sweeney. "This is only hearsay. And who knows, maybe they are all just passing on something that didn't happen. But the rumor mill is that they sometimes control people with sex and drugs. They blackmail the people. Sometimes they get them started on the drugs and with sex parties."

Lohman said, "God works in mysterious ways. That covers anything done by the religious. Anyway we get their business, so don't bad mouth them."

"Hey Dude, I know about getting business," said Sweeney. "Anyhow, I'll be there. Maybe I can scare up something."

Tuesday Lohman dropped in on Sean Featherbottom. He reviewed the facts with Sean. So far Sean was the only person who saw the messenger alive. His brooch, or at least probably his brooch, was found on the body. Lohman asked, "So what do you have to add to all this? How can we tell if it was your brooch? Or not your brooch? Did anyone see you or talk to you?"

Sean just did a little pouty pucker with his lips and turned his head to one side and did a little butt wiggle in his chair. Then he lifted a hand to his head and began twirling a few strands of his hair. "It looks like my brooch. The police showed me a photo of it. I don't know of who else would have one around here. It would be a coincidence."

"Crap!" said Lohman. "Anything else?"

Sean thought for a while. Then his facial expression changed for the better. "Yes! Yes there is. I left the building after I saw her up there. I went home. Kevin was standing in the lobby. He saw me. We nodded to each other. This was right after I saw her. I went to the elevators and down to the lobby and home."

"Who is Kevin?" asked Lohman.

"Kevin Bainbaum," said Sean. Lohman still looked blank so Sean added, "He works here. He's a few years ahead of me. Mostly litigation I think. I don't think he likes me."

"Ah yes," said Lohman. "I think I've met him." In a firm the size of F, P & C not everyone knew everyone else very well and some had never met some of the others. "Why doesn't he like you?"

Sean shrugged his shoulders. "Don't know. He's not very friendly. At least not to me. Anyway, he was down in the lobby. He was talking on his phone."

Lohman said, "Let's see if we can find him." He motioned towards Sean's phone and Sean handed it to him. He called Tete and got Bainbaum's extension and called him. He was in and Lohman asked him to come to Sean's office.

Lohman and Sean talked about what Lohman knew about the events of that Monday and what Sean had heard on the rumor mill until Bainbaum got there.

After a while Bainbaum came in. Lohman recognized him as someone he had seen around the firm as well as a name he had heard of. Bainbaum, and most other people in the firm, knew the name of the Managing Partner was Bumper Lohman, whether or not they had ever met him.

Lohman and Bainbaum greeted each other. Sean said, "Hi Kevin." Bainbaum just glanced at him and sat down.

Lohman repeated to Bainbaum what Sean had said about passing him in the lobby that Monday night. Bainbaum shot a glance at Sean and said, "What kind of fairy piddle it that?"

Lohman thought, "Well, so much for why he doesn't like Sean." Then he asked Bainbaum, "Were you there that night?"

"I was there," Bainbaum said, "But I didn't see him." He motioned towards Sean with his head.

"But you nodded at me," said Sean.

Bainbaum looked at Sean and then turned to Lohman. "Why would I be going all noddy with him, if you know what I mean?"

"You didn't see him? You weren't talking on the phone?" asked Lohman.

"No Mr. Lohman," responded Bainbaum. "I was going home."

Lohman dismissed him. Then he said to Sean, "That didn't help. You're sure he saw you?"

Sean was a little bewildered. "He was there. He was looking at me. We nodded. Maybe his mind was just on the phone conversation and he wasn't really aware of me."

Lohman sighed. "Well, I don't know what's going on here. Anyway, I have to get back to my office."

Lohman took his leave and got back to his office. Tete was there going through some records. She looked up when he came in. "I have some responses on those things you wanted to find out," she said.

"Good," said Lohman. "So far all I can find out just makes for more of a puzzle. The body was in St. Charles' office. But now I find out before the body was found there   Steven Stonegold – you remember he has the office next to Graybourne's – he found the body in his office in the wheeled bag Tuesday morning and he took it out and put it in Graybourne's office and he put the bag in the hall closet. Then he took off. Or so he says. And Levin and Camelman appear to have been around the night before and then Sean. He is the last one who says he saw the messenger alive. He was up there on 55. He says someone saw him leave in the lobby downstairs, but that person denies it. Christ!"

Tete said, "That Featherbottom! He's always involved. You're always saying he's a smart kid. Maybe he is outsmarting us on all these killings. You think so?"

"I don't know what to think," said Lohman.

"Well, anyway," said Tete, "I got Charlie's bill from the Pullman club for that Monday night. At least it has his member number on it. Big bill! He was not alone. Or if he was he ate and drank enough to kill three elephant herds. It also has his room charge on it. Then Geeley down in the business office had the building log checked for that Monday for Levin, Stonegold, Beale, Camelman, Sean and Charlie. Sean came in after dinner but, if he left after that, he did not check back in again. Levin and Camelman checked in around nine. Geeley told me they said they came back from dinner and then Camelman says he left shortly after that. Levin says he got a document he was looking for and then left. Their timesheets show an associate met with them around nine and that associate confirmed it. After that Pigman found that someone met with Levin down on another floor about ten. Beale was supposed to be in New York. He didn't check in that night. He did check in early the next day. On Tuesday. The people he supposedly met with in New York won't talk. The none of your business it's confidential bunk, but an associate who the time records show was with him confirms she was with him in New York. Stonegold was in Seattle. That checks out. He didn't check in that night. He came in early the next day. They also checked time records and phone calls for everyone else with offices on 55. None of them appears to have been there that Monday night. At least there is no evidence of it and they talked to them all and they all say they weren't there. None of them admits to being there after eight. Except of course Camelman and Levin. And Sean. But he wasn't officed on 55. Someone from another floor could have been up there too, Hon. You know, Geeley, Henner and Wiggy have been busy. They want to know if this is a law firm or a detective office."

"I can see why," said Lohman.

19 HE HASN'T GOT A LEG TO STAND ON

Wednesday Lohman had to appear in court early in the morning on a routine matter. After that he came back to the office and started reviewing a file Sean was working on involving the sale of a business by one of Lohman's clients. He had a question about the wording of one of the warranties in the contract and he picked up the phone and got Sean and told him he was coming there to talk to him about it. Lohman then went to Sean's office.

They greeted each other and Lohman sat down. "What's with this limited warranty Sean?" he asked. "We're saying the company has litigation? What litigation? I didn't know there was any material litigation."

Sean said, "Yes there is. You remember that guy who is suing for losing a leg when the client's truck ran him over. You remember. That guy who was making millions playing for the Bulls. Huge damages! Mr. Camelman was handling it. He had me work up a brief on a jury instruction matter so I was aware of it."

"Good old Winston," remarked Lohman. "But he lost. There is no pending litigation. It is a liability maybe, but not pending litigation."

"Yes, but we appealed," said Sean. "Now he wants me and Tambola to work on the brief. Didn't he tell you? It was just a few weeks ago."

Tambola was Tambola Cook, who had previously almost run Lohman down in the hall. Miss Leftwitch. She had a crush on Sean.

Lohman thought that this was typical of Camelman. Maybe Lohman would have wanted another lawyer to handle the appeal, but Camelman would be that much further from contact with the client so he was not going to tell Lohman anything about it. Lohman didn't say anything about Camelman's client stealing. But Sean's telling him about what was happening made him remember one of the many incidents from the past.

"You know Sean," he said, "This is like an old case from the street car days. I was once, way back in the last century when I was a kid, I was once talking to an old plaintiff's lawyer who told me a story about a suit against the street car company by a guy who claimed a street car ran over him, causing him to lose his leg. The evidence was presented and the lawyers were arguing the case to the jury. The street car company's lawyer summed up by saying, 'In conclusion, ladies and gentlemen of the jury, I submit that the plaintiff does not have a leg to stand on'."

Sean didn't laugh. He just looked at Lohman with wide eyes. After a while he said, "Was Mr. Camelman there?"

"No. Why?" asked Lohman.

"Because that's what he told the jury in this case," said Sean.

Lohman couldn't believe it. Then again, he could. He just did not say anything because for once he could restrain himself. All he said was, "So we lost. I see."

Then Lohman changed the subject. "Well apart from that, tell me Sean, what were you doing up on 55 that Monday night?"

Sean said, "As I told you. I was there to deliver a document to Mr. Levin. It was a letter from a file that he wanted. A letter from the SEC about one of his clients. I got the request for it on my email earlier in the day and that night when I got back from dinner I looked for it and found it and took it up there and put it on his desk. Then I went home."

"Where else did you go on 55?" asked Lohman.

"I didn't go anywhere else," said Sean. "I came up on the elevator, went down the hall to his office, put it on his desk, and went back out in the hall. Then I headed for the elevators and saw her – the messenger or whatever she was. I answered her question and went on to the elevators and downstairs to the lobby and home."

"So how did your brooch wind up on her?" asked Lohman. "Did you have it then?"

"I thought I did," said Sean. "I had my bag with me. But when I got home I noticed the brooch was missing. I don't know where it went. I had it when I was up there though. When I was coming out of the elevator coming up I felt my bag was hanging wrong and I picked it up a little from the bottom to readjust it. I felt the brooch. I remember I felt it. I know what it feels like. I pick my bag up like that a lot. It always gets into such an unfashionable position when I walk."

"Did you see it?" asked Lohman.

Sean thought for a while. "I don't specifically remember, Mr. Lohman."

"So," said Lohman. "You were there when the messenger was there, you had your brooch, she was murdered and your brooch was found in her boots. It doesn't sound good. How did that happen if you had nothing to do with it?"

Sean pursed his lips. He moved them to his left and held them there. He moved them to the center and un-pursed. Then he pursed them again and moved them to the right where they did not stay. They came back to the center and un-pursed. He wiggled his butt. He fiddled with his hair. He looked at the ceiling. He looked at the floor. He turned and looked out the window. Then he turned back to Lohman and said, "I don't know."

"Great," said Lohman.

Sean said, "Well, I lose them sometimes. They usually have a hinged pin on them. This comes all the way across the back and it fits into something to hold it on the other side. You pull the pin out so the pointed end is at a 90 degree angle from the back of the brooch and then put the pin through the fabric where you want the brooch to be. Then you fold the brooch back parallel to the pin and fit the pin in the holder. The holder is two circular rings with a third ring between them. The two outside rings are fixed and they have an opening on one side of them. The inside ring has an opening too. The inside ring rotates between the outer two. It's like three washers placed together. The inner ring rotates and they all have an opening. Each has an opening through the metal circle that surrounds the empty center. You rotate the inner circle so the three openings are together and then you can put the end of the hinged pin through them. Then you rotate the inner circle again so its closed part covers the opening where the pin came through the outer ring. The inner ring has a little raised piece on it so you can move it. A lot of the time the pin works loose and the inner ring comes around on its own so all the openings are together again. I suppose when you put the brooch on and wear it for only a short time this doesn't happen so much. But I put them on my bags and leave them there and sooner or later this happens. I've lost several that way. And I put them on my bike bags too. They glitter in the sunlight. It's a very nice effect. I lose them there too."

Lohman thought for a moment and then asked, "Do you remember anything particular about the brooch after you lifted up your bag?"

"No," said Sean. "Wait. I dropped the document when I took it out of my bag and I bent over to get it and my bag hit a corner of the desk. Maybe that did it. Dislodged the pin. But I don't remember anything in particular."

Lohman looked at him for a while and then said, "Well, try." Then he got up and said, "I have to go. I'll talk to the buyer's lawyer about the suit. Write me something describing it and how much is involved and we'll see what they want to do about the warranties."

As Lohman was getting up he asked, "By the way. Did you go to Mr. Stonegold's office when you were up there?"

"No," said Sean.

Lohman continued on up and left.

20 CLIENTS

Lohman spent the rest of the day dealing with clients, starting with George Klineberg, a director of Winky Titter Systems who chaired the board's compensation committee. This was a large publicly held company that was a software producer. Oddly enough, no one ever asked how it got its name. Perhaps they were afraid to.

Winky Titter was a client of Camelman's. It was his largest client. When he was a younger lawyer one of the other partners in the firm had the client. Camelman did most of his work for the client. The partner left to join another firm and he and the other firm thought Winky Titter was going to go with him. It didn't. It stayed with F, P & C and Camelman was the one they wanted to talk to so he got credit for the business. Camelman was there with Klineberg.

The company's CEO was retiring and they were negotiating with a new CEO candidate they wanted to hire. There was no disagreement as to how much they were going to pay. The more the better. Public company directors are mostly officers of other public companies these days. They usually do not sit directly on each other's boards so the situation was not one where they would say, "I will vote to increase your pay if you vote to increase mine." However, as a group they sat on boards that determined their compensation. Therefore, as a general rule they voted to pay big bucks to fellow corporate officers. All the companies had something like compensation committees. The purpose of these committees was not to pay enough to get and retain the best talent, at least not the best talent to handle production, sales, procurement, product development, finance and general management. As a general rule these people could not even find the john on their own and when they did find it they needed ten of the brightest MBAs in the land to go and hold their weenies. No, the purpose of the committees was not to pay just enough to get the best. The purpose was to figure out how much they could pay and how to justify it to the stockholders and the public.

Actually they did figure out how much they had to pay to get the talent to run the company. That much lesser sum is what was paid to the more junior people who reported to the great CEOs. All this is not to detract from the CEO types. They did have one outstanding talent. A talent shared with politicians. They had the talent to get elected and stay elected. It is hardly their fault that this usually was correlated with total incompetence in other areas.

Klineberg himself was a director of many companies also. He was also the head of a private equity company that took investors' money and put it in other companies and charged the investors a lot of money to do so. He was making way more than most CEOs and thus he didn't think that what they got was out of line.

F, P & C and Camelman had people in on the negotiations as they were progressing and they had informed Lohman in advance of generally what was going on. The CEO candidate and the company had agreed that he was to get incentive compensation on top of his "base" pay and benefits such that if the company increased its profits, he would make out like a bandit. Now, you may think he was being hired to get the company to make out like a bandit. Certainly, that may be a theoretical part of his job, but if you really wanted him to do his job you had to "incent" him. We all have pay plans like this. We come in on time, most of the time, we are there, and we go home at quitting time. When we actually lift a paper or carton or tool, we get incentive pay. Lots of it. Far more than our base pay. Or at least it would be nice if we did. And so it is with CEOs. You want them to do something more that come in to the office once in a while, you gotta pay extra. And why not tie their incentive pay to results. After all, they are entirely responsible for the results.

The negotiations with the candidate had reached a stage where a specific proposal had to be written up. Klineberg wanted it by the end of the day. Incentive pay deals are fairly standard so ordinarily there would not be too much problem with this. Just the ordinary rush job done by large law firms. However, there was a twist to the deal. The parties had agreed that the candidate was to make out like a bandit if profits went up, and he was to make out like a bandit even if they went down. Putting makeup on that pig to make it look like – well – anything else would take some doing. It also had to pass muster with the regulatory authorities that required the facts of what was going on to be disclosed to investors.

The accountants and lawyers on the job had already figured out how to structure the compensation to make it look good, but Klineberg was the rare client who knew that you don't get rush jobs done without some special intervention. He also knew that Lohman controlled who was assigned to what in the firm. Camelman also knew that. That is the reason they were talking to Lohman. They were talking to the guy who could order the job done and commit the manpower necessary to do it.

Lohman asked Klineberg how the pay was going to be structured. This had just been figured out so Lohman had not read the report on it yet. Klineberg explained that the CEO candidate's accountants had examined the Winky Titter financial records and found that one of their major supply costs was correlated with profits, but not on a direct basis where a 1% change in profits would cause a 1% change in the cost. Instead, a 1% rise in profits would cause a 0.9% increase in the cost. And a 1% decline in the profits would cause a 1.1% decline in the cost. Therefore the candidate was to be offered incentive pay for either increasing profit or decreasing that cost. This would result in his getting the extra pay whether profits went up or went down. And there would be justification for it. After all, one way to increase profits is to cut costs.

This did not surprise Lohman. Nor would it surprise anyone in the world of large public companies. The only little thing the company had to do was not to state publicly to all the sucker investors and the SEC that what they were doing is to make sure the CEO got big pay regardless of results.

Of course all this pay was to be in the form of stock so it could be turned into capital gains income at a lower tax rate and so the company could pull the usual accounting and share buy-back tricks to hike the earnings per share and thus the potential price of the candidates' stock after it was given to him.

Lohman let Klineberg know that he would do everything possible to get out a draft by the end of the day. Klineberg said, "No Bumper. You know what I mean. I need to get it to the candidate and his lawyers and accountants by 5."

"I understand, said Lohman. So I'll have to say good bye now and get on the stick."

The meeting broke up and Lohman started calling people and assigning them. Whether or not this would be done and delivered by 5 was an open question, but he got the best and put the screws to them. As the Managing Partner he sometimes had to do things like this. He had to drop everything and make things happen for someone else's client who would get the credit for the billings. Lohman did so and then finished up a few other matters and went home.

Thursday, as Lohman was coming in to the office he remembered he wanted to see Cohenstein about something so he headed for 55. When he got off the elevator he ran into Levin who was headed for Camelman's office.

Lohman greeted him. "Wanzer. Morning. Where you headed?"

"Winston's office," he said.

Lohman said, "I have to drop in Zenon's. You guys wait for me. I want to talk to you. It won't take me long."

They headed to their separate destinations and when Lohman was finished with Cohenstein he headed for Camelman's office. They all greeted each other and Lohman sat down. "Did you get the draft yesterday?" he asked Camelman.

"Seven o'clock," said Camelman. "You know, we really do need better people around here. I had to wait till seven."

Lohman sympathized with him. He probably had to wait around with nothing to do except bill Winky Titter for waiting. Actually he suspected that getting the draft that day was a big surprise to everyone, including to Camelman who's billing for waiting around was thereby cut short. So he said, "I'll bet Klineberg didn't think we could do it. I guess the deal's still on, right?"

"Of course," said Camelman.

"Good," said Lohman. He didn't add "Dip stick." He continued with, "I want to talk to you about that Monday night the messenger was killed. You guys were on the floor that night. How come you didn't tell us up front? And I want to find out if you know anything more about it than what you told me. For instance Sean Featherbottom says he delivered a document to you Wanzer. Says he left it on your desk. Just before that he saw the messenger coming in, or at least someone who seems to have been her."

"Yes, I got the memo the next day," said Levin. "I forgot about him. That queer kid. We have too many of them around here."

Lohman continued. "I won't ask you how you know who is – uh – gay and who isn't. Anyhow, he may have lost a purple brooch he had up here. It was pinned on the bag he had with him. He had it earlier and noticed it was gone later that night. Did you see anything like that?"

"Here? You mean in my office?" asked Levin. "Of course not. Now that you mention it though, I remember he always has something like that showing somewhere. Can't you tell him that's for women?"

"He'd just tell me it's for him too," said Lohman matter of factly. "So another thing, we find that the document you say was delivered by the messenger that night was delivered the next day. It was notarized the next day. What gives?"

Levin looked at Lohman for a while before he answered. "As you know documentation is a detailed and often voluminous aspect of our practice. We need documents for one thing and as soon as we have them we find we need other documents for other things... ." He went on. Blah, blah, blah, and so on.

This was not responsive to the question. Lawyers make objections on this basis in court. Nevertheless Levin went on for several minutes with more mouth noise. He concluded with, "So you can see how that happened."

Lohman did not want to be rude which saying, "No," would have been so he just said, "So how did the document you got that night get notarized the next day by a notary who is not in our office?"

Levin looked at him for a while again. Finally he said, "The document I got Monday night was unusable. I threw it out. I got another one the next day."

"Why the messenger service?" asked Lohman. "Can't drafts be emailed or faxed?"

"Yes," said Levin, "But they were originals. I had to get the originals. The first one had a mistake so I called and got another the next day. In the morning."

"Why the different messenger services?" asked Lohman.

"How should I know?" said Levin. "The sender sent them. Ask her."

"Ms. Bruce?" asked Lohman. "I did. She said she left it for pickup. Tuesday morning. She didn't mention a draft the night before. Did you get a messenger service to pick it up? Which one?"

Levin was impatient with this menial detail. "I have people who handle these things for me. I don't know."

Lohman wondered why people who pretended to Godly status never asked themselves what God would say if asked about the details of the Creation. Would he say, "I don't know. I have people who handle these things for me?"

"So who handled it for you?" asked Lohman.

Levin looked pained. "I don't know. You think I keep a log of who does every little menial detail?"

Lohman said, "The Monday night messenger was from Zoom Shot. The Tuesday morning delivery came from our regular service, Ready?-Sent!. They billed us for the Tuesday delivery. Does that refresh your memory?"

"No," said Levin. "Ask my secretary. Maybe she knows."

"Did either of you see the messenger Monday night? Did you see Sean?" asked Lohman.

They both looked at each other and then back at Lohman and shook their heads.

"What about Steven? Did you see him?" asked Lohman.

Camelman and Levin looked at each other and then back at Lohman. Together they said, "Who?"

"Steven," said Lohman. "Stonegold."

Lohman looked at Levin who said simply, "No."

They got off on to other little time wasters and then Lohman left. He went to Levin's outer office and asked his secretary if she knew who contacted the messenger service and she did not. Lohman then headed back to his office.

When Lohman reached his own office suite he asked Tete to find out who ordered the delivery Tuesday morning and then went on in to his private office. There he called Seladora Bruce from whom the Tuesday morning document came. He asked her if she had sent and earlier draft the night before and if she ever heard of Zoom Shot and she was no help with either question. All she knew was she could have had a prior draft and if Wanzer said it, she must have. Just as Lohman put the phone down it rang and Tete told him that she had checked with Ready?-Sent! and their records showed that Levin's secretary had ordered the pickup of the Tuesday morning document. They didn't have any orders from anyone to deliver something to F, P & C the night before.

Lohman did not have time to continue on with these inquiries since he worked for a living at something else. He got to that something else and was tied down by it the rest of the day and for most of Saturday and Sunday too.

21 IS IT A LAW FIRM, A ZOO OR A BOOBY HATCH?

Monday morning Lohman met with a principal of a potential new client. The client's accountants had referred him to Lohman. The client was trying to raise investor money to develop a new product. A lot of large law firm time is taken up by projects such as this. A lot of complicated things need to be documented and the client has to be told what laws he has to comply with and how or how he can evade the laws and the best tax treatment has to be figured out and if possible there must be patent and copyright protection. The client was currently named the ABX, LLC. They would probably end up with a lot of other entities and names when all was figured out, but ABX was the entity currently developing the product. Two main people were involved in ABX. One was one of those private equity guys who go around finding something that could interest investors who he would get to finance the whole thing. For big fees and part of the profits too if the thing was successful. This was Zenith Dumont. He was one of the owners. Or, that is, another entity he controlled was one of the owners. The other was Henry Fauret, a lawyer with an engineering degree who had practiced patent law at one time.

The client was going to be ABX, but F, P & C had done work for Dumont before and that is why they were there. Fauret and ABX had never had anything to do with F, P & C and Dumont and companies he was involved with had used many other law firms besides F, P & C. A big part of why they were there was to see if everyone was comfortable with working with each other and for a preliminary discussion of the issues.

If this meeting had been with most other partners in the firm they would have had a lot of other lawyers with them. A single person army is not impressive. When one sees many generals together one assumes they must have vast and invincible forces at their command. Nor is one idiot impressive. Many idiots together, though, are impressive. Especially to other idiots. However, Dumont knew Lohman and he did not need any more man power just to discuss the matter in general. Fauret, on the other hand, was a lawyer himself. At first he wanted to know where Lohman's other partners were, but Dumont told him he wasn't going to pay for the whole firm and Fauret laid off that topic and shifted to how he always had cut costs in his legal practice too.

Lohman and his guests engaged in small talk for a while and then Lohman asked them what sort of venture they were contemplating. He fully expected to be treated to an hour or so of talk about business models, systems, solutions, matrixes and so forth, but Dumont merely said, "We got a law machine."

Lohman thought of all the jobs in the modern economy that had been replaced by software and robots. He even was reminded that law firms were now using software to search documents rather that hiring low paid contract lawyers to do it. He was glad he was old enough and had enough money that he could just retire. "What sort of law machine?" he asked.

Fauret jumped in. "A real law machine," he said. "I mean, not just something to search documents or law or anything. I am creating a machine that you feed information in and in response it gives you a result. Think of it. What happens now is that we have hordes of lawyers getting the facts and documents from clients and other people and then reviewing them and looking up the law and then presenting a case to some tribunal and getting a result. It is horrendously expensive and only the rich can afford it. And to the extent you can afford it, the result cannot be predicted. You might as well flip a coin. The result would be just as accurate and just. And it would be far cheaper and faster. With my machine people who have a dispute with each other can feed the facts of the matter into a machine. The machine will review what is fed in by both sides and determine what extra facts it needs, either to make the submission complete or to answer questions it has about the veracity of facts it has already been fed. All the material about what is relevant will be programmed into the software. The law will be in the software. All of it. A huge database about the use of language, human behavior and the rules of physics and chemistry and other facts of life will be programmed into it. A Huge database of all the facts we can get. The machine will compare the facts it is fed against these other things to check reliability and veracity. It will analyze all that has been submitted to it and give a result. The right and just result under the law as it exists. Just think of it. You can do the same thing with questions of what you must do to comply with the law. Regulatory filings, negotiations, everything lawyers and judges do now. It will do it all. Most of our legal system's people and other costs will be eliminated. It'll just be us. We'll be the law. Think how much we can make, even if society's legal costs are drastically reduced."

"What about the human element and judgment?" asked Lohman.

"We'll program that in," said Fauret.

"How are you going to get society to accept this?" asked Lohman.

Dumont chimed in. "We'll offer it for mediation to begin with. You know, where parties hire a mediator to help them settle their differences."

"That's interesting," commented Lohman.

"It'll be far cheaper," said Dumont.

"Is all this ready now?" asked Lohman. "How long did it take you to develop?"

Fauret said, "It's not fully operational yet. We just have a prototype. Our first job will be to get investors to finance the development."

"It's an idea we can sell," said Dumont. "Just think of all the money we can point to. The entire cost of the present legal system. We can offer investors a large portion of that as the revenue that will be theirs. And we patent the machine and software. No one else can compete. And we have figured out a way to get a head start on everyone else."

"What's that?" asked Lohman.

Fauret said, "Remember that flipping a coin is as good as the current system. Well, for things we don't have programmed yet, we just flip a coin. The software will opt to a random choice solution."

That will be in the patent application?" asked Lohman.

"Certainly not," said Fauret. That would tell everyone what is involved. We will patent other parts of the system. That part will be secret."

"How are you going to do all this?" asked Lohman.

Fauret said, "Oddly enough we are going to need lawyers to advise our programmers what facts are relevant and how to find law and other legal things. Then the programmers will take it from there. It will take time, but it shouldn't be too hard."

Dumont added, "And in the meantime we will get successive rounds of investors to finance the whole deal. The pot at the end of the rainbow is huge. We can keep going with the money raising for a long time. And think of all the fees that will generate. This is a real winner whether or not it ever pans out."

"It will," said Fauret.

"What about out spending the other side?" asked Lohman. "One feature of our legal system is that few people can afford it. As a consequence you can win by outspending the other side. Your system would eliminate that possibility."

"No, no, no!" exclaimed Fauret. "That's the big one. Yes, it eliminates it for most people, but it would still be possible to outspend the other side in figuring out the system and gaming the inputs. It would just be horrendously more expensive. Only the really big guys could do it. The hundred billion a year companies can wipe out all the ten billion a year companies. That's the big potential money maker. We just have to figure out a way to capture their dollars."

To himself Lohman thought that there has always been a simple and far cheaper way to do that. It has been called bribery. To Fauret he said, "I see."

Lohman then talked to them about what things would have to be done. He would have to get detailed information from them about the product, its development, the costs and who they contemplated raising money from and when and then the firm could give a plan for meeting all the legal requirements. He told them what lead lawyers he would assign to the various legal areas involved in their matter and he started discussing the potential costs. He went through all the conventional steps in such an initial meeting. His heart was not really in it though. It sounded like a con to him. But then many new business ideas lawyers handle are cons. In large law firms they are not called that, but they are.

Lohman eventually got rid of these masters of the modern world. He had to get to a meeting of the lawyers working on one of his client's deals and since it was a very large deal with a lot of lawyers on it the meeting was to be held in one of the larger conference rooms on the 41st floor. Lohman was a little late so he hurried out of his office and down the hall towards the elevator. Just as he did so 15 kids came running down the hall screaming and laughing and chasing each other. He had to step aside and wait. This was one of the hazards of negotiating the halls at F, P & C. The firm ran a nursery and pre-school for the employees' children. Pre-schools take the kids out for group walks. Usually they are holding on to each other because they are outside with the rest of the world. But at F, P & C the walks were often around the firm. This was especially true on 44 where the nursery was. Since they were not outside they were not holding on to each other or in any way restrained. Very often what resulted was a mass kiddy flash mob. Lohman usually did not mind since he liked kids. A lot of the 44th floor was occupied by the firm's business, clerical, file and IT offices and not lawyers so the other lawyers in the firm were not often inconvenienced by the kids. Sometimes though, Lohman felt like – well he felt like he should not be feeling like that. Eventually the kid mob passed and Lohman got over it and he made his way down to 41 for the meeting.

When Lohman got to the meeting the participants were already engaged in talking about the problems of the deal. They filled Lohman in and they all went on from there. Lunch had been prepared by the firm's conference room staff and they worked through lunch. Soon after lunch they broke up and they all went back to their offices, as did Lohman.

When Lohman got back to his office he found Pincus Ruhlman, one of the equity partners, waiting for him. He had got there just before Lohman did and he was standing up talking to Tete. As Lohman came in they greeted each other and Lohman said, "What's up?"

"My dog," said Pincus. "Have you seen Rottweiler, my dog? Did you get any reports from anyone about where he is?"

"No," said Lohman. He turned to Tete. "You?"

"Nothing," she said.

Ruhlman just looked frustrated and then left. Lohman went on into his inner office. Neither he nor Tete acted as if this was anything unusual. And it wasn't. While not every large firm has dogs running around, and while it is more accurate to say that none do, F, P & C did. Real dogs. Ruhlman had a Rottweiler, the name of which was Rottweiler, which he often brought in. Sometimes it got lose and wandered around the place. It was usually quite friendly and most people in the firm were used to seeing it around. At times like these, though, Ruhlman usually went into a tizzy trying to find the dog. Ruhlman was an equity partner with loads of business. He did what he wanted.

No sooner had Lohman got into his office than Sweeney came in. Lohman had a client who was interested in getting involved in a film project and Lohman wanted Sweeney working on the matter because of his show business credentials. Just as Sweeney came in Lohman's cell phone rang. Since Lohman was an old thing, he pulled the phone out and sent the call to a message rather than talk on the phone in front of a guest in his office.

Lohman had one of those simple old style cell phones. Not a smart phone. It handled calls, but it did not have internet access or a lot of things called apps. Sweeney took one look at the phone and said, "Hey Dude, you got a dumb phone!" Sweeney knew that already, but this was his form of greeting this day.

"Yeah," said Lohman. Then he described the client and his interests to Sweeney. "His name is Ting Pan Feelawitch. I don't know if you've ever heard of him. He has never done anything in show business before. He sells rubber gaskets. It's a pretty big business. He doesn't make them though. He buys them from manufacturers in China. Nowadays he is getting them cheaper a lot of times from other countries. Anyway, the key to his success is that he finances his own business. He pays for the gaskets on delivery. All his competitors are financed by the gasket makers. They pay when they sell the gaskets. Naturally they pay for the financing with a higher price for the gaskets."

Lohman continued. "He's a nice guy. He works on the basics. He knows the basics of the business. He makes his own specifications for the gaskets too instead of just selling what the manufacturers supply. He's easy to work with too. He doesn't make problems. Everyone calls him TP."

Sweeney said, "TP! Well wipe my ass, Dude."

"Christ!" said Lohman. "Get serious."

"Well, what kind of name is that?" asked Sweeney. "I gotta call him that? I mean – oh Dude – Man – Oh Mother of Mary!"

"So now you're a Catholic?" remarked Lohman.

"Oh fuck Mother of Mary, you know what I mean," said Sweeney.

"Well," said Lohman, "You better be Catholic so you can confess your way out of that one." Lohman went on to explain the matter to Sweeney.

After he had done so Sweeney said, "I hope good old TP is easier than Camelman. He sounds more organized. Camelman, Dude! I was doing a deal for him. I hope you remember you sent me there. Just 'cause shooting TV ads was involved. Well it turns out it was really a new client who was referred to St. Charles. Somehow Camelman got involved. Couldn't get anything done. It involved a series of stage productions for the ads and there was this big disagreement over what kind of production and how expensive it was going to be. This finally got off on whether or not the star – they wanted a big one – was going to wear real jewelry or costume. Big cost difference on that one. That was just one of the cost points, but that was where we got hung up. I even got Sean in to tell them how they could get cheap real jewelry or make fake look like real. No use. No agreement on anything. Stupid Man! The real problem was that it was going to be a shitty show."

Sweeney went on. "But God sometimes makes fuck-ups for a reason. In this case God made Camelman. It's like, Dude, like he throws all the papers up in the air and if you're fast enough you can run around and catch them and put them all down where you want them. At least that is how I work with the mess makers. Let them make the mess and then I can rearrange things. So one day the deal blew up. You know how it goes. Everyone threatening to call it off and blaming it on the others. But I knew the star. I called her. Turns out she was the one who was insisting on the real jewelry. And the deal was that she could keep it after the shooting. It also turns out that she and Camelman – well - I don't want to say this. We didn't represent her. We represented the advertiser. The company making the products. She and Camelman, now this is just something I heard, they were up to something. So I just suggested to her that I had heard about it and that she ought to wear costume jewelry and tell her lawyers that. Then I changed the documentation to reflect that. Stayed up all night, Man. Next day we got over that hang up and got on with the deal."

"What's with her and Camelman?" asked Lohman.

"I hear things, Dude," said Sweeney. "On the circuit, you know. I didn't really hear about him. I heard about her. The rumor is that she is a wild one when you give her the right – inputs let's say."

"What?" asked Lohman. "Drugs?"

"Yeah, Dude. And money," said Sweeney. "So some of her, let's say, acquaintances are mentioned and it turns out I hear the name Camelman. I am interested. You know I keep up on the party scene. Drugs, sex, rock and roll. It all sells. Fatass Levin goes to orgies."

Lohman looked surprised. "Yeah, Dude, orgies," continued Sweeney. Some of the parties are orgies. And how much would you pay for sex with a big star? And how much would she charge? Of course payment does not have to be in drugs or cash. It can be in hiring the provider for something or getting a big part."

Lohman put his elbow on the desk and put his hand up to his forehead and rubbed it. "Just out of curiosity, what have you heard about me?"

"Oh shit Dude, you don't – another world, Man. If you move in these circles – well I'd shit if I heard that."

Lohman was relieved. "So what is Levin doing at these, what, orgies?"

"I wasn't there," said Sweeney. "Not at the same ones anyway. I just heard about him. He likes to watch. And you know what. I asked around when I heard about Levin. Guess whose name also came up?"

Lohman looked blank. But he was guessing. No names came to mind.

"Guess," prompted Sweeney.

Lohman shook his head.

"Camelman," said Sweeney. "Tiny Tim Camelman. And guess what they say he likes to do?"

Lohman was looking blank again. He wasn't much upon orgies.

"Show!" said Sweeney.

"Show what?" asked Lohman innocently.

"He likes to have sex in front of the others. Like an exhibitionist."

Without thinking Lohman asked, "Who would watch?"

"Hey Dude, it's the perv world," said Sweeney.

"They go to orgies and do this?" asked Lohman.

"Well I never heard they were at the same orgy. And I never saw them at one."

"You go, do you?" asked Lohman.

"Business, Dude," said Sweeney. "And pleasure. But I never mix business with pleasure. I'm either there for one or the other. Not both."

Lohman was a bit jealous and regretful that he had not heard about all this when he was younger.

"And another guess what," said Sweeney. "Guess."

"More?" asked Lohman apprehensively.

"Yeah, Dude. That messenger. I saw pictures of her the cops were showing around. They came and showed them to Sean while I was in his office. I think they're trying to pin it on him. Maybe he did it.

Anyway I saw the pictures. He identified her as the messenger he saw that night. Man, he saw her he says. He was there. His pin on her. Well, anyway, I saw her too. I've seen her before. Not around here. I've seen her at orgies too. One of the working girls. Hot!"

"Did you tell the police?" asked Lohman.

"Naw," said Sweeney. "They seem to know about her already. No one else from the firm was there. As a matter of fact I have never seen anyone from the firm at any of the orgies and hardly ever at any of the other parties and events, let's call them. And, to be honest with you, I don't want to spread it around in the upper world that I work the boards at these places."

"I don't want that to get around either," agreed Lohman. "You know, I can't imagine explaining this kind of thing to Graybourne. While we're at it," he added, "Have you heard anything juicy about Steven and Lincoln?"

"Stonegold and Beale?" asked Sweeney. "No. I wouldn't expect I would. But then I would never expect I would hear anything about Camelman and Levin."

Lohman and Sweeney finished up talking about TP and the gossip and Lohman got back to the work on his desk. Later in the day he had to go to a meeting of the Management Committee. It was an emergency meeting called on short notice. One would think it involved a matter of supreme importance and so it did, at least a matter of supreme importance to St. Charles and his waspy faction. It turns out that someone had touted St. Charles on a new marketing gimmick. St. Charles and some of the other partners were often found on golf courses with clients or potential clients.

Of course there were other people at the courses too. Influential people, at least at the courses patronized by F, P & C partners. It turns out that some golf equipment salesman had got St. Charles' attention and convinced him that the hottest marketing technique would be for all the firm personnel to adopt a distinctive color for their golf balls and to place the firm logo on each ball with distinctive and contrasting colors. St. Charles wanted to discuss this important and urgent topic and so an emergency meeting was called. He wanted a pink ball with deep purple markings.

Lohman looked over the papers for the meeting and sighed. What crap! Well, he had plenty of experience with things like this and the best way to deal with them was to show up and keep his mouth shut until it was over. He went up to St. Charles's conference room for the meeting and did manage to keep his mouth shut most of the time, but there came a time when he could not avoid making a sarcastic comment. He suggested that it was such a great idea that they should require all firm personnel to drive pink cars with the deep purple firm logo. No one else thought this was sarcastic. They took it seriously and thought it was a great idea. They only question was what colors should they choose. Thankfully that question got deferred until later and Lohman got to go home and feel sorry for the fact that God was going to punish him for opening his big mouth by making him drive a pink car. He thought that at least Sean would like driving a pink car, but then he remembered that Sean didn't have a car. He was a biker. He would like a pink bike.

22 TECH ISSUES

Later in the day Lohman had arranged to meet with Henner Pigman in IT. He went to the business office and walked into a small conference room where they were going to meet. Pigman was there with two of his assistants. He called them assistant trainees. They had to have been adults, but Lohman couldn't tell from what he heard. One of them was saying. "So like, Dude, I told him, Wow, like, I said Oh My God Man! That's awesome!"

Pigman said, "And what did he say?"

"What?" said his assistant.

Pigman said, "I said, what did he say?"

The assistant said, "What. He said what."

Pigman said, "Is that what it is?"

The assistant said, "What is that?"

"What is what?" said Pigman.

"What it is, Man. It is what it is," said the assistant.

"I see," said Pigman. "That clears things up a lot. So next time give him a LOL SHI PIMP."

Lohman did not understand a bit of this. He wondered if they did either. He said to Pigman, "Laughing out loud at something pimp?"

Pigman gave him an annoyed look. The assistant said, "So hard I peed in my pants Old Man."

Pigman said to the assistant, "Mr. Lohman. He's the Managing Partner. The one we're supposed to meet. Remember?"

The other assistant said, "He's that old?"

Someone else might have been upset with this, but Lohman knew enough to expect it every time he wandered into the IT department. "It's a good thing you'll never get to be an old man," he said to the assistant.

The assistant said, "Yeah Dude."

Lohman then started in reviewing what they had been doing in searching through the firm records. The firm's records were stored on a central computer with several backups located elsewhere. Client records, documents, business records, personnel records, correspondence, even records of phone calls and records of what each person's computer terminals had been used for and when. There was a lot of data to go through if someone was searching for something in general instead of a specific thing that they knew the location of. There was also a complication in this case which Pigman explained to Lohman. The firm computer records did not record things done outside the system. For instance it did not record things people did on their laptops and other mobile devices unless they were later fed into the system or unless they used the firm's Wi-Fi. Nor did it record phone calls people made on their cell phones to places outside the firm. If someone used a cell phone to call into the firm, that would be in the records, but if they used it to call somewhere else, that would not be in the records.

Lohman told Pigman that he wanted a search made of things involving Kevin Bainbaum who Sean said he had seen in the lobby that Monday night when he was leaving. He had said Bainbaum was talking on the phone and Lohman wanted to see if perhaps he was calling someone upstairs. He asked Pigman to get everything he could on Bainbaum that day and the Sunday before and the Tuesday after.

Then Lohman asked Pigman if he had found out anything about the apparent user name and password they got from the police.

"No. Nothing," said Pigman. "You need to know the site before you can do anything. You can't find out what the site is from the user name and password. I sure would like to see that site."

"What about the people I asked you to check out?" asked Lohman. "Anything on them?"

Pigman said, "We checked them out. I put together a log of all their phone calls for a week before and a week after and id'd the phone numbers we could. I sent it to your office just last night along with the time records we could get for those guys. I didn't see anything unusual, but you would know more about what the entries mean than us."

"What about their computer records? Did you get anything there?" asked Lohman.

"Do they know we're doing this?" asked Pigman.

"I hope not," said Lohman. "Did you find anything?"

"Nothing that I can tell is interesting," said Pigman. "You know those guys are big shots here. They don't even know how to use computers. You should see. Their data is just a mess."

"You checked out Levin, Camelman, Beale, Stonegold, and Featherbottom? How about Mr. St. Charles?"

"Yes," said Pigman. "Nothing interesting, except perhaps Camelman. He's been looking at some killer porn sites."

What's that," asked Lohman.

One of the assistant trainees knew. He said, "Like where the whore gets offed. That's where you cum, Man."

Lohman said, "Camelman?"

"Don't know," said Pigman. "It's on his terminal records. Maybe the cleaning crew is using it after hours. Anyway, the user name and password didn't work on those sites."

"Anything else?" asked Lohman.

"No," said Pigman. "Oh, that Featherbottom kid. All he does, besides the work, is he looks at news and weather and then fashion sites. That's what I'd call them. Clothing, jewelry, interior design, antiques. What's with him? Do we have clients like that?"

"He's just interested in that sort of thing," said Lohman. "Did you find anything else? What about Mr. St. Charles?"

Pigman said, "He doesn't even use the thing."

Lohman took his leave and went back to his office. When he got there Tete told him Wiggy Rodriguez, the investigator, had called. Lohman called him back. Wiggy had finished talking to all the people the firm records could identify as billing after six on the Monday night in question. Just as he had predicted, some had refused to tell him anything or even to talk to him. But in those cases Tete had intervened. If the national security fairies that protect our fair nation knew about her, they would not resort to water boarding. All was revealed. None of them admitted to being on 55 that night and there was nothing in the records to contradict them.

Wiggy and Tete had also talked to everyone on 55 – or their secretaries – and nothing was revealed that put anyone other than Sean, Levin and Camelman there after 9 or so.

23 WHERE WAS OUR LEADER?

No sooner had Lohman got back to his office then the phone rang. Detective Bongwad was calling to tell Lohman that they wanted the firm's help in checking out where St. Charles had been on the night in question. Bongwad had been told St. Charles was at the Pullman Club, but the manager was telling him that they would not talk about their members and that Mr. St. Charles probably was not there anyway.

Lohman told Bongwad that the firm had a bill from the Pullman Club for that night. He said he would have Tete email a copy to him.

"How do you know who it's for?" asked Bongwad.

"They have signatures for things. You order something in one of these clubs and when you do you sign for it. I'll have Tete get it. It'll take a while probably. They only release them to the member who signed."

"So I'll ask Mr. St. Charles to get it," said Bongwad.

"No, don't," said Lohman. "He'll shit. I'll have Tete get it. She can get things like this."

"How?" asked Bongwad.

"I'm afraid to ask," said Lohman.

They hung up and Lohman went out to talk to Tete and ask her to get the signed slip from the Club. Then he returned to his office and got back to work preparing for a meeting the next day.

Before he left he called Sweeney. "You remember you told me you knew a waiter at the Pullman Club?'

"Yeah, Dude," said Sweeney.

"Well," said Lohman, "it's the same this time. I want to check on St. Charles again. You remember you told me that they have big time gambling there. Maybe he was doing that again the Monday of the murder. We got a bill for way more than just him or him and a few guests. See what you can find out. I don't care what he was doing there. I just want to find out if he was there and when."

Sweeney said he would.

Tuesday Lohman spent the whole day in a meeting with a client's officers and some of its accountants working out their negotiating strategy for a deal. They finished up around six and they all headed for home.

Lohman had the time so he hoofed it. He headed straight North up Dearborn. At first the sidewalks had a lot of traffic. As he crossed the river there were a lot of young women headed in the same direction. They would come into the sidewalk from side streets or buildings along the way and they would go two or four blocks and then turn off on a connecting street. They were usually dressed to the hilt and had quite high heels. Nevertheless, each and every one walked faster than Lohman could even imagine. He basically had to keep dodging them, since most were not going to walk around him. Through him, yes. Around him, no. This kept up until he got about a mile north. Beyond that the girl traffic subsided and things were more normal. That is, from there on home he had to run for his life every time he crossed a street. At one point he came to a four way stop. There were stop signs for all the traffic in both directions. Just as he stepped into the street four cars came up to the intersection, one in each direction. They all arrived at once and they were all in a hurry. None stopped. The one nearest Lohman, to his right, slowed a little and swerved to go around him. This was not a very effective maneuver and the car was going to go through Lohman, not around him. Lohman grabbed his hat and ran. The drivers had all come to the intersection at the same time so, naturally, each had the right of way. All laid on their horns and accelerated. Wham! A four-way in the middle of the intersection. A four-way is good in sex. Bad here though. Lohman got to safety and looked back at the crash just as it happened. There were four new cars. A Mercedes, a BMW, an Audi and a Bentley. Lohman looked at them and saw about $400,000 of car loans that now would not be paid off because the so-called rich can just barely afford the monthly car payment with nothing left over for insurance.

Lohman felt a sense of satisfaction. Should he call the police or the emergency number for an ambulance? What if the car contained lawyers? Would that make a difference? Anyway, Lohman felt quite secure that someone else would and he went on towards home. Up the street he went until he was a few blocks from home. He was walking past the Squash Club where he knew the doorman who was standing outside, just having helped a member into a cab. Lohman stopped to chat. As he did so another member came out. Lohman recognized him. They didn't know each other well, but they had met at social events. The guy was an offensive snob and he had let Lohman know in the variety of ways that snobs do, that he talked to him only at sufferance. Lohman said, "Hello."

24 THE PANTIES AND THE BITCH WHO MOANS

Wednesday morning Lohman no sooner got in than he was told by Tete that one of the partners was demanding to see him. It was Moira Weiner. Moira was one of the estate and trust lawyers who handled only the wealthy. Moira was in Lohman's office frequently complaining about one thing or another. When she wasn't there she was calling Tete with complaints. Her secretary was as big a complainer as she was. Her secretary is the one who had found the panties in the waste basket. Ms. Weiner loved to be offended. She loved to complain about the outrages that cursed her daily life. Oh how she would have loved Hell! She was not named Weiner for nothing. Actually her nickname within the firm was "The Weiner".

She stomped in to Lohman's office saying, "Bumper this has got to stop. The language I am exposed to on these premises is disgraceful. It is abhorrent. And if I am exposed to it, just think what our clients are exposed to. Many times they have told me how they have experienced disgraceful language in our halls."

Lohman knew what the answer would be, but just for the record he asked, "Who? Which client complained?"

"That's confidential," she said. "This time people have told me that they were going down the hall on 55. That, you know, is where our top people are. They were passing the men's room when someone had just gone in and the door was still open. It was disgraceful! The language!"

"What language?" asked Lohman.

"I'm not going to tell you a thing like that," she said indignantly. "Suffice it to say it was shocking!"

"In what way?" asked Lohman.

"Oh, it is stressful to even think of it," she said. "References to elimination and urgency."

"So who did you say complained about this?" asked Lohman. He well knew that she was the complainer, but like most such people she claimed that someone else had complained to buttress her case.

"That's confidential," she said.

Lohman said, "I see. Well that certainly is shocking. I'll bring it up at the next Management Committee meeting."

"See that you do," said The Weiner. "And one more thing. We have a young associate around here named John Sweeney. Do you know him?"

Lohman almost cringed. "I know who he is."

"Well," said The Weiner, "he was there passing by at the same time. I - the client - I was with the client - we were shocked and we exclaimed so. He just said – I can't believe he would address me – the client – this way. He said, 'Cool it Doll. It's just,' --- I cannot tell you what he said. More words about elimination. Well, I would not put up with that. I said, 'You're crazy'. Then do you know what he said?"

Lohman did cringe this time. He asked tentatively, "What?"

She said, "He said, 'Could be, I'm talking to you.' What outrage! I want him disciplined."

The Weiner never demanded that her offenders be fired. She wanted to keep them around. You don't want to lose a good offender.

"I'll see to it," said Lohman.

When Ms. Weiner left Lohman called Sweeney and told him about it and told him to stay away from her for a while.

Sweeney said, "There wasn't any client there, Dude. Just her. The door was still open and someone said, 'Gotta shit man.' That's all. Then she started in so I just said, 'That's what we talk about in the crapper.' She was like, I'm gonna die."

"So just stay away from her," said Lohman.

"Sure will Bumpy," said Sweeney. "I don't wanna go anywhere near something that ugly anyway."

Lohman hung up and spent the rest of the day working on his own clients.

Thursday morning Lohman took Louie for his morning walk. Lohman loved the walks. Louie was the friendliest dog in the neighborhood and he got to meet and greet a lot of the neighbors this way. No sooner did they hit the sidewalk than they ran into The Rev. Pratton Cuthbert and his little poodle. The dogs headed straight for each other dragging their owners with them.

The Rev. Cuthbert was the pastor of St. Tom's of Christ, the Gold Coast's fashionable Episcopal church. He and Lohman were friends and The Rev. Cuthbert was often out to convert Lohman, even though he knew Lohman was a Presbyterian. Lohman had been raised a Presbyterian and thus knew that all other religions were composed of people on the down road to Hell. On the other hand he knew that people who put out that crap were leading the charge on the same road. He maintained his connection to the church for social reasons. Cuthbert knew this and he knew most of the people in the neighborhood were like this so he was always out trying to bring them into his fold.

In fact, the neighborhood people were often in all the local churches besides the ones they belonged to because of their connections to each other so Lohman was often found at St. Tom's.

They greeted each other and got to talking while the dogs slowly lost interest in each other. Cuthbert said, "I'm so sorry to hear all the furor about your recent misfortune. I'm sure it must be very stressful, you being the Managing Partner and all."

"Yes," said Lohman, "it's quite a distraction."

"Did they find out who did it?" asked Cuthbert.

"Not yet," said Lohman. "I suppose you know the sordid details, or some of it. The police are still working on it."

"Any suspects?" asked Cuthbert.

"I don't know," said Lohman. "They just ask us things. They don't tell us much."

"Well," said Cuthbert, "I hope none of your top people are involved. I was talking to the Cardinal recently and he said that vast sins occur in high places." At this he paused and looked significantly south and east towards a 2500 foot high tower called the Aspire that housed The Prophet and ECOTAG.

Lohman skirted the subject. He asked, "Are you going to the ASPS fundraiser Saturday night?"

"Oh yes, I'll be there," said the Reverend. "We can use the money. We all get a small percentage of the receipts, so we all go there. But you know it is really run by Cardinal Sammy and The Prophet. They get most of the receipts and everything is oriented towards them. Are you going?"

"Of course," said Lohman. "Probably for one of the same reasons you go. It's a party and a place to meet and mingle."

They pledged to see each other there and they went on in separate directions with their dogs. Lohman finished the walk, took Louie home and headed for the office where he spent the day on his own clients' matters.

25 ETHICAL MATTERS

Friday morning Lohman was reviewing a client's file when he learned that Will Emery, one of the equity partners, wanted to see him. Emery came in and they greeted each other. He sat down and said, "Bumper, did you hear about those motorcycles that blew up yesterday?"

"I think I heard something about it on the radio news," said Lohman. "But I wasn't listening very well. Who is riding a motorcycle in February?"

Emery said, "It got up to 50 yesterday. I understand that the hard core riders are out when it gets that warm, winter or not. Anyway, they didn't go much of anywhere. Apparently they just turned the cycles on and gunned them a little and they blew up. They were killed by the explosions. I have an ethical problem."

Lohman was a little taken aback. How could he have an ethical problem about it? It sounded like a good thing to him. "You were involved? What's the problem?"

Emery said, "Do you know Deng Farnum? He's one of my clients. You may have heard of him. He invents a lot of things and he had got a lot of publicity. He doesn't like motorcycles and the noise they make. So he comes in to see me and he tells me he has invented a device that you can place in a motorcycle's tail pipe and as soon as it starts making noise the cycle explodes. He wants to patent the devices. He told me he had planted the devices on those bikes. He works at home and these guys pulled up near his house and parked their bikes and walked down the street. Who knows where they were going. Farnum tells me he planted the devices while they were gone. They came back, got on the bikes and Boom!"

Lohman just looked at Emery. After a while he said, "So?"

Emery said, "So do I turn him in? How does the attorney client privilege apply?"

"Ugh," said Lohman. "I don't really know. I think the exception covers cases where the guy is going to do it again. I don't know. So we have an ethics committee. I'll get them on it. Did he say he was going to do it again?"

"No," said Emery. "He just said he was trying it out and these two guys deserved it."

"How can you patent a murder weapon?" asked Lohman. "Well, I suppose you can, like a gun. How could he make any money off this?"

"That's one of the things he asked me to look into," said Emery. "He thinks you can justify planting one of these devices by the law of nuisance. Then you can put a sign on the motorcycle so they are warned that if they start it and make noise it will blow up."

"Did he put a sign on these motorcycles," asked Lohman. "Would people read the signs? Would they believe them? Couldn't they get the device and remove it?"

Emery said, "He did say he put a sign on them. And he told me that he is working on a mechanism that causes the bike to explode if someone attempts to remove it. "

Lohman referred Emery to the head of the ethics committee and called the guy to tell him Emery was coming. He spent the rest of the Friday and Saturday morning on normal client work. Then he went home to get ready for the ASPS fundraiser.

The fundraiser was an annual event. The American Serenity Providers Society was supposedly an ecumenical association of all the religions in the Chicago area. However, in its earlier years it seems the only serene haven was Christian. Muslims and other "fringe" religions were not included. Jews were invited, but they would not join. In time, however, attitudes changed and proper financial arrangements were made and all were included.

ASPS was organized with the financial industry as its model. The organizers were The Prophet and the Cardinal and guess who made out best. All the religions shared the fund raising proceeds and they used the organization to develop prospects they could concentrate on individually. However, just like with the financial industry and the investment bankers and the hedge fund managers, the organizers raked off fees for their services in putting the organization together and managing its assets. It had large endowment funds and they needed investment management and guess who provided it. ECOTAG just happened to have its own investment management company which generously provided its services to ASPS for modest charges, at least modest compared to its "normal" rates which it never charged anyone to begin with.

The event was a fundraiser and only rich people were invited. This was part of the modern equivalent of high society and those invited came because it was a grand social event. This meant they wanted to socialize with and schmooze each other. They did not want to hear a bunch of malarkey coming from a stage. They were there for the party. It was one of the grand events on the social calendar.

Since the persons who came were there for the party, they were not necessarily there to give or to in any way support ASPS. So how did ASPS get the dough? It published a list each year of who was invited, who attended and who gave what. So why would anyone bother with the event if they were just going to have to give money? Simple. If you were not on the list you were a nobody. To avoid unseemly competition among the attendees which could hike giving to levels where they really would stay away, ASPS suggested the proper level of giving to each attendee in private communications. On top of this, tickets were $1000 each.

The interests of those in attendance also made for an odd format. The event was always held in a hotel ballroom. There were tables and chairs scattered throughout in miscellaneous locations. There were bars and buffets for snacks around the sides as well as waiters and waitresses circulating through the crowd. The people came to mingle with each other and that is what they did throughout the event. No one was much interested in hearing the presentations. The event opened with a presentation on the stage from either the Cardinal or The Prophet. They took turns each alternate year. They started out with a prayer and everyone just kept talking. It went on this way throughout the evening. Each presentation would be followed with a representative of another religion saying something. Then at the end either the Cardinal or The Prophet would present an ending prayer. The only time the crowd ever quieted down was when some very wealthy person was presented on the stage and his or her large donation announced.

While all this was going on the various religions had their high ranking representatives mingling with the crowd to scout out prospects. Each religion also had a booth around the sides of the room intermingled with the buffets and bars where people could register. Once again, who registered and where was published in the list.

This list was something like the Social Register of old. Those who cared about such things referred to it as "The List". Anyone who aspired to be considered important or wealthy, no matter how much they owed, wanted to be in The List. And to see who was who you had to pay $1000 to get a copy. God does work in mysterious ways. The Devil do too. Which is which? God does, the Devil do, that's who do be which.

This year's fundraiser was to be held at the Gander Hotel, one of the grand old Chicago Hotels right at the north end of Michigan Avenue where it turned into Lake Shore Drive. The Lohmans and a lot of other high ranking lawyers were invited because they were well to do. They were also invited because F, P & C often did work for The Prophet and sometimes for the Cardinal.

Naturally Lady Fitch-Bennington was there with her boy toy. Her place was just a block away from the Gander and she had the after-party at her place. And across the street from her building was the 7th Presbyterian Church, purveyor of the one true religion to Chicago's social climbing Presbyterians. While other Presbyterian churches are attended by those in closer contact with God than are found in the Heathen churches, among Presbyterians there are degrees of closeness to God and social rank. Those Presbyterians most in possession of these qualities were to be found at 7th Pres.

Anyone else who would put some big money in was welcome too. This night 7th Pres. was open for continuous prayer for those in need of renewing their contact with God after the evening's events. It was billed as an ecumenical prayer service and it was open just to the ASPS attendees. There were greeters at the Church who attempted to get contact information for further follow up. Many people stopped in at the Church either on the way to Lady Fitch's or after going there.

There were other churches in the area, but they were a little too far away to get the after-party crowd. One was Holy Name Cathedral, the Cardinal's top outlet. It was open, but hardly anyone showed. The Cardinal was infuriated, but when he had a nun kneel down for him while he prayed God answered and said, "Next time Sammy. We'll get 'em next time." So he felt better and slept well that night.

The Lohmans made it to all three places and still managed to get home before midnight. At their age this was not just late, it was after the end. They collapsed.

Sunday was busy. For some it may be a day of rest, but for many the days of rest are just days of different kinds of work. The Lohman's were due at a client's home for lunch. The client was a member of 7th Presbyterian as were the Lohmans so they all met at the Church and attended the service before going to lunch at the client's house.

After that they went to two wakes and made a hospital visit to a sick friend. Then they went on to dinner at another client's home. This is the life of a professional who is developing business. They key to enjoying it was to enjoy people and mingling with them.

26 THE BROOCH

Monday morning Sweeney stopped by Lohman's office to tell him that the waiter he knew at the Pullman Club said St. Charles was there gambling on the Monday night in question. "The same as last time when he said he wasn't there at all, Dude." By "last time" Sweeney meant the last murder in the firm.

Lohman sighed. "Well at least this time he said he was there. I don't know how he is going to explain how big his bill was when he says he was there alone. How come all this isn't common knowledge. You'd think someone would squawk to the press."

Sweeney said, "I think they have press people there too. To shut 'em up. They certainly have some of the top cops and politicians there too."

"They probably let them win big too I'll bet," said Lohman. "Well, anyway, what else is new?"

"Not much," said Sweeney. "Gohr thinks he has some financing lined up for Trisha's film. We're working on it."

"Good," said Lohman. "Then she can find someplace else to dance around and find bodies."

Just then Sean Featherbottom came in to deliver some papers to Lohman. They all greeted each other and Sean handed the papers to Lohman.

Sweeney said, "Hey, Dude, I got some action on Trisha's film. I gotta get a draft of an agreement out on it. Come back to my office with me. We'll go over it."

Lohman said, "Yes, you guys get on it. The world needs the – whatadoodle?"

"Pimpadoodle," said Sweeney.

"Pimps. Whores. Doodles. I think good old Fenton and Pettigrew are spinning around in their graves. As for Zenon – well he could figure out how to sell the plague," said Lohman. Then he turned towards Sean and asked, "Did you remember anything else about that Monday night? Do you remember where you lost the brooch? How did you lose it?"

Sean said, "No. I don't remember anything except what I told you. I had it on the way up there and I only went into Mr. Levin's office so I must have lost it in the halls or in his office. Unless I lost it on the way home or in the lobby and someone picked it up and then – well – brought it back and put it on her. You remember I told you I seem to remember brushing up against something in his office. I'll bet that's where it went. I lose them a lot. That's why I only use costume jewelry."

At this Sean picked up his bag which he had put down on Lohman's desk and showed it to Sweeney and Lohman. "Here, look. See." He moved his hands over the glass pieces on the brooch on his bag. "See. They're glass. Do you like it? I put on a new one this week. See. It's a simple piece. Actually I got it new at, now you won't believe it, I got it at Sears over there on State Street. It started raining all of a sudden when I was coming back here and I went through the store to get a block of dry walking in. I saw this on the way through the store. I couldn't resist it. See. Look at the beautiful and intriguing color of the glass pieces and see how they change color as the light changes." He angled the bag to catch the light from the windows and he moved it around.

Lohman and Sweeney followed all this intently because it was interesting and the reflection of the light on the piece was intriguing.

Lohman said, "Well Sean, it doesn't look too good for you. It would be a big help if you could come up with something. All I can say is that it seems some other people have some explaining to do too."

Sean just looked at him.

Lohman continued. "You were up there. You saw her. No one else says they saw her. Alive that is. You admit your brooch was up there. On you to begin with. Then it was found on the body. Your prints were in Mr. St. Charles' washroom where the body was found. You say Bainbaum saw you leave around 10. He doesn't remember it. The police seem to be focusing on you. I can see why. I don't believe you are a killer, but look at it from an objective view. You see what I mean?"

Sean just looked back at Lohman and pursed his lips in and out a little.

Lohman said, "Well at least others are involved. The body was found in Mr. St. Charles' office. His gun was used to kill her. He says he lost it earlier, but it was his. His prints were found in her blood on her bag in the hall closet and in his washroom. Now how does that look?"

Sweeney interjected, "So who's gonna be the Chairman when we get rid of him?"

"Don't get ahead of yourself," said Lohman. "He apparently was at the Pullman Club while all this was going on. And Mr. Stonegold now tells us he came in Tuesday morning a little before 9 and found the body in his office and he says he moved it to Graybourne's office and put her bag in the hall closet. Remember that his office is next to Mr. St. Charles'. So when Mr. St. Charles tells us the body was not in his office earlier that morning when he came in, he apparently is telling the truth."

At this point Lohman stopped and called Tete. "Tete," he said.

"Yes Hon," she said.

Lohman said, "Take a look at the records and see if you can find when Mr. St. Charles first came into the building on Tuesday after the killing." Then he looked around at Sweeney and Sean and added, "Where did he stay? He's at the Pullman Club till late and he says he is here early the next day, so where did he stay. He lives in Lake Forest. Maybe at his in town condo? At the Club? I think he said he stayed there."

He heard Tete on the other end of the line. "Are you talking to me Hon?"

Lohman couldn't help himself. It just slipped out. "I'm like the old guy who just got laid. I'm talking to everyone about it?"

This didn't bother Tete. "At the Club," she said. "I remember that big bill for Monday night. It included a room charge. That's where. Don't you remember how some of you partner guys stay at the downtown clubs or hotels on late nights?"

"Right," said Lohman. He put the phone down and said to Sean and Sweeney, "He probably stayed at the Club. We got a room charge in the bill."

Lohman looked at Sean. "So, it's you or Mr. Stonegold. I don't mean I think that, but look at it from the point of view of the police. What are they going to think? Your brooch was in her boots. How did it get there? And, now that I think of it, there was a piece of paper there with what the police think is a user name and a password. Do you know anything about that? Well, anyway, the sex angle seems to let you out."

Sean just sat there and looked up and sideways with pursed lips. "What do you mean?" he asked.

"You like men don't you?" said Lohman.

"I like girls too," said Sean.

"To screw, Dude," said Sweeney. "He means to screw."

"Oh," said Sean. "Yes."

Then Sweeney turned towards Lohman. "What's that about the user name and password? What site were they for?"

"I don't know," said Lohman. I asked Henner to check it out, but he says he can't find a site from them. He also searched our computers for any use of them and didn't find anything. I can't remember them offhand, but it was some kind of sexual language."

"I heard something about that Zoom Shot outfit," said Sweeney. "They supposedly have their own porn site with bad stuff on it. Supposedly it works on Wi-Fi. They have their own van where they put it out. Broadcast it, you might say. We usually think of Wi-Fi signals as coming from fixed locations, but they are supposed to be able to move the van around to suit the customer locations. I hear they use it for payment too.

"Now that's all we need," said Lohman. "Murder is one thing. Now we have a sex scandal. Oh well, at least Zenon thinks we can play it for good publicity. I don't know how."

"Yeah, Dude," said Sweeney. "They are supposed to have all kinds of porn. Stuff that would be illegal. Anything you want, even death porn and animal porn. Kiddie too. Dogs – that's the most popular I hear. Next thing you know I'll hear they're doing puppy death porn."

No one said anything. Sean wiggled in his chair and puffed his cheeks out and looked up and to one side of the room and then the other. Eventually he said, "He's joking."

"He is?" said Lohman.

"Yes," said Sean. "You can tell. When he's joking about serious things I feel like passing gas."

"You farted?" asked Lohman.

"No," said Sean, "but I felt like it. I held it."

"Dude, he's right," said Sweeney. "Whenever I make fun of something, no matter how serious I put on, he can tell. He wiggles around in his chair and then his cheeks puff out and he blows it out. Stinks Man!"

Lohman didn't say anything. He did not move. He pulled his glasses off, looked at the lenses, pulled out a tissue and wiped them and put them back on. Then he said, "Could you get me one of the puppy death ones for tonight. I'm feeling kind of horny."

All Sweeney had to say was, "Oh shit, Man, now I'm gonna fart."

Sean started giggling. Soon after that the meeting broke up and Lohman was able to get back to his work and prepare for a meeting coming up at the Pullman Club with the Cardinal and The Prophet.

27 THE CARDINAL AND THE PROPHET AT THE CLUB

A little before noon Lohman and St. Charles got together and walked over to the Pullman Club for a meeting with the Cardinal and The Prophet Andy. The subject of the meeting was a "deal" which might produce some legal work. St. Charles never attended such a meeting by himself. Only the unimportant go about by themselves. Also, while he was a lawyer, he did not do legal work. That was beneath him. Some said it was above him, but in any event he needed a lawyer with him.

The Cardinal and The Prophet were continuing their cooperative ASPS venture. They had rounded up someone who headed a company that owned a lot of manufacturing plants in the US. The guy was worried that terrorists might attack the US and might attack his company's plants since they were symbolic of the American Way. The guy was convinced that all terrorists are Muslims so he was going to protect the plants by putting up money to build mosques near them. The guy did not know any Muslims and did not want to. However, he needed to contact them to embark on the company's great charitable venture. They were going to bill it as something involving outreach to the Muslim community to show how America appreciated Muslims. Naturally the idea had to be refined. He had approached ASPS, the great ecumenical organization, for help with the venture.

The Prophet and the Cardinal knew what the guy was up too. They had similar feelings about Muslims and they wanted a show piece of cooperation too. What luck to find a sucker to finance it. All they had to do was put together a plan for approaching their Muslim contacts to get the ball rolling. That was what was going to be discussed over lunch.

When St. Charles and Lohman got to the Club they found their guests waiting for them in the lobby. The Cardinal and The Prophet were on the verge of putting on an unseemly show. It seems The Prophet thought that the Cardinal had kept a separate prospect list at the ASPS fundraiser and he wanted it surrendered for all to use. The Cardinal was denying that he had one. Thankfully the arrival of St. Charles and Lohman cut this short before it got out of hand and the group went up to the dining room.

Once there they reviewed the menu before the waiter came to their table and started through the specials. St. Charles ordered Cornish Hen Gizzards with Mustard Dill Timbitari sauce. The rest ordered food. As the waiter left with their orders, the Cardinal said to St. Charles, "Where is Winston – Mr. Camelman?"

"Why would you ask me?" asked St. Charles.

The Cardinal said, "He's the expert on this isn't he. He told us that."

St. Charles gave him a blank look. Then he looked at Lohman. Lohman said, "He does know about these matters, but the superior expertise is here." He was kind of proud of coming up with that kind of bullshit.

"I see," said the Cardinal. "You fellows have so many lawyers. Law is so complicated. Earthly law, that is. And with so many lawyers look what happens. I don't mean to belittle lawyers as is the fashion these days, but the more people you have the more the odds are that you will have some wrongdoers. Why, even in the Church we have – well – some of those."

The Prophet smirked.

The Cardinal knew better than to return the attack, but he did want to shift the focus of wrongdoing. "For instance, take that recent incident in your firm. You see how wrongdoers can infiltrate anywhere?"

"Why that's certainly true," said St. Charles. "This – this – little tart infiltrated into our sphere. Talk about wrongdoers. And her name! What was it Bumper?"

"Wendy Laymen," said Lohman dryly.

"Who?" asked the Cardinal.

"Laymen. Wendy Laymen," repeated Lohman.

"Oh, I know her," the Cardinal blurted out. Then he looked around at the others at the table with an odd look of surprise at what came out of him.

"You do?" asked St. Charles. "How?"

"From deliveries," said the Cardinal.

Lohman asked, "Of what?"

"Oh, it must be some documents," said the Cardinal. "I've seen her name in the delivery records."

"Zoom Shot? That is the messenger service. Or her name, Laymen?" asked Lohman.

"Uh, both," said the Cardinal.

The Prophet said, "Well I never heard of that service or her either."

The Cardinal asked, "What service do you use?"

"I told you," said The Prophet, "I never heard of her or the service. Why would I have anything to do with evil?"

"Who said anything about evil," said the Cardinal testily. "I only asked about the service – Zoom Shot or whatever they are called."

"There," said The Prophet, "you did. You mentioned the evil."

Lohman interjected, "Well it's not important. What about the mosque idea?"

This got them back to the intended subject and that occupied them for the rest of the meeting. After that they broke up. St. Charles and Lohman went back to the office and the Cardinal and The Prophet went off on their own worshipful pursuits.

Lohman spent the rest of the day on his own clients' problems

Tuesday Lohman met with Tete when he came in. "Tete," he said, "have Wiggy check on Stonegold again. He says he got in here early Tuesday and found the body in his office. What was he doing here early in the morning when he was in Seattle the day before? How did he get back here so quick? Ask Wiggy to find out."

"I think he did Hon," said Tete. "I think, well he gave me a lot of information on everybody. And Henner and McDade have been giving me a lot of stuff too. They gave me files on a lot of people and I had Henner put them together. They're on the computer. Here, I'll look."

Lohman waited while she looked for the file on Stonegold. At first she had trouble with a special password. "You know, Hon," she said, "I'd like to find out who invented passwords. I'd kill the guy. And Hon, you can bet it was a guy. I'll probably never find out though because I'll bet his name is password protected." She fiddled around some more. "There, I got it." Then she looked through the pages until she came to one. "Here it is. Wiggy found out his flight. He came back here on an early evening flight. This says he got to O'Hare around ten. So he had time to get home and sleep and get here early. I think he lives not too far from there."

Lohman said, "He had time to get here too. She was killed after ten, the police say. Does that show anything about where he went after landing – wait – what do the building entry records show? He doesn't show as checking in that night does he?"

"I don't think he was one of the ones coming in that night. You had us check on that. I'll check again." She fiddled with her keyboard and mouse some more and came to a page where she rested. "Here. I have the list of all our people who checked in late that night. He's not on it."

"So maybe he came back here earlier and was already in the building. Is there anything that tells us he was actually on the flight Wiggy checked?" asked Lohman.

Tete looked through some more computer pages. "I have his file again." She looked through the information. "Here," she said. "It says here Wiggy checked with the person he said he met with out there and that person says they did not break up till 4 in the afternoon. He couldn't have got back here earlier than 10 or so."

"So," said Lohman, "Maybe he's in the clear. But why was the body in his office? Assuming he is telling us the truth. How did the body get there? It didn't get there earlier in the day if the police are correct about the time of death. Who killed her? Was she killed in Stonegold's office? Somewhere else? Stonegold says her body was in the wheeled bag when he found her."

"Well, Hon." said Tete, "I'm not an expert on these things. Why don't you ask Sean?"

"Do you really think he is involved," asked Lohman.

"Isn't he always?" said Tete.

"I hope not," said Lohman. "He's a nice kid."

"Yes," said Tete, "and he always whacks the right people."

Lohman looked at her and sighed. "Well anyway, what about Levin? What was he doing here? He says he was going to a show with his wife, but she was sick so he came in after dinner. Do we know what he was doing here? Check out his files and time records and what he says and those people who said they saw him here. Camelman too. And Sean. See if the files show anything about what he was doing and where. If we didn't go through all these records looking for that information, have Wiggy do it again. Then let me know if they find anything. And, I almost forgot. Sweeney. John Sweeney was here too. And he had gone to dinner with Sean and came back with him. Try to find out what he was doing."

"Why don't you just ask all these people, Hon?" said Tete.

"I want to see what we can find out without asking them. Then I can ask," said Lohman. "So find out what Sweeney was doing."

"Probably screwing someone or something," said Tete off handedly.

"What? Here?" Lohman blurted out.

"You're lawyers. You screw people." said Tete.

"Oh," said Lohman. Another one of her jokes.

"But him – him I mean sexually. You should hear what people say about him," said Tete.

"Yes, well, find out and let me know if you find anything. Now, I have to get to that meeting you scheduled for me at The Bank," said Lohman. He went into his office, got ready for the meeting and left.

28 BILLING

The meeting at The Bank lasted through Wednesday morning. The meeting was ostensibly between St. Charles and Swifty to review all The Bank's legal matters that F, P & C were handling. Naturally there were a lot of other people there because while the Saint and Swifty were perfectly capable of discussing anything, they were seldom limited by reality. Lohman was there to supply legal expertise and show everyone that St. Charles had high level subordinates. Camelman was also there because the General Counsel of The Bank insisted on it. More and more this was happening. The Bank's General Counsel insisted that he had to talk to Camelman about certain matters. St.Charles did not like this, but what could he do? The meeting went on until mid-morning.

The meeting had been held in a large private room at the Pullman Club because Swifty was scheduled for a lunch meeting there later. St.Charles liked to walk between the Club and the office. He, Camelman and Lohman walked back towards Swifton Plaza. On the way they came to the Chicago branch of Cooks & Brothers, the high level men's furnishings store. Most men wore clothing. The wealthy, apparently, wore sofas.

Camelman said, "Let's go in Cooks. I have to get something. They have a sale on shirts today. I really need some."

St. Charles sniffed, "You use ready-made?"

"Sure," said Camelman. "What do you wear? Where do you buy your stuff?"

St. Charles straightened up. He did not take kindly to interrogation by his inferiors. "You know perfectly well that I buy my furnishings on Saville Row in London, or what is left of it for those of us who are discriminating. Each garment is tailored to my own contours and fitted by hand." He sniffed. "Each fabric is of limited production and of superior texture and pattern. I can't imagine wearing what you call ready-made or, do they say, ready to wear." He raised his shoulders a little and gave a slight closed eye shake of his head and shoulders.

Despite the fact that they might as well have been entering a charnel house, the three went in to the store. Camelman started looking at shirts and ties. As he did so Lohman decided to take a chance.

"Graybourne," he said, "I found out where the body came from."

St. Charles gave him a scared look. "What?"

"The body in your chair. Steven told me that he found the body in a wheeled bag in his office Tuesday morning. The time seems to correlate with when you were out at the meeting. He says he panicked and put the body in your office. He carried it. Then he put the bag in the hall closet."

St.Charles said, "There. I told you I didn't know how it got in my office."

"Yes," said Lohman. "We have that explained now. And we found something else. I haven't had a chance to tell you this and I don't think the police have got to you yet on it. At least it doesn't sound that way. The bag had your fingerprints on it in the dead girl's blood. And one of your prints in your washroom is in her blood. I know this sounds bad, but we're going to have to explain this."

St. Charles became still. He didn't move.

"Well," said Lohman. "We're going to have to explain it."

St. Charles was still. Lohman knew this did not mean he was thinking. With St. Charles it meant he had shut down. The circuits had overloaded and shut down.

"Well?" prompted Lohman, "we are going to have to come up with an explanation."

"Yes, do so," said St. Charles. "Oh look, Winston has found something." He took off towards where Camelman was looking at a shirt being held up by a salesman. Lohman followed.

Camelman saw them coming. "Look at these," he said. "See." The salesman held the shirt for all to see and Camelman pointed to it and to one laid out on the counter. Both had ties on them, one being held on the shirt by the salesman. "See," said Camelman. "These are great. $250 for the shirt and $150 for the tie. They're on sale. $800 for both pairs. Where else can you get that kind of value?"

Lohman thought, but didn't answer. The true answer was that you probably could not find such a bad value anywhere else.

St. Charles had taken off. He didn't want to be around Camelman or Lohman. He said as he left, "I'm going upstairs to look at the suits. I will see you two back at the office."

As Camelman and Lohman were waiting for the shirts and ties to be wrapped Camelman said, "Who are you going to bill for this?"

Lohman had not been thinking of billing anyone for his shopping, or watching others shop. However, he knew damn well that most of his brethren did. He said, "Oh, I don't know."

"Well," said Camelman, "I'm not billing The Bank. Who gets credit for those billings? Not me. Him." He gestured with his chin towards the elevators where St. Charles had gone. "I think it'll be my new client, Amalgamated Pussy Wipe."

"Pussy Wipe?" exclaimed Lohman.

"Yes," said Camelman, "I ran it through you for a conflict check last week. You remember. The pet products company. Remember. I'm doing a financing for them."

"Oh yes," said Lohman. He didn't remember it because there were so many, but he was wondering if he was becoming senile in not remembering a client with a name like that. On the other hand Tete and Pigman did much of the spade work on the conflict clearances.

Eventually Lohman and Camelman got back to the office and split up.

29 PHONE RECORDS

When Lohman got back to the office he went to the lunch room for a quick bite and then went to his own suite. As he came in Tete told him that Pigman wanted to speak to him. Lohman was a bit rushed for time so he called Pigman. "Henner," he said. "This is Bumper. You wanted to talk to me?"

"Yes," said Pigman. "I got a call into the firm around 10 that I can trace to Bainbaum's phone. I came into the office. A land line. The firm phone system, so we have a record of it."

"Where did it come from?" asked Lohman.

"From Bainbaums' cell number," said Pigman. "We have everyone's cell numbers you know."

"No, I mean what location did he call from?" asked Lohman.

Pigman answered, "That we don't know. Not with a cell phone."

"So how could I find out?" asked Lohman.

Pigman said, "Ask the other person on the call. We have the phone it went to. It went to one of the associates. Blondella Dumay. She's one of the new associates from last fall."

"That's her name?" asked Lohman.

"You hired her," said Pigman dryly.

Lohman got her location and phone extension from Pigman and then went to her office. He found her in, buried in a pile of papers.

He knocked on her open door and went in. Guess what? She was a blonde. And gorgeous. And she certainly looked a bit dim. On the other hand, she had been tenth in her class at Harvard. "Miss Dumay," Lohman said.

She looked up and bit her lip and squinted as if she were still considering whatever had been occupying her attention.

"Yes," she said.

"I'm Bumper Lohman," he said. "I'm the Managing Partner here."

She just looked at him without comment. Most of the associates, especially the newer ones, had never met the Managing Partner. After a while she said, "Hello." That's all she said. What would you say if you were a newbie in a big place and all of a sudden the big boss appears in your space?

Lohman was aware that his unexplained presence could frighten the new associates and he was accustomed to putting them at ease. "It's nice to meet you. We have had favorable reports about your work. But I'm here about something else. We have some internal firm matters that you may know something about so I'm just here to find out."

She just stared at him blankly.

Lohman felt a little uncomfortable in the gaze of this gorgeous, hot, young thing. He was a little surprised to catch himself thinking, "Down boy." What he said was, "You have heard about the dead woman we found a while ago, I'm sure."

She continued to stare at him. Just then her phone rang and she picked it up and engaged in a phone conversation that seemed to have something to do with an upcoming nail spa appointment. After a while she hung up.

At this stage Lohman pulled out his phone and asked her for her number and dialed it. She picked up the phone. "Hi," he said, "this is me. Let's talk in person." Then he put the phone down without hanging up so she could not get any more calls.

"So," he continued, "You remember it was in January. We found the body on Tuesday morning. January 15th. She had died the night before. Do you remember?"

She just continued to stare at him.

"Well," continued Lohman. "No one really knows what happened, but we have been trying to find out. In the process we tracked down a call to your phone that night. It came from Kevin Bainbaum, or at least his cell phone. Do you remember that? Did you talk to him then?"

"You know that?" she finally spoke. "You are spying on us?"

"On no, no, not at all," Lohman said. "In this case we were looking for calls and we found this one."

"You have a record of my calls?' she said incredulously.

"The firm computer system records the numbers," said Lohman. "We don't record the calls." He didn't want to add that they could if they wanted to. "It helps with billing."

She just stared at him.

"So do you remember talking to Kevin Bainbaum that night?" Lohman continued.

She averted her gaze to the pile of papers in front of her and looked like she was forcing thought. After a while she said, "Yes."

"About what?" asked Lohman.

She didn't bat an eyelid when she responded, "You know if you were a hillbilly and I was a cop and pulled you over for speeding and asked you if you had any id then I could understand you saying 'About what?'. But that's private."

"Yes," said Lohman, "I can understand that. But do you know where he was calling from? That's really what I want to know."

"Why?" she asked. "Are you spying on him?"

"No, no," said Lohman. "Do you know where he was calling from?"

"The lobby," she said. "I was supposed to meet him down there and I was late. He called and reminded me and I went down and we left."

"When was that?" asked Lohman.

"I was supposed to meet him at 10. I was a little late. I don't know how well you know him, but he's not a big waiter. He wants it now."

Lohman could imagine what. "Thank you," he said. "I know this all sounds intrusive. I can tell you that we ordinarily stay out of our people's private lives, but this is related to that event on Monday night."

"How?" she asked.

Lohman answered. "Sean Featherbottom. Do you know him?"

"Him?" she said. "Yes, I think so. Someone pointed him out to me in the lunch room. He's cute."

Lohman continued. "He says he was leaving about then and that Kevin saw him in the lobby. Kevin says he didn't see Sean, but Sean had said Kevin was using his cell phone so we checked out the calls. So now you confirm that Kevin was on the phone in the lobby and that seems to confirm what Sean said."

"So what does Sean have to do with the murder? It was murder wasn't it. That's what everyone says."

"Nothing I hope," said Lohman, "but we are checking out people who were in the place that night."

"Oh," said Blondella, "Well, I wouldn't know."

Lohman thanked her and left. On the way back to his office he was thinking that at least Sean had some support for his version of the events. But he asked himself if Sean could have killed the messenger anyway. He thought that Sean wouldn't have had the time to do it if she came in around the same time he left.

30 CLIENT STEALING

Thursday morning Lohman met with an associate named Joe Showman in Lohman's office. This time the meeting was in Lohman's office because he had materials there he had to refer to. Showman had been working on a deal for one of Lohman's clients that had recently closed. The client had bought a fairly large company from its sole owner. Then the client had fired the former owner. The former owner was now claiming that part of the deal was that he was going to continue on as a consultant at an exorbitant yearly fee. The legal basis for this was not exactly clear since none of the deal papers called for it, but the guy was claiming he had been promised this as part of the deal. Lohman wanted to fill Showman in on the claim and have him get to work on investigating it.

As soon as Lohman described the nature of the problem to Showman, he said, "Sounds like McG's Depot. Have you heard about that one?"

"No," said Lohman. "What's that about?"

"McG's was owned by Bill McGillicudy," said Showman.

"Oh, yes," said Lohman. "I've met him at parties at Mr. St. Charles' house."

"Yes," said Showman, "he's a client of Mr. St. Charles. Or at least McG's Depot was. It wasn't the biggest company, but we did a fair amount of work for it. I was assigned to a lot of it. Mr. St. Charles didn't get too involved beyond dealing with Mr. McGillicudy. He had other partners handling the work. Usually not one of the equity partners. Then on one deal Mr. Camelman got involved and after that McGillicudy seemed to be talking to him instead of Mr. St. Charles. Nothing had to be cleared through Mr. St. Charles anymore it seems. The few times I talked to McGillicudy after that he kept referring to Camelman instead of St. Charles. Before that whenever he talked about who he was talking to on deals he said St. Charles."

"This is sounding familiar," said Lohman.

"You know about it?" asked Showman.

"Not this deal," said Lohman. "Our Mr. Camelman seems to be after Mr. St. Charles' clients."

"Well," said Showman, "in this case maybe it worked. McGillicudy sold his company and the new owners demoted him. They didn't fire him like your deal, but he was no longer the boss. The deal said he would be continued and his compensation was specified, but it didn't require him to be the boss. We didn't cover that detail. So they sidelined McGillicudy and he was furious. He came in to see Mr. Camelman. I was there. Mr. Camelman told him that he had suggested that the deal papers require him to be kept on as Chairman, but that Mr. St. Charles had said there was no need for that. I doubt that. Mr. St. Charles never got involved in the details of anything else I worked on with him. The few times when I was there and he had to make a decision he called someone else and asked them. I remember once, it was you."

"Yes, he does that," Lohman said. "Well, anyway, we're on the other side of the question with this one. What is McGillicudy doing now?"

Showman said, "He's set himself up with a private equity outfit. He's trying to attract investors for new deals. What he really wants is to be the boss of something. Mr. Camelman's handling all his work now. I don't think Mr. St. Charles knows anything about it. And from what I can tell he is doing things like this with other St. Charles clients too. It looks like he is making a major move on them. I've even heard him tell Mr. Swifton that Swifton should call him direct and that Mr. Charles said he should do this."

Lohman considered this. Then he said, "Look, I want to find out more about this, but I don't have time right now. Review all the facts of the matter and then we'll talk. Let's see--." He looked at his calendar and the two of them made a date to talk about it. Lohman still used a paper calendar.

Showman got up to go and then said, "You know, I want to be a partner here and I know I have to develop business. But I always thought other people's clients were hands off. And if I say anything about the guy who has the client I am supposed to talk him up. Is there a lot of this going on here?"

"No," said Lohman. "When a wolf turns on other members of the pack it gets killed, unless of course it gets to be the dominant wolf. We usually don't turn against each other in getting business. It's self-defeating. But some guys try it. It's a standard character type in law practice."

Showman said, "Some of the things I see around here surprise me." He paused and they asked, "Did Mr. St. Charles kill that – um – messenger?"

Lohman was surprised, not only at the question, but its wording. "You're the first person who hasn't called her a little whore. Is that how people in the firm are referring to her now? That's an improvement."

"No," said Showman. "Little whore seems to be what everyone calls her. I was just trying to be polite. Did he kill her?"

"Why are you asking me?" asked Lohman. "Should I know? I wish I did. Why do think he killed her? Why do you ask?"

"Mr. Camelman told me he did," said Showman.

"Well then," said Lohman, "let him tell us all about it."

"He is," said Showman. "I heard him tell someone over at a committee meeting at The Bank. The suspended payments committee."

"What's that? What do they do?" asked Lohman. The Bank, and any large client, usually had many mystic committees.

"I don't know what it is either," said Showman. "It was just a lunch meeting and they didn't seem to talk much business. They were mainly discussing the wine."

"I know the drill," said Lohman. "Anyway, I don't know what basis he has for saying Mr. St. Charles did it. I'll talk to him about it." Then he added, "I hope he didn't tell the police."

Showman left and Lohman got back to immediate concerns which occupied him the rest of the day. One of the concerns was the upcoming President's day party. President's day was on Monday, February 18th and F, P & C always had a big party to celebrate. They had many parties and celebrated any occasion they could. Everyone of importance was invited and the parties were grand schmooze events. This time the party was to be held on Saturday and they had rented all the public rooms of the Swifton Palace Hotel. Several times in the distant past they had actually had then current or past presidents at the event, but they had no such luck in recent years. They were, however, going to have the Secretary of the Treasury present as the President's emissary. Since the President was not likely to attend these days, the firm had dreamed up something they called the President's Award, given each year to the person who a committee selected as being of the most aid to the President in the past year.

The gathering involved a cocktail hour followed by dinner. Then the program usually opened with a blabber-mouthed presentation from some firm twit who introduced the recipient of the award and presented it. Then the recipient gave an acceptance speech. Then some of the firm lawyers presented a musical. Then the formalities ended and the drunken mingling commenced in earnest.

Winter Goren, the Firm Fruit with the large entertainment clientele, was the head of the firm's entertainment committee. This year the show was going to be a cross dressed musical. All the male parts were played by women and all the female parts were to be played by men. So why not call it a dual drag show? Because the performers actually sang. They did not lip-sync. Anyway, the show was "Priscilla And The Magic Prince". Priscilla is a princess who will turn into a commoner at midnight unless she marries someone of royal rank. It is getting late and she is sulking about her fate in the woods when she sees a frog staring at her whilst sexily licking its lips. She picks it up and kisses it and it turns into a Prince. A magic prince who can make a church and a priest appear. They get married before midnight and live happily ever after which is not good for divorce lawyers.

Levin could sing. He loved it. He wanted to play the part of the princess. There had been controversy about it. No one wanted a princess that big. Levin was an equity partner, but on the other hand there was someone who was perfectly fitted for the part of the prince and everyone insisted that she have the part. She finally put her foot down and said she was not going to be the prince if Levin was going to be the princess. Levin was furious and had her investigated. What he found out was that she was actually born a man, a gay guy, and she had had a sex change and had then become a lesbian. All this happened before she had gone to law school. Levin knew this would scandalize some, but he also knew that these things cannot be used these days to discredit someone formally. Therefore he rested his case on the claim that she was not a she and did not qualify for the part of the prince. He lost. He was relegated to being a member of the chorus.

If Levin was going to be in the chorus, he was going to be the star of the chorus. In the center. In the front. Final dress rehearsals were going on and that is where he placed himself. However, with him in the front most of the other chorus members were obscured. He had been placed in the back row and he was furious.

Friday morning Lohman had gone to St. Charles' office to meet with St. Charles and Cohenstein concerning what to do about Camelman's client stealing attempts. Levin's office was next to St. Charles' office and while Lohman and the others were talking they heard increasingly loud sounds coming from Levin's office. The sounds grew to shouting and there were sounds like something hitting the wall. Finally Lohman said to St. Charles and Cohenstein, "Christ!" Then he went to the door between the offices and went in to Levin's office. Levin and Goren were engaged in a fight.

Goren had just picked up a pile of papers from Levin's desk and thrown it on the floor. "There!" he screamed as he gave Levin a backward flip of his wrist. "If you can't control yourself, you're out. We'll sing without you. It's Priscilla And The Magic Prince, not The Fat Turd And The Prince!"

Levin lunged for him and Goren screamed. Lohman shouted, "Can it! Shut the fuck up! What's going on here?" Both stopped in their tracks and looked at Lohman with open-mouthed, wide-eyed, shocked expressions.

After they had calmed down they told him what was going on, both with their own versions. When they had settled down Lohman said, "The show is tomorrow night. Winter is in charge of it. Wanzy – you have to realize that. You move to the back row. We can go into whatever you want after the show, but right now what Winter says goes. As for you Winter, get back to your office or whatever, just get out of here."

Goren left in a huff and Lohman tried to talk Levin down. As they were talking Levin looked down at the papers and pointed at them. Then he turned towards the wall between his office and St. Charles' and pointed to a mark on the wall. Below it was a cell phone on the floor. Levin said, "I hope it still works. I missed the little I queer, but I'll bet it would have shut him up if I'd hit him."

Lohman continued to calm Levin down. After a while Levin called his secretary in to pick up the papers and the cell phone while he and Lohman were still talking. It was manual labor and beneath him. Besides, he couldn't really bend down to the floor and if he went down on his knees he couldn't get up. Some princess! What good is a princess who can't get down on her knees for her prince?

As the secretary was picking up the cell phone Lohman noticed that Levin seemed to have a new rug. He had a massive patterned rug in his office over a bare wood floor. "Is this a new rug?" asked Lohman. "Didn't you have a reddish and beige one before?"

"Yes,' said Levin. "I got a new one. Someone spilled shit all over it. You couldn't see it too well against that pattern, but I could tell."

"Who spilled what?" asked Lohman.

"Don't know," said Levin. "Someone must have got in here. Maybe the cleaning crew. It looked like a lot of coffee. It ruined the rug."

Lohman said, "Isn't this expensive? Did you get it cleared? I don't remember getting anything on this?"

"I'll get it in to you later. I just wanted it fixed."

"OK," said Lohman. He continued talking to Levin for a while until Levin had calmed down and then he left and went back to St. Charles' office and explained to St. Charles and Cohenstein what was happening. In the process he explained to them what the show was going to be and how the dispute arose. They were not privy to these matters. St. Charles had nothing to say.

Cohenstein merely remarked that the show should be about putting on the Priscilla And The Magic Prince show and Goren and Levin should be the stars. He said, "Their fight should be part of the show. It would be one of those actual reality shows."

31 THE PRESIDENT'S DAY PARTY

Saturday was the day of the big party. Lohman was in the office in the morning, but he came home in the afternoon for a nap. The entire aged portion of the Western World is napping half the time. If we could only get the crooks to nap away the day think of how much more peaceful life would be. This is never going to happen, but oldsters know how to deal with the situation. The crooks may not be napping and out of action, but those who are napping are not bothered by whatever else is happening.

In late afternoon Lohman arose and he and Gloria relaxed for a while. Then they got ready and left for the Swifton Palace Hotel where the party was to be. They got there early because, as the Managing Partner, Lohman was ultimately the one who would take the blame for anything that did not go right, even though the whole affair was handled by a President's Day Committee headed by Mititz Gladman.

When the Lohmans arrived some other early arrivals were already there. And the cocktail hour had already begun. The Lohmans began mingling and talking as more and more people arrived. After a while they came upon Penelope Whitehead and her entourage. Penelope was an old white haired thing who fancied herself the leader of Hinsdale society and probably the leader of Chicago society. Hinsdale was the nearest thing to an old line upper crust suburb west of Chicago. While it did not have the tone and age of the North Shore suburbs, such as Lake Forest, it did have wealthy people and people who pretended to wealth. And it had horses. It had the horsey rich people. Penelope had horses. Because of this she had moved from Lake Forest to Hinsdale. So, she did not take second place to the North Shore set. In fact, she maintained her Lake Forest estate for social events.

So there she was, out with the horsey set and with her horses. She couldn't ride a tricycle, but she had horses. They were mostly polo ponies which she put in the local polo matches, and matches all over the county as well, with a team of suitably socially ranked riders. In effect, she lent the ponies to other snobs. She also had some riding horses for her attendants and carriage horses for the carriages she rode in whilst watching the matches. Penelope's great grandfather had been one of the consolidators of the wholesale grocery and meat packing businesses and she had a lot of money.

Penelope was socially aggressive. She was a good salesperson. What she was selling was herself and her superiority and her social standing. Her nickname was The Duchess of Hinsdale. St. Charles loved her.

The Lohmans were taken into the group by The Duchess and they began listening to the Duchess' continued story about her visit to the Palace in Monaco, The Duchess described how the Prince told her about his polo ponies and how he made quite a lot of money betting on the matches, both for and against his team. At this one of the old guy's in the group said "Poppycock! I know him well. He wouldn't do that."

Just then Sweeney passed by with Trisha DeLang in tow. She heard the "Poppycock" and came over to the group and said, "Oh Man, I don't think you should be talkin' like that. I mean it's lewd Man. Talking about your cock poppin'."

This would have been quite a difficult situation for ordinary mortals, but The Duchess was not one of them. She knew how to handle the matter. "What do roosters have to do with it?" she asked.

Sweeney grabbed Trisha and said, "She's just joking." He started to pull her away.

The old "poppycocker" said, "How can you tell?"

Sweeney said, "You think she's really offended?" He then did drag her away and those in the group continued their conversation about the Prince and the polo ponies.

The Lohmans managed to excuse themselves from this group and went on meeting and mingling with others until the time for dinner when everyone went into the adjoining Grand Ballroom for dinner and the program. There was a big stage set up at one end of the room and tables for all the guests in front. The show was going to be on the stage which was set up for a program to be presented in front of the curtain which covered the show set. The Lohmans, as usual, sat at a table in the front and corner of the room where Lohman could sit facing both the stage and the audience so he could keep on top of what was going on.

As everyone got seated the wait staff started serving the dinner. It was not something you would find in a restaurant of note, but then it tasted better. Lohman never ceased to be amazed at how some large hotels could feed masses of people in a short time period with good food. Nor did he cease to be amazed at how they could consistently make good meals out of ordinary things. Tonight the Hotel was serving a choice of chicken breast with wine sauce, prime rib or baked whitefish. All good. None of it fancy. The only regret Lohman had was that "prime rib" was the name of a cut of meat these days. "Prime" used to be a grade of meat. The cut was called roast beef or standing rib roast or some such thing. These days "prime rib" was very often not the prime grade of meet. However, tonight it was. The only problem with that was of course that what is prime these days would often not have qualified for the commercial grade when Lohman was a kid. The Lohmans had the prime rib and, whatever the grade, it was good.

The stage had a podium on it with chairs for those who would participate in the festivities. All this was in front of the curtain and could be easily removed when the show was to start. After dinner the wait staff got busy taking more drink orders while the participants in the presentation moved to the stage and took their seats.

St. Charles, of course, was going to lead off. However, he could not be subjected to the indignity of getting the audience quieted down so the firm had selected Monica Platt to do that. She assumed the podium and started talking. She knew no one was listening so she just went on with platitudes until things quieted down a little. Then she went on for a while about how great St. Charles was and introduced him.

St. Charles assumed the podium and started blabbering. Mostly he started name dropping and pointing out dignitaries in the crowd. Finally he turned things over to Monica Platt who got down to introducing the chair of the event, Mititz Gladman. Monica described her as, "The 2012 American Scrap Dealers Association Lawyer of the Year, Adjunct Distinguished Professor of Law at

Northwestern University Law School, and author of 'Legal Aspects of Scrap Metal Commoditization'. I give you Mititz."

Mititz was a short little thing with big bazooms. She came up to the podium and started talking. Naturally she couldn't get too close to the microphone. People in the crowd started shouting, "Can't hear you."

Mititz then remembered that there was a little step stool that had been put near the podium for her. She moved it into place, stepped up on it and lifted up her – parts – and put them on the podium and learned closer to the microphone and said with quite adequate volume, "If you'd shut up you could hear me." They did shut up, mostly out of shock, but partly because shutting up was such a novel idea that they decided to try it. She then went on to start talking about their distinguished guest, the Secretary of the Treasury and his accomplishments. After telling everyone how wonderful he was she called him forward and presented him with his award. Just as he was about to assume the podium for his words of thanks and wisdom all the doors to the Grand Ballroom swung open, flooding the darkened room with swaths of light. At the same time the curtains on the stage behind Mititz and the Secretary swung open to reveal the costumed cast assembled and ready for the opening number. Swat team police officers were coming in and guarding all the entrances to prevent anyone from leaving. Bongwad and Gilbert (or is it Wilbert?) were leading a team of police coming in behind the cast and moving them forward to the front part of the stage.

Bongwad came out from behind the cast and came to the podium. As he motioned for some of the officers from the back of the stage to go out into the audience he said into the microphone, "All right, where is he? Where is the little Poofbaum? Featherbaum! That's it."

By this time Lohman, ever on the alert, had come up on the stage to the podium. "What's going on here?" he asked.

"We're arresting Featherbaum," said Bongwad.

"Featherbaum? Who's he?" asked Lohman.

"Poofy," said Bongwad "This time we're gonna' nail him."

"Featherbottom?" asked Lohman. "Where do you get Featherbaum?"

"Ain't you guys all half Jewish," said Bongwad.

Lohman just said, "No."

Bongwad addressed the microphone. "All right. Nobody goes anywhere until we get him. You all stay in your seats. He's a murderer. He's probably desperate and we're here to protect you as well as to get him. Everybody stay where you are, stay seated and stay calm." Then he looked around the room and asked his men, "Do you guys see him?" Then he addressed the crowd. "Whoever knows where he is, tell us."

Nobody did know where he was. Actually one person did and that was Winter Goren and he wasn't telling. At the last minute one of the chorus members had come down sick and Goren had got Sean to fill the part. Sean was costumed as a particular character and he was the same size as the person who he was replacing. He had not dressed with the other cast members and he was put in just at the last moment so not even they realized who was in the costume. There Sean was, standing on the stage, just to the left of Bongwad and looking like a pretty young girl while officers were going around the room searching for him.

Lohman was fed up. Sean probably wouldn't harm a fly. "Poppycock!" he exclaimed.

From somewhere in the middle of the room everyone could hear Trisha shouting, "Yeah, Man!"

Lohman continued. "Look here Detective," he said, "Sean Featherbottom did not do it. He's not the one."

"Oh yeah," said Bongwad. "Then who did?"

Lohman didn't know, but he said, "It's obvious. I'll tell you." Here he came to the podium and pushed Bongwad aside. He addressed the crowd. "I think we all want to see an end to this so we can get on with the show. I know I want to see it. So let me tell you who did it."

Fine so far, old boy, but who did it? Lohman began his Chanification. Charlie Chan always started talking and the whole thing was made clear. So Lohman began.

"Let's look at what happened," he said. "A group of us found the victim, a messenger for a service called ZoomShot, dead one Tuesday morning in the desk chair of the Chairman of our firm, Graybourne St. Charles. Her name was Wendy Laymen. She was a young thing and naked except for thigh high shiny black high-heeled boots. There was a waste basket liner over her head stuffed with bathroom tissue and towels and some clothing articles. Some congealed blood was coming down from the bag. I myself was one of the people who witnessed this. As for the waste basket liner we know that there was a fresh one in Mr. St. Charles' office at the time. There were several parallel lines on the carpet beside his desk. We found out later that she had been shot in the side of the head right above her left ear with a gun that belonged to Mr. St. Charles."

At this stage St. Charles had turned into stone with a look of horror on his face. Luckily, not too many people were looking at him.

Lohman continued. "Along with myself, Mr. St. Charles, Trisha DeLang, who you all have heard of even if you do not know her personally, John Sweeney, her lawyer, and Sean Featherbottom were there too. Now, our firm has a messenger service we use regularly and it is not ZoomShot. But then, other people often are responsible for selecting the services they use to send things to us."

Lohman continued. "Now, this young woman apparently had a record of prostitution and drugs. She was only 18." St. Charles began sliding down in his chair towards the floor. "The service, ZoomShot, is known to provide prostitutes, as least so I am told by people who know about these things. The police tell us she was killed between ten at night and four in the morning with the probable time of death around midnight or a little earlier. Under that bag on her head, along with the other materials, there was a pair of lace panties rolled up with the end of the roll stuck in her ear, apparently to stop the bleeding. There was a sexually suggestive note found in her boots, apparently a user name and password. No one has found a site for this, but I am told, once again by people who know about such things, that ZoomShot has its own web site broadcasting in Wi-Fi from mobile locations."

Lohman paused, then continued. "She checked into our office around ten at night or a little before. She was seen by Sean Featherbottom coming in on the 55th floor where her body was found the next morning. She had a big wheeled bag with her and she asked for Mr. Levin, one of our partners." Lohman looked back at the show cast and motioned towards the big one in the back row. "Sean had just been in Mr. Levin's office delivering a document. The wheeled bag was later found in a hall closet. Her prints, as well as some others, were on it. When found, the bag was mostly empty."

"One other thing," he added. "Sean was there when she came in. He is the only one we know who saw her on 55. Something of his was found on the victim. In one of her boots the police found a purple brooch belonging to him. So perhaps it is no big mystery as to why the police think he did it. But he didn't."

Sean was standing near Bongwad looking up and rolling his eyes around and pursing his lips in and out and swaying around like he was about to dance. He darted his glance to the left. Then to the right. However, no one knew it was Sean who was getting so goosey. Bongwad became aware of this and turned to him and placed his huge hand on Sean's shoulder and said, "Take it easy little lady. Everything will be all right. You're safe when I'm here."

Sean just gave him a wide-eyed stare.

Lohman continued. "Some unusual things happened that night. In addition to the murder I mean. There were complaints about the towels missing from the 55th floor washrooms. These complaints came in on Tuesday. Ordinarily the towel containers are filled at night by the cleaning crew and periodically through the day by the people cleaning the washrooms. There were also complaints that the cleaning crew did not empty the copier waste baskets on 55. What appeared to be dirty women's panties and darkened paper towels were said to be in there. The cleaning service tells me these waste baskets were emptied Monday night. They usually do so around six or seven. They tell me the washrooms were also serviced. The wastepaper baskets by the copiers were also emptied Tuesday night. At that time the cleaner noticed the sound of some hard objects coming out. No special notice was given to this because I am told there are often solids in the waste baskets. Nor would I imagine that the cleaners like to sift through the trash."

"Now," said Lohman, "match this up with some other things. The wheeled bag was found in one of the closets on 55. It was mostly empty. It had the victim's blood on it and her prints. It also had other fingerprints on it in her blood. It had the prints of Mr. Stonegold and Mr. St. Charles. Perhaps the contents went into the copier wastebaskets. Perhaps some of the clothing items in the bag were used with the washroom towels to stuff in the bag around the victim's head to stop the blood from coming out. The few remaining items in the wheeled bag were mostly of a sexually oriented nature. Why the bag was emptied is another question though."

"Here," said Lohman, "I might add that prints in the victim's blood were found in the private washroom of Mr. St. Charles. Also found there, but not in the victim's blood, were prints of Sean Featherbottom."

Lohman continued. "Let's look at what else we know. Who else was on the 55th floor where the victim was found? We're lawyers. We have people working in and out of the office at all hours. What do we know about who else was there? We have billing records showing that three of our lawyers who have offices on 55 were billing after eight that evening. One was at home, one was out of town working on a deal and one was our partner Lincoln Beale. Of course these records are not always up to date for our more senior partners." Here Lohman reconsidered what he had just said and got in a modifier as he continued. "They are so busy they cannot always keep up to date on the clerical matters." Good save Bumper. "And we did have many people on other floors whose time records indicate they were present that night. A few even billed past ten. Now, we cannot be sure any of them did not go to the 55th floor, but we have inquired and none had any apparent reason to."

"So, anyway," Lohman continued, "we have two more facts to deal with. One is that the gun used to kill the victim belonged to Mr. St. Charles. Another fact is that Mr. Stonegold says he found the body in his office Tuesday morning. He says she was dead and in the wheeled bag and he panicked and took her out and carried her to Mr. St. Charles' office. He says he is the one who put the bag in the hall closet. And he knew that Mr. St. Charles had the gun and where it was kept. On the other hand, many other people in the firm knew this too."

Lohman went on. "Now we have another potential suspect. Mr. Stonegold. The messenger checked in to see him and asked for him when she came in to the lobby. The only trouble with using this to implicate Mr. Stonegold is that he was in Seattle till about 4 in the afternoon and he did not get back to O'Hare until around 10. We have confirmed that. He says he left a building pass for her and he did. There is no record of him checking into the building on Monday night. So what do we make of the fact that his prints in the victim's blood were found on the bag and in the 5th floor washroom? Perhaps what he says is true. He says he came in a little before 9 on Tuesday. He says he found the bag in his office, which was a mess as he puts it, and he took her out and moved her to St. Charles' office which adjoins his. He tells us that there were tracks left by the bag on his carpet. He says he moved the bag to the hall closet when no one was looking. No doubt the prints in the washroom came about when he went in there to clean up. The prints on the bag would have got there when he was taking her out and moving it."

Lohman concluded, "We can see that, while Mr. Stonegold looks implicated, he just wasn't there. His story also tells us how the body got to Mr. St. Charles' office. So why did the messenger check in to see Mr. Stonegold? What he says about that is that Mr. Beale told him that he – Mr. Beale – was supposed to let the messenger in, but he got called away and he asked Mr. Stonegold to let the messenger in. Now, Mr. Beale could have left a pass too, but many of our top partners are not up on the mechanics of things like this and he may not have known he could leave the pass or he may not have had time to do it."

"Now," said Lohman, "that brings us to Mr. Beale. What did he have to do with the messenger? Well, he tells us that Mr. Levin had told him to accept a delivery because he – Mr. Levin - was not going to be there. Mr. Beale says he wound up in New York on a deal and he asked Mr. Stonegold to let the messenger in. We have confirmed that Mr. Beale was in New York Monday night. Now, we do know something else in regards to Mr.Beale." Here Lohman realized that he had to watch it again. "Mr. Beale is diligent in paying attention to the quality of work we get from our cleaning service. In this regard he has told us that there was no liner in the wastebasket in his office on Tuesday. On the other hand the cleaning person for his office says she put one in on Monday night. Remember that the victim had a wastebasket liner on her head."

"Now," said Lohman, "Let's look at what we know about our firm leader, Mr. St. Charles." Lohman motioned to St. Charles. St. Charles straightened up in his chair and lifted his chin and nose, and thus his whole visage, to his usual look of highly placed disdain. Mr. Stonegold had absolved him. He was back to sainthood. "We now know that, while the victim was found in his office, the body had been moved there by Mr.Stonegold who took it out of the wheeled bag in his office and carried it into Mr. St. Charles' office. This was done when Mr. Stonegold got in around 9 on Tuesday morning. Mr. St. Charles had been in his office earlier and tells us the body was not there then. This is supported by what Mr. Stonegold says. So why, I ask, were Mr. St. Charles' prints in the victim's blood in his washroom and on the bag?"

Lohman went on. "Two other curious facts. The waste basket in Mr. St. Charles office had a liner in it Tuesday morning and there were two parallel marks on his carpet near his desk. Like marks that could be made by the wheels of one of those bags. Then," Lohman added, "it was his gun that killed her. And where was it found? It was found by the cleaning crew later in the week under the filler in his cat box. We all know and admire the beloved Pussy he keeps in his office. It was a small gun with a silencer. He ordinarily kept this in a drawer in his office. He tells us this was missing some time before the murder. The drawer the gun was in was wiped clean of prints. Now this brings up the question of how he knew it was gone. He would have had to open the drawer to know it was gone." Here St. Charles started turning green. "Who took the gun and when is an open question. Anyway, someone wiped any prints off the drawer."

Lohman looked around the audience as he thought for a moment. Many people in the audience were unfamiliar with thought so they did not know what he was doing. "So," he continued, "where was Mr. St. Charles on Monday night? That is when she was murdered, not Tuesday morning. He says he was at the Pullman Club and we have a bill confirming that and the Club has his signature on the chit. We have also confirmed through confidential sources that he was seen there. So with respect to our Chairman, how did the parallel marks get on his carpet if the bag was not in his office? How did his prints in the victim's blood get anywhere? There is no record of his checking in on Monday night, although he could have stayed after hours. It's a puzzle."

"Now some other people did check in that night. Two were Sean Featherbottom and John Sweeney, one of our prominent younger lawyers active in the entertainment area. They came in together after eating dinner. There is no indication Mr. Sweeney was on 55 and he says he went home around 9:30. Nothing contradicts this. On the other hand he says he saw a purple brooch on Sean's bag. Sean is fond of decoration. You will remember that Sean's purple brooch was found in the victim's boots." Now Lohman was beginning to wonder about Sean.

"So let's look at Sean. It's too bad he isn't here to perhaps explain some of this," said Lohman.

At this Sean started getting antsy again and rolling his eyes and puffing his cheeks. Bongwad reached over and hugged him and said, "Don't worry Hon." Sean just looked up at him with the wide eyed look. Bongwad kept his arm around Sean as Lohman continued.

"Sean's prints were in St. Charles' washroom. He says he had used it earlier. On the other hand his brooch was found in her boots. He admits he saw her when she came up to the 55th floor. He says he was up there to deliver a document to Mr. Levin which he put on Mr. Levin's desk and then left. He says he was walking down the hall towards the elevators when the victim was coming towards him wheeling her bag. He says she asked for Mr. Levin and he pointed out his office to her. He says he then left and went home. Who is to say he did? He says another associate saw him leaving in the lobby. If so, that would go towards exonerating him since there is no record he checked back in. He says it was Kevin Bainbaum who saw him. Mr. Bainbaum denies this. Sean says Bainbaum was talking on his cell phone. We checked the phone records. As an aside," said Lohman, "NSA isn't the only one tracking phone calls. Anyway, we found a record of a call coming to one of our other associates around 10. This was Miss Dumay. She confirms that Mr. Bainbaum did call her then and that he said he was in the lobby. How would Sean know this if he had not been in the lobby then? As for his brooch, he says he felt it on his bag as he was coming out of the elevators on 55 so he had it then. He says he brushed up against Mr. Levin's desk and that is where he could have lost it."

Lohman paused. Then he said, "One complication after another. So far they all look like they did it, but could they have? So who else was there? Mr. Camelman. He and Mr. Levin came in late Monday. They checked in around 9. They say they were coming back from dinner. They both met with one of our associates around 9. This was on another floor."

Lohman paused again. He briefly wondered if he should go on with what he was thinking. However, it seemed relevant and, as Zenon would probably say, it would add interest. "There has been some controversy between Mr. St. Charles and Mr. Camelman recently about who is responsible for which clients." Lohman wondered briefly if he had actually said Camelman was trying to steal the St. Charles clients. "There has been some tension between them as a result. Bearing that in mind, Mr. Camelman has told some people at The Bank and one of our associates, Mr. Showman, that Mr. St. Charles is the guilty party. That Mr. St. Charles is the murderer. I have not had a chance to follow up on this yet, but one wonders how he knows. At any rate, Mr. Camelman tells us that a car dealer had delivered a car to him to test. The dealer had left it in the building garage on Monday. The keys were delivered up to Mr. Camelman. He says he picked up the car around ten that night and went home. He says it was a DB B24, whatever that is. He says it is a coupe with a seven speed transmission. He says he got it from Midwest Luxury Motors. He says he drove it home. His wife cannot confirm or deny this because she says she was away visiting relatives. We do have someone who knows something about this and that is the dealership. They say the car is not made in coupe form and that it does not have a seven speed transmission and that they did not give him one to try out."

Lohman then paused again. Should he or should he not bring up what he was thinking. "Well who knows," he thought, "maybe it could be relevant and Zenon would say, once again, that it would add interest." So Lohman said, "We have to consider the sex angle now. I think it is going to come up anyway. The angle, that is. So what am I talking about? There are some facts we know about Mr. Camelman. Sources, which will have to remain confidential, say they have seen Mr. Camelman at orgies where he likes to show, if you know what I mean. These are show business sources of course. And, just like NSA, we can look at computer records and there are records of sexually oriented sites on his computer. On the other hand we tried the user name and password we found on those sites and it did not work."

Lohman then summed up Mr. Camelman. "We know he was there around 10. His story about driving home is malarkey, but on the other hand Mr. Camelman is often trying to impress people with his cars and possessions. So while we hear the poopoo of the bull, it does not necessarily mean he had not left the pasture."

"So who else was there?" asked Lohman. "Our Mr. Levin is who else was there. He came in with Mr. Camelman that night. He tells me that he had been planning to go to a show with his wife that night, but she came down with a cold. He went out to dinner with Mr. Camelman instead and came in to get the document he had asked Mr. Beale to get when he had thought he was not going to be there. Mr. Beale passed on the task to Mr. Stonegold as we have seen. Now we also know that Mr. Levin met with others on a lower floor after he came back from dinner."

"What was the messenger delivering?" asked Lohman. "Mr. Levin says she was delivering a document he needed for a hearing the next day. He says he came in and got it and went home. He says the general counsel of a client, Ms. Seladora Bruce, sent it. We checked the file and the document was notarized on Tuesday. But it was supposed to have been delivered on Monday. When asked about this Mr. Levin tells us that the document he received on Monday night was unusable so he got another on the next day. Ms. Bruce cannot remember the details of what day she sent what. The messenger service used on Tuesday was our regular service which is Ready?-Sent! and not ZoomShot. Ms. Bruce at first said she left the document for pickup, but once again, she can't remember the details. Mr. Levin's secretary says she did not remember if she arranged it, but our service says she ordered the pickup on Tuesday. Couple this with his asking others to let the messenger in. Then I just found out recently that he got a new rug in his office and he says someone spilled something there. And his office is across the hall from the copy room on that floor. Further, consider the arrangement of the offices on 55. Mr. St. Charles' suite is between the offices of Mr. Stonegold and Mr. Levin. And Mr. Levin's has Mr. Beale's office on the other side. Let us consider where the bag on the victim's head came from. Did it come from Mr. Beale's waste basket that had no liner Tuesday morning? And consider Mr. Stonegold moving a body around. If he can move a body around, so can other people. And what else have we heard from our show business sources? Mr. Levin has been seen at orgies too and he likes to watch. On the other hand, how did Mr. St. Charles' prints wind up on the bag in the victim's blood? Was she killed in Mr. Levin's office with the gun obtained from Mr. St. Charles' office? Did the murder then get the trash bag from Mr.Beale's office and stuff it with towels from the washrooms and other items? Were the contents of the bag then put in the copier waste baskets? Was the body then put in the bag and moved elsewhere? I hate to say this, but was it moved to Mr. St. Charles' office? And did he come in early Tuesday, find it and then move it to Mr. Stonegold's office and did Mr. Stonegold then take it out of the bag and put it in St. Charles' chair? After all, no one wants to have a dead body found in their office. And do we have any record of where Mr. Levin was that night? And who knew Mr. St. Charles kept a gun in his office and where he kept it? We have found out that Mr. Levin and Mr. Camelman knew."

Lohman paused. "Now consider this. Whoever was sending what to whom and whoever the messenger said in the lobby she was checking in for, it was Mr. Levin who the messenger asked for when she got to 55. And consider this. Everyone else we know was there, no matter how deeply implicated, is exonerated by certain relevant facts." Lohman turned and pointed towards Levin, who by now was huffing and puffing at the back of the chorus line. "Wanzer Levin – you did it!"

"No! No!" shouted Levin. "Not me. All we were doing was a little sex. I didn't do anything. We were in my office. Winston likes dangerous stuff. Gets off on it. He went and got Graybourne's gun. Winston was in the arm chair. She was going down on him and he was pointing it at her head and making threatening talk. Just when the – well just at that time he pulled the trigger and – well – she just collapsed in his lap. After he recovered his senses he told me to go get towels and stuff for the blood. He started stuffing her panties in her ear while I got some paper and stuff from Lincoln's office. He always has some napkins in there. I got the trash bag too.

We put it on her and I went to get more. Christ. And she dropped her brooch too. I picked it up off the floor and shoved it in one of her boots. Then Winston said, 'Let's get her out of here. It's Grabby's gun. Let's just put her in his office and we'll be in the clear. We can pin it on him and finally we can get rid of him.' So we emptied the bag and put the junk in the copier room baskets and we put her in the bag and put her in Graybourne's office. I didn't do it. I swear. I wouldn't lie to you. He told me if I ever said anything he'd nail me too."

All of a sudden there was a commotion out in the audience. Camelman was up and running towards the doors. As he was running past Tete she stood up and grabbed him by the neck and lifted him up. He was swinging and thrashing his legs and arms and trying to swear at the same time. She held him until some of the swat team could come and get him. Then she sat down and said to those at her table, "You think the stage show will be better?"

After everything had calmed down Monica Platt was hugging Lohman up on the stage. "Good going Bumper. You did it again."

Tete then said to her tablemates in general, "Look at that will you. They're always at it."

As for Sean, he was rather disappointed that Bongwad had released him.

And the show? Goren slipped into Levin's role and the show went on, as it always must.

DON'T COMPLAIN! YOU WERE WARNED UP

FRONT. ON THE OTHER HAND YOU HAVE

BEEN RENDERED ILLITERATE AND PROBABLY

CAN'T READ THIS SO WHO CARES!

For more trash like this see

DONNIESYELLOWBALLBOOKS.COM

Made in the USA
Charleston, SC
23 January 2015